# THE ADVENTURESS

## ALSO BY TASHA ALEXANDER

# THE
# ADVENTURESS

A

LADY EMILY

MYSTERY

*Tasha Alexander*

Minotaur Books ☙ New York

THE ADVENTURESS. Copyright © 2015 by Tasha Alexander. All rights reserved. Printed in the United States of America. For information, address St. Martin's Press, 175 Fifth Avenue, New York, N.Y. 10010.

www.minotaurbooks.com

Designed by Omar Chapa

The Library of Congress Cataloging-in-Publication Data is available upon request.

ISBN 978-1-250-05826-3 (hardcover)
ISBN 978-1-4668-7607-1 (e-book)

Our books may be purchased in bulk for promotional, educational, or business use. Please contact your local bookseller or the Macmillan Corporate and Premium Sales Department at (800) 221-7945, extension 5442, or by e-mail at Macmillan SpecialMarkets@macmillan.com.

First Edition: October 2015

10  9  8  7  6  5  4  3  2  1

*For Jane and Andrew, remembering our wonderful trip to the south of France. I am glad it was less eventful than Emily's.*

# ACKNOWLEDGMENTS

Myriad thanks to . . .

Charlie Spicer (a dream of an editor!), Andy Martin, Melissa Hastings, Paul Hochman, Sarah Melnyk, April Osborn, Tom Robinson, David Rotstein, and Anne Hawkins. Working with you all is the best.

Kate Dyson, my wonderful friend who has proven essential when it comes to naming English estates. Thank you for finding Woodsford for Jeremy.

Jane Grant, more dear to me than any sister could be, for traveling with me to the south of France while I was doing research for this book. It would not have been half as good without your insights.

As always, my writer pals and dear friends, who make every single day brighter: Brett Battles, Rob Browne, Bill Cameron, Christina Chen, Jon Clinch, Charlie Cumming, Jamie Freveletti, Chris Gortner, Nick Hawkins, Robert Hicks, Kristy Kiernan, Elizabeth Letts, Carrie Medders, Kelly O'Connor McNees, Deanna Raybourn, Missy Rightley, Renee Rosen, and Lauren Willig.

Xander Tyska, research assistant extraordinaire.

My parents, who make everything better.

Andrew. Everything, always.

*He must needs go that the Devil drives.*

—WILLIAM SHAKESPEARE, *ALL'S WELL THAT ENDS WELL*

# THE
# ADVENTURESS

# 1

"The English duke is dead."

The words, muffled and heavily accented, hardly reached me through the voluminous duvet that, while I slept, had somehow twisted around me with such violence that it now more closely resembled mummy wrappings than a blanket. Struggling against its bonds, I managed to extricate one hand before realizing my head was under a stack of pillows. I flung them aside and sat up, turning to discover my husband was no longer next to me. The words came again, and this time vanquished in an instant all of the confusion clouding my mind after being awoken from a deep slumber.

"Monsieur, the duke, the English duke, he is dead."

"Jeremy?" I leapt from the bed, dragging the duvet with me (I had not been quite so successful in the removal of it from my person as I had hoped), and started for the narrow patch of light coming into our room from the door, held open by my husband, his dressing gown pulled around him. A chasm seemed to open inside me, as if my heart were splitting and filling me simultaneously with intolerable cold and heat. Jeremy Sheffield, Duke of Bainbridge, my dearest childhood friend, who had tormented me in my youth not quite so much as I had tormented him, could not be dead. I tried to step forward, but my limbs would obey no commands.

"Is he in his suite?" my husband asked. The man standing in the corridor nodded. "I shall come at once."

He must have closed the door, but I have no memory of him having done so. I collapsed in an undignified heap, my legs no longer able to support me.

"Emily." Colin knelt at my side, scooped me into his arms and deposited me back onto the bed. "I must see what has happened and will return as quickly as possible. Will you be all right?"

"Yes, of course." I rubbed my face. "No. No. I must come with you."

"I don't think you ought." His dark eyes locked onto mine, and I could see pain and worry and just a bit of frustration in them.

"I have to see him. I—"

"No." He squeezed my hand and slipped the dressing gown from his shoulders, finding and putting on the stiff boiled shirt he had discarded earlier in the evening with entirely no regard for its subsequent condition. After retrieving his trousers from the back of a chair and locating his shoes—one had disappeared under the bed— he shrugged into his tailcoat and walked to the door, pausing to turn back and look at me as he opened it. Had I not been so upset, I would have better appreciated the handsome dishevelment of his cobbled-together evening kit. "I am so terribly sorry, Emily."

The tears did not come before the door clicked shut behind him, but then my eyes produced a worthy monsoon. Sudden storms are short, however, and this was no time for succumbing to emotion. I splashed water on my face and pulled on my dressing gown. There could be no question of returning to my own previously discarded garments: Ladies' gowns are designed to require assistance, and while this may allow for a more beautifully designed bodice, it proves an immense frustration when one finds oneself on one's own.

Fortunately, no one saw me slip out of our room as there were not yet other guests meandering through the Hotel Britannia, the most fashionable place to stay on La Croisette in Cannes, and arguably on the whole of the Côte d'Azur. A clock near the curved marble stair-case told me it was nearly half five in the morning. Anyone awake now would either be a servant or someone staggering in from a long evening, probably spent playing baccarat at the Cercle Nautique. I climbed one flight to the top floor, where Jeremy had insisted on staying. The view, he said, was incomparable. His door was closed and locked, so I tapped on it, and a man I did not recognize opened it without delay.

"Madame, you would not wish—"

I pushed past him and went straight through the sitting room to the bedroom, where I saw my husband standing with two other men. On the bed was the prostrate form of a gentleman in evening kit.

I recognized the wiry individual closest to the supine figure as the hotel doctor. He adjusted the tortoiseshell pince-nez on his long nose and placed his unopened bag on a bedside table. "We will need to further examine him, of course, but there is no question—"

"There is no question," I said, stepping forward with no regard for any of them, "because this is not the duke."

"Emily—" Colin reached for my arm, but I pulled away and moved to the opposite side of the bed, closer to the body, determined to confirm the identity of the man. It was harder to move him than I had anticipated, but I managed to roll him over and reveal his face, the eyes staring and vacant.

"Chauncey Neville." I was shaking rather violently now, and realized that I was barefoot and my teeth were chattering. "It is not Jeremy. Not Jeremy." Mr. Neville, a shy, soft-spoken gentleman from Cornwall, had always seemed an unlikely friend for Jeremy, but the two had been close since their days at school. We often joked that they tempered each other, Chauncey reeling in Jeremy when he got too out of hand, and Jeremy prodding Chauncey to embrace joviality. Shy though he was, Mr. Neville never proved awkward in social situations, but instead was kind and thoughtful, always on hand to support his friends in any of their schemes.

"Come, my dear," Colin said. "You will catch your death of cold. You know how chilly the seaside gets at night."

Any person who has had the privilege of forming even the barest sort of acquaintance with Colin Hargreaves knows he is not the sort of gentleman to make such trite remarks. Rather, he is the most trusted agent of the Crown, a particular favorite of Queen Victoria's, and the individual most frequently called upon by the palace to assist in delicate matters that threaten the state of our great empire. My eyes focused better on the room now, and I saw the manager of the hotel wringing his hands.

"Fear not, Monsieur Fortier, this is not the first body I have seen," I said. In fact, I had seen many. The work my husband and I shared—sometimes in official capacities, sometimes when we chose on our own to help those in need of assistance—had led us to reveal the identities of no fewer than nine cruel murderers. I was not a stranger to violent death. Whether my words soothed the concerned hotelier, I do not know. Colin removed me to our own suite of rooms before I could gauge the man's reaction. Regardless, the untimely demise of one of our party would dramatically alter what had been intended as a celebratory holiday on the Côte d'Azur.

Nearly four months ago, at Christmas, I had received a telegram from Jeremy, announcing his engagement to Miss Amity Wells, an American heiress who had realized her parents' dearest hopes by catching an English duke. Miss Wells's mother, a veritable battle-axe of a woman, far better suited to roping steers on the range than moving in high society, insisted on throwing an engagement party to celebrate the match, but would not content herself with a ball in Mayfair. Instead, she had planned a trip to the south of France, where all the closest friends and family of the bride and groom would spend a fortnight, culminating in a party she assured us would be more spectacular than any we had ever seen. England, she explained in a coarse whisper, was such a little island it could not possibly be expected to hold all her big ideas.

Colin and I had met mother and daughter over New Year at Jeremy's estate in Kent; the Wellses had cut short a trip to Egypt for the occasion. While Mrs. Wells could be described as a force of nature, one had to accept Amity as something akin to a dream. Her fresh-faced beauty, enviable figure, flair for fashion, and quick wit made her a favorite in London society. A favorite with the gentlemen, that is. I am sorry to say that my own fair sex proved far less generous with her, a judgment firmly footed in the lair of envy. I scorned this, knowing it to be unfair, but must acknowledge that my reaction to Miss Wells proved somewhat more complicated than I should have liked.

The estate of the Duke of Bainbridge lay adjacent to that of my own excellent father, and Jeremy and I had been inseparable as children. When it came time for him to leave for school, I cried for three days straight, and marked on my calendar when he would be home between terms, counting the weeks until I would see him again. By the time he had finished at Harrow and was leaving for Oxford, we no longer climbed trees together, instead finding great amusement in the knowledge that both our mothers longed to see us (and our families) united in marriage. Neither of us could think of anything more ridiculous, for although we adored each other, our temperaments and our interests could not have been more at odds. I had grown up studious and intellectual; Jeremy had championed the goal of being the most useless man in England. When his father died suddenly during his son's second year at university, everyone hoped the new duke would undergo a transformation à la Prince Hal and adopt a more solemn and appropriate demeanor. This served only to spur him into more questionable behavior.

Jeremy played the rake with consummate skill, but, at heart, his kindness and steadfast loyalty prevented him from ever becoming truly profligate. He claimed this to be his greatest disappointment. He took splendid care of his mother, refusing to let her be holed up in dowager quarters, and, knowing both what an asset she had been to his father and how much she had enjoyed helping to run the estate, insisted that she continue her work. He did as little as possible, squeaked through Oxford with a degree he claimed disgraced every Bainbridge ancestor, ran with a fast set, and, perhaps, drank too much on occasion, but he never got himself into irreparable trouble. Everyone in society fawned over him, particularly the legion of mothers who longed for the dashing, fun-loving duke (whose fortune was even more attractive than his bright blue eyes) to someday propose to one of their daughters.

Over the years, Jeremy's steadfast resistance to marriage became the stuff of legends. He did everything in his not inconsiderable powers to avoid it, including pretending to court my close friend Margaret Michaels, née Seward. Their deception was borne out of mutual need. Margaret, an American, had been sent to England, much like Amity Wells, to catch a titled husband. She, however, had no interest in such things, wanting instead to study at Oxford. She and Jeremy spent a season pretending to be in and out of love. Eventually, when he threw her over (at her insistence, of course), she pled a broken heart and convinced her parents that they must not try to force her into marriage until she had quite forgot the duke. Jeremy let it be known (quietly) that he felt an English peer ought not marry an American, a sentiment lauded by the aforementioned legion of mothers. Their daughters vied for his attention with such implacable nerve that it began to make him quite unable to enjoy all the social functions in which he used to take such pleasure. Finding this condition unacceptable in the extreme, he decided to direct all of his affections toward me, his oldest friend.

At the time, I was a young widow, my first husband having been murdered only a few months after our wedding. Out of mourning and back in society, I had fallen in love with Colin Hargreaves, and even after I had accepted his proposal of marriage, Jeremy refused to stop pressing his own suit. Not, mind you, because he actually loved me, but because he knew I would go along with his scheme. He viewed my engagement as a gift from the dear Lord himself. Society believed him to be heartbroken and devoted to a lady he could not have, and the legion of mothers could tolerate with relative equanimity waiting for him to recover from the blow my second marriage struck.

Colin accepted this arrangement with good humor, knowing full well Jeremy had never been a threat to our marital happiness. He also knew that one day, Jeremy would have to marry. He might play the profligate, but he would never leave his dukedom without an heir. Much as I enjoyed Jeremy's little game, I had rejoiced when I read his telegram and knew it was over. I longed to see my friend as happily settled as I.

Then I met Amity Wells.

I am, perhaps, not being entirely fair. She failed to make much of an impression at our first meeting, but balls do not provide much of an opportunity for deep conversation. Our trip to Cannes was to offer us that. Yet almost from the moment I stepped into La Croisette with her, I knew we could never be friends. And I feared Jeremy would never forgive me for that.

# Amity
## Twelve months earlier

India did not suit Amity. The oppressive heat reminded her too much of her grandparents' plantation house in Natchez, Louisiana, where she had spent more than one unhappy summer while her parents retreated from New York's Fifth Avenue to their mansion in Newport. This arrangement came at the insistence of her grandmother, Varina Beauregard Wells, who was as unhappy at the Confederate loss in the War Between the States as she was that her Harvard-educated son had abandoned all his breeding and married a Yankee. She had always objected to sending him north for an education. The fortune he earned in copper tempered her displeasure, but she was not about to let her only granddaughter grow up with coarse northern manners. Her daughter-in-law made no effort to dissuade her. Learning to simper in that charming southern way could do nothing but enhance Amity's value on the marriage market, and Birdie Wells had every intention of seeing her daughter married to an English nobleman. So far as she was concerned, this outcome was nonnegotiable. Her husband had no interest in arguing with her regarding this or anything else about which she felt strongly.

"She must be a duchess, don't you think?" Birdie—Amity had never been able to think of her mother as anything but Birdie—made a habit of talking about her daughter as if she were not there.

"I am sure you know best, dearie." Amity's father loved to indulge his wife, who was delightfully unlike the southern belles his mother had traipsed before him, hoping he would take one of them as his bride. Their superficial charms were many, but none could compete with his Birdie, who spoke with a shocking degree of directness. The day they met she had looked him in the eyes and said, *You are less of a fool than I expected, Wells*, and he knew he had found his partner in life.

"I am doing this all for you, my dear. Vanderbilt's daughter caught a duke and we cannot tolerate falling beneath that family. I should be unable to take so much as a step out of the house. We have got to take her abroad without delay."

"I would never deny you something you want so badly, Birdie." Mr. Wells folded up his newspaper and left for his office, where, after finalizing a deal that nearly doubled the family's already enormous fortune, he set about making plans for their trip. That he chose to start with India reflected his priorities. An old friend who had wrangled himself a plum position after the dissolution of the East India Company had invited him to visit, with the object of convincing him to invest in what he was certain would prove a most profitable arrangement. They would be in India by February, and stay until the following winter, when they would remove themselves to Egypt, and form all the acquaintances necessary to make an appropriate splash in London the following spring. Birdie would have preferred to start in London, but understood her husband too well to suggest an alternative to his itinerary.

Within hours of their arrival in Bombay, Amity was being heralded as the belle of expat society. Invitations poured in, and the family found themselves in even greater demand than that to which they were accustomed in New York. Birdie's exuberant parties proved a great success with the British community, although Amity noticed more than a few ladies looking down their nose at her mother, especially when she insisted they ride camels to the site of one of her picnics. Regardless, Amity allowed herself to be escorted to countless events by a series of young men Birdie had vetted, but she took little pleasure in the company of any of them. She did not object to making a good marriage, but felt that she ought at least to be allowed to like her future husband. Her new friend, Miss Christabel Peabody, shared this view. Miss Peabody, a young lady whose British manners and affability were approved of by Birdie, had traveled to India to visit her brother, who was serving there in the army. Within a fortnight of their introduction, she and Amity were inseparable.

"I do not think I shall ever adjust to being here," Amity said, as she and Christabel lounged in the courtyard of the villa Mr. Wells had taken for their stay. "The humidity is intolerable." She stretched out on a chaise longue and waved a large ostrich fan in front of her face.

"And it is not yet summer," Christabel said. "You will adore Simla, though. Everyone spends the summer there. The society is incomparable."

"Incomparable society in Simla?" A stocky man in uniform approached them, Birdie's housekeeper following behind, doing her best to announce the visitor. "Christabel, you are giving this young lady the wrong idea altogether."

"Captain Charles Peabody, Miss Wells!" The servant made a slight bow, her hands pressed together as if she were praying.

"Very good, thank you," Amity said.

"And Captain Jack Sheffield as well."

Amity thanked the housekeeper again and inspected the new arrivals. Christabel's brother, Captain Peabody, was a bit of a disappointment; Amity preferred her officers to cut rather more of a dashing figure in uniform. Fortunately for her, his companion filled the role admirably. Tall and lanky, Captain Sheffield moved with careless ease, and Amity was taken at once with his easy humor and self-deprecating ways.

"The society in Simla is the worst sort of colonial balderdash,"

Captain Peabody said. "If one is to be in India, one ought to *be* there, not set up some sorry version of England instead."

"Going native, Peabody?" Captain Sheffield's grin brightened the room.

"I take all my opinions from you, old boy, so you ought not criticize me."

"Quite right." Captain Sheffield tugged at the cuffs of his bright red jacket. "India is magnificent: exotic and mysterious. How many forts have you ladies visited thus far?"

"Forts?" Amity asked, pursing her perfect lips and raising her eyebrows. "Why should I have even the slightest interest in visiting forts? Unless you can promise me more officers as charming as the two of you?"

"Not that sort of fort, Miss Wells," Captain Sheffield said. "I speak of the ruins of ancient citadels, the towering walls and heavy gates that kept safe the maharajas and their jewels. You do know about the maharajas and their jewels?"

"What girl worth her salt wouldn't?" Amity smiled. "Daddy promised me emeralds while we are here."

"Good girl. Insist on rubies as well."

"Sheffield is a terrible influence," Captain Peabody said. "But you could not put yourselves in better hands should you want a guide to show you the area. I am afraid, Christabel, that I will not have quite so much liberty as I had hoped during your visit. Mother is furious, but I must do my duty."

"Of course, Charles. No one would expect less from you," Christabel said.

"I have brought my friend along as a peace offering. Mother has no interest in doing anything beyond taking tea with her old friends, and I do not wish to see you trapped doing only that. So far as she is concerned, she has already seen the best of India."

"She and father were here for nearly a decade."

"Yes, but she is very keen on you having a wander around, so long as it does not interfere with her routine. Sheffield is as good a bloke as I know. He will look after you well."

"I am still in the room, Peabody."

"Right. Well. I must be off. I shall leave the three of you to formulate a plan for your adventures."

From that day forth, Captain Sheffield spent every waking hour not required of him by the army with Amity and Christabel. Birdie initially balked at the young man. Captain Sheffield would never make an acceptable candidate for her daughter's husband—he was a dreaded younger son, and, hence, without title or fortune—but once she learned he was the brother of the Duke of Bainbridge, Britain's most desirable bachelor, her feelings warmed slightly. That is to say, she no longer did her best to discourage the acquaintance.

Amity, Christabel, and Jack—for none of them required formality of the others any longer—began to refer to themselves as the Three Musketeers. They traveled (chaperoned, of course, by Birdie) to the Golden Temple at Amritsar, where Amity threatened to become a Sikh, but only if she would be allowed to wear a turban and carry a dagger. The dagger, Jack assured her, was a requirement. They lamented the sorry state of the Lake Palace at Udaipur, where the damp had taken hold and ruined much of the fine interior.

"I shall make it my mission to return here and restore every corner of this place," Amity said.

"I have been laboring under the impression that India did not suit you," Jack said. "It would impossible to count the number of times you have told me you would prefer to be in Paris or London—"

"Or the Alps," Christabel continued, crossing to her friends after she had finished photographing the remains of a frieze on one of the walls. Her brother had given her a camera for Christmas, and she had become something of an expert at using it. Carrying it on their trips often proved problematic, but they all agreed it was worth the aggravation when they saw her pictures. "Or Rome—"

"Stop, you wretched beasts! I repent," Amity said. "I repent wholly. The subcontinent has grown on me. When are we to see the tigers?"

Birdie categorically refused to allow a safari of any sort, tigers or not. This did not give Amity more than the slightest pause. She appealed to her father, who never could resist her, and he organized a hunting party for them. Christabel very nearly begged off coming, but was persuaded in the end, although she was convinced, up almost to the last moment, that it was a wretched idea.

"Come now, Bel," Amity said. "Think of us, camping in the wild, riding on elephants—"

"I do quite fancy riding on an elephant," Christabel said.

"I promise you will never regret it."

"Oh, Amity, I can never say no to you!"

"Why would you want to?" Amity smiled. They departed for the Rajasthani hills the next morning.

# 2

The celebration of Jeremy's engagement to Miss Wells began on board a special train in London, hired by her father. The ordinary boat train was not good enough for his little girl, nor was the ordinary boat that ferried ordinary travelers to Calais. We made our crossing in the lap of luxury—even the weather cooperated, treating us with bright sun and smooth seas—and we were then ushered onto a second special train that whisked us south toward Cannes.

I resented everything about the trip, particularly having to be away from my twin boys, Henry and Richard, who were now two years old. They, together with our ward, Tom, brought joy and laughter to our home, along with trails of muddy footprints, dogs hidden in the nursery, and more than a few casualties among the breakable objects in our possession. Tom's mother was a former friend of mine who had turned out to be a cunning murderer, and his parentage had raised more than a few eyebrows in society. That is, his maternal parentage. His father, a dissolute wastrel to my mind, was considered superior because he came from an old and noble Italian family. Fortunately, neither Colin nor I cared a bit for anyone's opinion on the subject, and we held Tom, who was a few months older than the twins, as dear to us as Henry and Richard. I missed them all terribly and longed to return home to shower their chubby cheeks with kisses.

When we arrived in Cannes, each member of the party was assigned rooms in the town's best hotel, located in the eastern end of La Croisette, the wide, fashionable avenue skirting the coast of the Mediterranean. To my mind, we were a motley party: English nobility, American robber barons, and a collection of nouveau riche from both sides of the pond. I hated myself for sounding like my mother, but in this instance, I could not help myself.

"It is not that I object to Americans," I said, doing my best to explain myself to two of my dearest friends. We had taken a table in the center of the hotel's terrace, a large, beautifully landscaped space, surrounded by graceful palms between which one could watch a steady stream of elegant tourists walking along the sea. Mimosas, orchids, and hyacinths brimmed over vases on each table, their bright colors contrasting with the deep azure of the sky and the seemingly endless stretch of water in front of us. "You of all people know that perfectly well, Margaret, but this American in particular—"

"She is even prettier than you are. I hated her the moment I laid eyes on her." Margaret Michaels, whom I had met while in the last days of mourning for the death of my first husband (and who had, as previously mentioned, once pretended to be in love with Jeremy), was a Bryn Mawr–educated American who had skillfully persuaded her parents to accept an Oxford don rather than a duke for a son-in-law.

"Heavens, Margaret, how I have missed you!"

"You are both jealous." Cécile du Lac waved for a nearby waiter and ordered more champagne. "It is unseemly."

"We are not jealous," I said. "It is just that, well, Jeremy is—"

"Bainbridge is no longer mooning over you and you feel the loss keenly. It is to be expected. I cannot count the number of times I warned you that it would, eventually, happen." Cécile, a stunning and elegant Parisian of a certain age, was my confidante, the one person other than my husband who understood every dark corner of my soul.

"When Jeremy did moon over me it was only for show," I said, frowning. "He used me as an excuse to avoid marriage."

"Perhaps." Cécile shrugged. "But who would not enjoy a constant stream of attention from a gentleman so longed for by the rest of society, even if he is not nearly so handsome as your own husband?"

"Her own husband is Adonis," Margaret said. "Even Mr. Michaels admits as much."

"I do wish you would stop calling him *Mr. Michaels*, Margaret. You have been married for how many years now?" I asked. I leaned over to make it easier for the waiter to refill my glass with champagne.

"You have met him, Emily. Could you call him Horatio? It does not suit him in the least."

"No, it does not," I admitted. Margaret's husband, a dear, serious man, and a scholar of Latin, rarely left Oxford. He and his wife were a perfect match, leading a life full of raging intellectual arguments and the exchange of semiobscene Latin poetry.

"Mr. Michaels would be mortified by Miss Wells," Margaret said. "She is everything he despises about Britain."

"She is American, *ma chérie*," Cécile said.

"Precisely. I would not have dreamed of letting him accompany me here. I do think Miss Wells would have pushed him so far over the edge that he may well have been unable to speak coherently again in any language other than Latin. Perhaps that is why I object so vehemently to her. Her mere presence would destroy my husband's will to live."

"That is unfair. She is a lovely girl!" Cécile drained her glass and signaled for another refill.

"She is," I said. "Stunningly beautiful. Bright. Refined when necessary, but otherwise in possession of a passion for life my mother would find wholly unacceptable."

"Rather like you, Kallista." Cécile had always objected to my Christian name and chose instead to call me by the nickname bestowed upon me by my first husband. "Perhaps you are too similar to get along."

"That is such a cliché." I bunched up my napkin, frustrated, and flung it onto the table. "I object to Miss Wells not as an individual, but as a spouse for Jeremy. She is a flawless example of studied perfection. It is as if everything she does has been carefully designed to attract him. Heaven only knows what she is really like. We are not bound to find out until well after the wedding."

"I cannot agree with that, Emily," Margaret said. "I think we are seeing her true self, and unfortunately that true self is intolerable. She is not like Emily, Cécile. She is obnoxious and crass and—" She stopped and smiled too sweetly, looking over my shoulder. "So nice to see you, Miss Wells. Won't you join us for some champagne?"

"I can think of nothing I should better enjoy. Garçon, another chair for this table please!" Her voice as she called for the waiter grated on my nerves. It was an octave too low and a level too loud. Furthermore, she had a manner with staff that bothered me. She was in every way technically polite, but at the same time managed to convey that she thought herself superior to them. I did not like it. "You girls must call me Amity. Jeremy is so fond of you all that I feel as if you will be like my sisters, and sisters ought not address each other in formal terms."

"Were I your sister, Mademoiselle Wells, I should be most concerned about our parents," Cécile said. "I am very nearly of an age with them."

"Oh, Cécile, you are simply too very! I don't know how I ever lived before knowing you."

"One shudders at the thought." Cécile drained her glass. "I fear there is not enough champagne in Cannes."

"Perhaps that is why I have always preferred whisky. Please don't share that with my mother." Miss Wells bubbled with sultry laughter. "Margaret, I must tell you how I laughed at Jeremy's story of your false courtship. I cannot remember ever before being so amused."

"Yes." Margaret pressed her lips into a firm line.

Amity gulped down her glass of champagne. "I have come to inform you that we are all going for a stroll along La Croisette this evening before dinner. The light is so lovely as the sun starts to set. I have promised the gentlemen cigars for the occasion. I do hope you can tolerate them smoking."

"I would prefer to join them," Margaret said.

Miss Wells grinned. "My dear, you really are simply too very. I would smoke with you but promised my darling Jeremy that I would only do it when we are alone so that his friends aren't scandalized. I imagine your own divine husband wouldn't look kindly on the activity, would he, Emily? Although I suspect he is far more enlightened than his dignified exterior suggests. Still waters and all that. At any rate, we shall take a turn along the sea before we eat. The boys are off to the casino afterward for a party I've organized. I thought it would be nice for them to have some time away from us ladies. I don't like to stifle them. Ah! I see them now. Ta-ta, girls!" She stood up and excused herself, flitting across the street to the edge of the beach, where Jeremy and some of his friends were standing.

"I cannot put my finger on what it is, precisely, that I don't like about her," I said, "but there is something that rings decidedly untrue. She is an extremely beautiful chameleon. She likes cigars when Margaret does, whisky when Jeremy fancies it."

"As I have already said, it is jealously." Cécile's smile resembled that of a cat. "And it is unbecoming in a lady."

Three hours later we gathered in front of the hotel, where Amity lined us up, two by two, like schoolchildren. "I want us all to get to know each other better," she said. "There's no fun in everyone sticking with their ordinary partners, so I have decided to mix us all up. Jeremy, darling, you walk with Christabel. Emily, you're to be with Jack." She continued on, and I wondered if Cécile's opinion of her high spirits and similarities to me would change after she endured this forced march on the arm of Amity's father, Cornelius Beauregard Wells. She had saved Colin for herself, saying that it was only fair the bride should be escorted by the most handsome gentleman, and flirted with him so shamelessly that his eyes danced with a mixture of mortification and amusement. Chauncey Neville, Jeremy's chum from his school days at Harrow, dutifully took the arm of Mrs. Wells, politely complimenting her on the rather extraordinary hat she was wearing, and as soon as Amity had finished pairing off the rest of the crowd, we set off along the pavement.

"Your brother has shocked us all," I said, leaning close to Jack as we strolled. "All these years he has sworn off marriage and then a handful of weeks in Egypt convinces him to abandon his principles."

"It shook me to my very core, Emily," Jack said. "Yet they were so very happy from the moment they met, I do not see how things could have ended any differently."

"I understand you made Miss Wells's acquaintance some time before Jeremy's arrival in Cairo." I shook my head. "It is difficult to imagine him agreeing to go to Cairo. I half suspect you dangled her in front of him as an enticement."

"I did, and I am not ashamed to admit it. She is such a wonderfully open girl. One gets to know her so quickly that before long one cannot imagine having ever not known her."

"You first met her in India, did you not?" I asked. He nodded. "Was it immediately apparent your brother would like her?"

"Without a doubt. They are so very alike. When I told her stories about him I was amazed by how readily she related to him."

"Yes, it is rather astonishing." I wondered if my tone shouted cynicism.

"Not so astonishing," he said. "They are both under a great deal of pressure to satisfy the desires of their families. You know how difficult that can be. I am pleased they have found each other and only hope they have a pack of sons as quickly as possible so that I am as far removed from the dukedom as possible."

"Jeremy does so wish you would return to England."

"And I do so wish I would be posted back to India. My brother and I have rarely wanted the same things for me." He flashed a bright smile. "Or for him, for that matter. Amity may indeed be the first."

"Then I am happy for him," I said. "He is deserving of every good thing, and if he is content that is what he has found in her, no one could be more delighted on his behalf."

Jack's grin widened, conspiracy in his eyes. "We both know he always wanted you, Emily. I may have only been six, but I saw him kiss you—"

"Don't be silly. We were children and any flirtations we may have shared in the past were mutually agreed upon performances to keep him from the bonds of matrimony for as long as possible. Now that he has found his heart's desire, he has no need for such games."

"Quite right. You were too good to him, you know. You may think him deserving of every good thing, but that can only be because he was far kinder to you during your childhood than he was to me. I think him a perfect beast."

"You two fought constantly. I remember it well."

"I recall your father taking him to task for bad behavior on more than one occasion," Jack said. "Perhaps we should warn Miss Wells. She may not be aware of just what she is taking on."

I smiled—warmly, I hope—but did not tell him I feared it was Jeremy, rather than Miss Wells, who was blissfully unaware of just what he was taking on.

We looped back along the promenade and returned to the hotel, dining before the gentlemen abandoned us for the casino. On their way out, they led us into the lounge, where Amity had organized coffee and sherry to be served to us ladies. Like the rest of the public rooms in the hotel, its walls were covered in a delicate porcelain-colored paint, trimmed with elegant gilt work. Shimmering Persian carpets softened the pale marble floors, and the Louis XIV furniture was upholstered in golden silk.

"I understand that some among us may prefer something other than sherry," Amity said, her perfect lips spread into a smile that lit up her face. "I have ordered port for you, Emily."

"You are very kind to have taken note of my wife's habits, Miss Wells," Colin said, standing behind my chair.

"My darling Jeremy insists that I take good care of her to make up for how abominably he treated her when they were small," Amity said, "and I make a point of always doing whatever he says."

"How did I get so lucky?" Jeremy beamed. If ever a man appeared truly happy it was he on that night. "Right, now, chaps, we must take our leave from these lovely ladies and console ourselves as best we can without them."

"I am certain you won't miss us for a moment," Amity said. "I have made arrangements with the management of the casino to ensure the establishment will cater to your every whim. Daddy, you must behave just a little, though. I cannot have Mother angry at me."

At this comment, Victor Fairchild, a tall, well-built man whose studious countenance belied a personality devoted to cricket rather than any academic pursuit, raised an eyebrow, and then leaned down to whisper something to Cécile. She whacked Mr. Fairchild's hand with her fan and shooed him away as the gentlemen departed. He skulked behind the others, but looked back twice as he crossed the hotel lobby. Cécile met his gaze both times.

"Really, Cécile," I said. "He is not yet forty and therefore does not meet your ironclad requirement for being interesting."

"Sometimes, *chérie*, a lady does not require interesting. There are other qualities that, on occasion, prove more important. I do believe that Monsieur Fairchild's devotion to cricket might prove to have some fascinating and unexpected benefits."

"If I understand you correctly, Cécile, you might want to take better notice of Jack," I said. "He ran the marathon in Athens in 1896, when the Olympics were reestablished."

"I shall take your suggestion under consideration," Cécile said, "although at the moment it is the patience cricket requires that intrigues me. Only consider what ramifications such a well-developed skill might have when applied in other situations."

"You are such a card, Mrs. du Lac." We had not spoken in a volume loud enough to be overheard, but Mrs. Wells must have been able to interpret some essential part of our exchange. "Nothing wrong with the young man that I can see."

"I am fortunate that my fiancé's friends have proven so delightful," Amity said, "although I fear the same could not be said about all of their wives. Are you girls acquainted with Mrs. Harrop? I find her a terrible bore and do not comprehend how her husband can tolerate her. I have met her only briefly, but it was long enough to know that I didn't want her here in Cannes with us."

"But Mr. Harrop is here. I assumed his wife was indisposed," Margaret said. "You refused to let her come?"

"Categorically," Amity replied. "Do not think me cruel. She had as little interest in being here as I had in hosting her. You, Margaret, like me, are used to American directness. Society is all well and good, and many of its mores are admirable, but I will never play false with anyone. I did not cut her openly, nor would I. I shall never be anything short of civil to her. We are not fond of each other, so why should we be thrust together simply because our husbands are friends?"

"You have no doubt made both Mr. and Mrs. Harrop happy through your decision," I said. "They have never been what one could describe as close."

"Another unhappy forced marriage?" Mrs. Wells asked.

"Quite," I said. "Both families wanted it." Amity's words about Mrs. Harrop were harsh, but accurate, and I admired her unwillingness to hide her true feelings, while at the same time maintaining civility.

"I would never have allowed my Amity to enter into such an arrangement," Mrs. Wells said, her wide bosom swelling. "Savage, really."

Amity's eyes flashed as her mother spoke, but she regained her composure with such speed I was unsure as to what I had seen. Our libations arrived and once they had been consumed, we all retired to our rooms. Colin returned from the casino only a little over an hour later. Gambling had never held much appeal to him, particularly, he told me, when there were far greater temptations at his disposal.

"Tedious evening, truth be told." He unknotted his white tie and pulled it free from his collar before draping it over the back of a chair and turning his attention to the studs on his shirt. "I am far happier here with you."

We both were, until the knock on our door came, informing us that death had interfered with everything.

# Amity
## Seven months earlier

Amity took to tiger hunting like a young Indian prince for whom it was a required right of passage. Anyone would think she had been born for it. She adapted quickly to riding on elephants, and, despite the obvious discomforts of camping in the wild, adored every minute of the experience. On the third morning, she killed a tiger. That afternoon, her father took out four.

"When is it enough?" Christabel asked, looking morosely at the animals' sad corpses. "Surely we do not need more than this."

"Does it trouble you?" Jack asked.

"Very much so, I'm afraid." Her voice trembled and broke. "I thrilled at seeing the noble beasts moving through the grass. It was at once terrifying and delightful. But the moment the first fell—do forgive me, Amity, I know it was a triumph for you—I was sickened. I refused to take your father's photograph with his trophies and he is most put out."

"You are a dear, sweet thing," Amity said, "and I shall tell Daddy that we are done here. I don't want you tormented for even a single minute more."

"You are so kind to me," Christabel said.

"Your friendship makes up for all the years I spent with nothing but brothers in the house."

"How many brothers?" Jack asked.

"Five, each of them perfectly savage. Augustus, the youngest, is perhaps the least awful of them, but I despise them all," Amity said. "Fortunately Daddy does, too. He fears for his business when he's gone. I think that is part of the reason he wants to see me well settled. He knows my brothers will do nothing but squander everything they have. What about your brother, Jack? Is he a savage?"

Jack laughed. "A savage? Not quite. Your father would, no doubt, object to his reluctance to do any sort of useful work, but in his case, that would only mean managing the estate, and my mother handles that. My father quite relied on her. I have never been able to determine whether Jeremy refuses to assist her because he wants to lead a meaningless life or if it is all just a scheme to let her continue. She and my father adored each other, you see, and his death left her heartbroken. If she were no longer needed on the estate, I am not sure what she would have to live for."

"Her sons, of course," Christabel said.

"No, she never much cared for either of us. She was too engrossed in everything to do with Father. At any rate, we were away at school most of the time. After that, I dedicated myself to the pursuit of adventure, something to which my mother never objected. It did not trouble her in the least when I set off to re-create the travels of Marco Polo, even when I told her I might be gone for several years."

"Did you succeed?" Amity asked.

"No, alas," Jack said. "We made it from Venice to Constantinople and then to Jerusalem, where, after visiting the Church of the Holy Sepulchre, my compatriots decided they wanted to return to Europe. They'd had enough of the East, they said, and not even Polo's descriptions of the palace at Xanadu could induce them to continue on. The only encouragement I got was from my mother, who told me in every brief letter she wrote not to worry that she was suffering from my absence."

"Is she kinder to your brother?" Christabel asked.

"Not in the least. She scolds him constantly."

"Yet despite this, your brother does all he can to ensure her comfort. Is it possible that he, whom you have previously mentioned only occasionally, but always in terms that made me believe him to be something of a dissolute cad, might, in fact, be of noble character?" Amity asked.

"There is a slim possibility," Jack said. "Nobility is in his blood, after all."

"Oh, you British and your aristocracy." Amity sighed. "I suppose it does make things awfully nice so long as you're the one inheriting. No need to work or be useful."

"That does not spare one from feeling the pressure to maintain the estate and take care of one's tenants," Jack said. "I, fortunately, need not worry about either. I much prefer the army."

"And India?" Christabel asked.

"Yes, although I am afraid I shan't be here much longer. I am being posted to Egypt next month."

"Egypt? Is this an attempt to follow us when we leave India?" Amity asked.

"You are both going to Egypt?" Jack asked. "I thought your mother was taking you back to England, Christabel?"

"Amity has persuaded me to stay with her."

"It was difficult," Amity said, "but Daddy saw to her. He called on her five times every single day until she relented. He wants me to be happy, and he knows I can't be if I don't have my Christabel with me while I explore the land of the pharaohs."

"This is outstanding news!" Amity noticed a slight color rising in Jack's cheeks as he spoke. "I shall be in Cairo before you, and will be at the station to welcome you upon your arrival. In the meantime, there is still more to be seen in India. Come, now, let us draw up a list of every place we must visit before we all depart the subcontinent. There is much to be done."

# 3

Mrs. Wells had arranged for us all to breakfast together each morning of our stay in a private section of the hotel's elegant dining room. Colin had gone down early, knowing that someone would have to inform the others of Mr. Neville's death. I followed him as soon as possible, wanting to be on hand to offer whatever help I could. For more than three-quarters of an hour, we were alone. The row of French doors that led to the terrace stood open, letting in a balmy breeze from outside. The air smelled of lavender, not surprising given the profusion of its flowers found in the vases on each table, and the sun warmed the room to a pleasant temperature.

"It seems the evening's festivities took a toll on the group as a whole," I said, looking at the sumptuous buffet Mrs. Wells had caused to be laid down for us and finding I had no stomach for food. All I could think about was the glassy look of poor Mr. Neville's eyes. "How long do you think they will all sleep?"

"Quite late, I imagine," Colin said. "A great deal of champagne had been consumed and Wells had already lost five thousand francs at baccarat when I left. I wonder how his wife took that?"

"I wonder if she knows?"

"Do you really think she allows him to hide anything from her?" Colin asked.

"A fair point." I sighed. "Amity has been up early every day that I can remember. She told me she likes to walk in the morning. Perhaps she is already out and we missed her." It was Margaret and Cécile who appeared first, however, both in high spirits that evaporated the instant we told them of the tragedy.

"How terribly sad," Margaret said. "I had not known Mr. Neville well before we came to Cannes, but I have grown rather fond of him over these past few days. He had such a calming effect on everyone around him."

"His kindness was extraordinary," Cécile said. "He took great care to make sure we all were comfortable and well looked after. He even offered to go to Paris to collect Caesar and Brutus for me when I mentioned feeling their absence keenly." Cécile adored her two small dogs, and rarely traveled without them. On this occasion, Brutus had been somewhat under the weather, and she felt it best to leave them at home. "A lovely man. What caused his death?"

"The doctor suspects overindulgence," Colin said.

"Overindulgence?" I scowled. "Does that not seem odd? Mr. Neville was a hearty young man, full of vigor and health. Are we to believe one night of excessive carousing put him under?"

"What are you suggesting, Emily?" Colin asked.

"That someone murdered him, of course," Margaret said, nodding with such violence I worried that her hair might come undone. "Capital idea, Emily. I quite agree."

"This is a very serious accusation," Colin said. "We must not make light of it."

"Apologies, Colin. I let my imagination get away from me," Margaret said. "It was wholly inappropriate."

"We are all on edge after this news," I said. "And it will behoove us to remember that reactions to grief range from tears to laughter and everything in between. Will there be an autopsy?"

"I imagine so," Colin said, peering at me through narrowed eyes.

"I assume we are to conclude that your own reaction to grief is to search for explanations?"

"Doing something productive will keep me from going mad," I replied. "I remember seeing a bottle of whisky next to the bed where Mr. Neville fell."

"Yes. There was a glass on the floor near his outstretched hand," Colin said. "A trickle of liquid suggested he was drinking before he lost consciousness."

"They must surely suspect foul play in such a case," I said. "Why else would a gentleman teeter over mid-drink?"

"It can happen, Emily," Colin said. "I have seen it, although it does not generally end in death. Perhaps we should hope for a straight-forward verdict from the coroner, given that Neville was found in Bainbridge's room. Accusations of foul play would not be pleasant for your friend."

"You cannot possibly be suggesting that anyone would believe Bainbridge would cut down one of his dearest friends?" Cécile said. "It is unthinkable."

"I quite agree," Colin said, "but murder investigations have a way of refusing to stay within the bounds of propriety. No one would be beyond suspicion if this were ruled a homicide."

Amity and her parents approached us, her sickly-looking brother trailing behind them. "Poor Augustus is exhausted, which makes me wonder just what you all were up to last night," she said. "I expect you, Colin, to look after him specially and make sure he enjoys himself today."

My husband did not reply to this inane command, and the young Mr. Wells made only the barest replies to our greetings before seating himself at a table and asking for breakfast. Evidently he was too fatigued to bother to go to the buffet himself. I knew Amity had other brothers—several, though I could not remember the precise number—and I wondered why none of the rest had come to celebrate her engagement. Mrs. Wells had made a multitude of comments about business and how time-consuming it was, but the expression on her spouse's face at the time caused me to believe there was some other reason they had stayed away. Colin pulled aside Amity's father and spoke to him sotto voce. Mr. Wells blanched at the hideous news and called for his wife. After an earnest-looking discussion, Mrs. Wells shouted—yes, shouted—for Amity, who was now sitting next to her brother.

"Mother, darling, can't you see I'm trying to look after poor Augustus?"

"You must come at once, child. Emily—help me."

"Enjoy your ability to summon me while you can, Mother. Soon I shall be a married woman and you will not be able to order me around any longer. I—" She stopped when she saw Jeremy walking toward her, still in evening kit. "Darling! You look a wreck."

"Long night, my dear. I have only just arrived, as you can see."

"Whatever happened to you?" Amity asked, crossing to him and offering him her hand to kiss.

"It is a rather complicated story, I am afraid. I—"

"Bainbridge, I need to speak with you at once," Colin said. "Will you come outside?"

"Now, Colin, don't you go taking my fiancé away from me in what I promise you will be a vain attempt to keep him from having to explain his appearance."

"I assure you, Miss Wells, I mean nothing of the sort." He gave her a neat bow before placing a firm hand on Jeremy's shoulder and steering him out onto the terrace through the French doors at the front of the dining room. Before they crossed the threshold, he turned back to me. "Emily, will you see to things?" He nodded subtly in Amity's direction.

The Wells parents were now standing in a corner, facing away from the group, apparently having given up on delivering the unhappy news to their daughter. I marched over to her. "A word, Amity?"

"After breakfast, Emily. Why are you being so uncivilized?"

"It cannot wait, I'm afraid."

"If you know something about what Jeremy did last night, I have no desire to hear it. So far as I am concerned, there are some things a gentleman should be allowed to keep private."

I wrenched her up from her seat and dragged her away from the table. "I have no interest in what Jeremy may or may not have done on any evening. This concerns another matter entirely. Mr. Neville was found dead last night—in your fiancé's suite. Colin is giving Jeremy the news now."

"In Jeremy's room? How is this possible?" Amity's eyes swam with tears. "Was he ill?"

"I do not at present know the cause of death."

"How can I help?" She dabbed at her eyes with a dainty lace handkerchief and stood up straight, her shoulders back. "We must arrange for new rooms for Jeremy at once, of course, but my father would be better suited to that task than I. Has anyone notified the family?"

"So far as I know he did not have any," I said. "Perhaps you could speak to Jeremy about how best to proceed. He will need you, Amity."

"What a grim task," Amity said. Colin returned inside and motioned to her. She went straight to her fiancé.

"Have you seen Mr. Fairchild yet?" I asked Colin.

"Yes, I stopped at his room on my way down. He took it very badly."

"As have we all," I said.

News of the death was quickly making the rounds through the hotel guests, as evident from the curious stares pointed in our direction from every corner of the dining room, and this was unsettling to our group. To all, that is, except Augustus Wells, who showed not the slightest concern at the turn of events. He had plowed through his breakfast and was now reading the newspaper with utter disregard for everything going on around him. I was about to admonish him when I caught a glimpse of two extremely serious-looking men striding through the lobby. Assuming (correctly) that they were from the coroner's office, I took the opportunity to slip away and hailed the men just after they had exited the hotel.

"You are here to investigate Mr. Neville's death?" I asked in French, standing beneath the columned porte cochère, where liveried porters bustled by with the luggage they had removed from carriages.

"You are French?" the taller of the men asked.

"No, English."

"But with a very good accent, madame," he said. "We are dealing with the matter of Monsieur Neville's death. If you were acquainted with the young man, I convey my deepest condolences."

"Thank you. We are all most distressed. My husband tells me the hotel doctor suspects overindulgence?"

"I am afraid it was nothing of the sort, madame. It was obvious to us at once that the man died after consuming poison. You must understand that hotel doctors always prefer to find something that will not raise any sort of scandal."

"Of course. Do you know what sort of poison?"

"Not yet, madame, but you should not trouble yourself with such unsettling details. Again, my deepest condolences to the duke and the rest of your party." He tipped his hat, muttered something to his companion, and walked away.

"Poison?" Mrs. Wells clutched at her neck and rose from her dining chair, sending her empty breakfast plate clattering to the floor, from whence it was collected by the same waiter who had earlier fetched food from the buffet for Augustus.

"Do try to keep your voice down, Mrs. Wells," Colin said.

"What a terrible thing," she said. "To have sunk so low as to believe there is no hope to be found except in death."

"It is tragic indeed," Colin said. "Bainbridge tells me Neville's only family is an older brother who moved to Australia more than a decade ago. They did not keep in touch. We think it would be best for the funeral and burial to be held here."

"Is there no one else we should contact?" Mr. Wells asked.

"I am afraid not. Neville's closest friends are Bainbridge and Fairchild, and they are both already here. He was not the sort of man who would want a fuss made over him."

"I shall ask the concierge to assist with the details," Mr. Wells said. "Am I correct in assuming that we should like the service to take place as soon as the body is released?"

"Yes," Colin said. "That would be best."

"Em, darling, may I have a word?" Jeremy came up behind me and spoke quietly, his face grey and his hands shaking. He had left Amity with Margaret and Cécile at another table, away from the others in our group's section of the dining room. They appeared to be chatting amicably, but I could read the tension on my friends' faces.

"Of course." I followed him to an alcove in the main lobby. "I am so very sorry, Jeremy—"

"Do you know what they are saying about his death? What they think happened? Suicide? I don't believe it for a second, Em."

"Why not?"

"Neville wasn't the despondent sort. Quite the contrary. Yes, he was quiet, but not in a depressed sort of way. I should have described him as the most perfectly content man of my acquaintance. This is not like him."

"What are you suggesting?"

"I should have noticed there was something wrong and stopped him."

"Stopped him? Jeremy, how could you have known what he was contemplating? You said yourself he wasn't despondent."

"He went to my rooms for a reason. He may have wanted to discuss something of critical importance, and when he didn't find me . . ."

"This is not your fault, Jeremy." I took his hands in mine.

"I left him alone to die."

"You did not know he was there."

"When I came in last night and was about to ask for my key at the desk, I stopped, because I saw that there was only one hanging on the hook beneath my room number. There ought to have been two, as I am not sharing the room. To be quite frank with you, I worried that Amity had the other and was waiting for me."

"Waiting for you? In your rooms?"

"Do not take that tone with me, Em," he said, his eyes darting as he watched a pack of louder-than-usual guests crossing the lobby. "It is most unbecoming. For a moment I had the misfortune of feeling as if I were attempting to confide in your mother."

"But waiting in your rooms? I am all astonishment, Jeremy."

"The thing is, Em, so was I," he said. "I never would have entertained such a notion if I hadn't had quite so much to drink. Instead of going upstairs, I went back out. That is why I only returned this morning. Of course, it turned out Neville had requested a key the previous night, and the desk clerk told me they had given it to him as I had told the staff on two occasions earlier in the week that he might have access to my room whenever he wanted. Had I been in a more lucid frame of mind, I would have assumed it was he, not Amity, who had the key, and I would have gone straight to my room, and then I could have—I might have—"

"Jeremy." I gently placed my hand on his cheek. "No matter what you did or did not do last night, you are not responsible for Mr. Neville's actions."

"I cannot tell Amity any of this. What would she think?"

"She would not blame you. She might, however, wonder where you slept," I said. He looked at the floor. "Where did you sleep?"

"I believe I am entitled to some secrets, am I not?"

I hardly knew how to respond. My mind reeled, but I managed

(I believe) to maintain my composure. "What made you think Amity would have gone to your rooms?"

"Nothing specific, Em, and in hindsight the idea seems preposterous in the extreme. You won't tell her, will you? She would despise me on two counts: first, for having entertained the notion that she would have such low morals, and second, for not having saved my friend."

"I can agree with you, but only on the first count. Really, Jeremy, to think such a thing! No unmarried lady, no matter how modern she may be, would ever wait unaccompanied in a gentleman's hotel room."

"I do recall a time in Vienna when you insisted I leave you alone in Hargreaves's rooms to wait for him, and that was before you were married."

"That was entirely different. To begin with, his rooms were not in a hotel." I could feel heat rising in my face. "In the midst of a murder investigation it is sometimes necessary to strain the bonds of propriety. Oh, never mind. I shall not torment you with it any further. The loss of Mr. Neville is a terrible blow, and I am here, as your friend, to offer any comfort that I can. Anything you need, you have only to ask."

"Thank you, Em. I never could do without you."

Mr. Neville's funeral was a depressing affair. Out of the fifty guests Mr. and Mrs. Wells had hosted in Cannes, only a handful of us stayed on to attend the service, which was held at the Eglise Saint-Georges, built in honor of Queen Victoria's son, Leopold, the Duke of Albany, who had died in Cannes in 1884. The rest of the group departed, many of them making no attempt to hide the fact that they were merely decamping to Nice, where, they believed, the society would not be so grim. Mr. Neville's shyness had kept many of the party from getting to know him, and they had felt nothing but discomfort at the news of his death. After the burial, Mrs. Wells hosted a subdued tea, where we all told stories about the deceased. No one there could doubt how deeply Mr. Neville's loss had affected his friends or have come away without admiring the man even more than they previously had.

"I hate funerals," Colin said later that afternoon, as we walked along La Croisette, doing our best to ignore a misty rain that seemed all too appropriate for the day. "Do remember, when the time comes, what I have told you in the past about pyres, will you?" He gripped my arm tighter and cleared his throat. "Bainbridge says he doesn't want to go back to England right away, and asks if we will stay on as well. I told him we would, of course. Mrs. Wells has abandoned all ideas of her party, although I can tell she mourns the loss of her fireworks more than that of Neville."

"To be fair, she hardly knew him, and although it is wickedly unjust, she blames him for taking away a piece of her daughter's happiness," I said. "Jeremy blames himself, you know."

"That is not unusual in cases such as this," Colin said. "None of us thought Neville was unsound of mind. I suspected nothing of the sort. If anything, he proved himself a steadying influence on Bainbridge time and time again."

"What happened that night at the casino? Do you remember anything that might have sent him careening over the edge?"

"I did not stay long, but while I was there it was the usual sort of thing. Conspicuous consumption of whisky and champagne, excellent cigars, a bit of gambling."

"Why did you leave so early?"

"I missed you." He squeezed my hand and we stopped walking. The benches lining La Croisette were too damp to sit on. I rested a gloved hand on the railing above the sandy beach as Colin leaned against it, carefully holding his umbrella so that the rain would not fall on me.

"I know you say that, and it is not that I doubt your veracity, but I do know you so very well, Colin. There is something more."

"Suffice it to say that I do not share all of the vices of my friends," he said.

"Meaning?" I raised an eyebrow and stared at him without blinking.

"Nothing that matters, Emily." He looked away, turning toward the sea.

"Pretty young things sent to entertain the lot of you?"

His body stiffened. "You should not discuss such things. It is unseemly."

"Perhaps, but it is also correct."

"You may think whatever you like." He tilted his hat back on his head.

"Amity mentioned to me that her father had brought dancers down from Paris."

"He told her that?" The umbrella swayed, but he steadied it at once.

"Perish the thought. She overheard him speaking to Jeremy about it and she found it riotously amusing."

"She did?" His dark eyes widened.

"I am not certain she understands that such women are, on occasion, called upon to do more than dance."

"Emily!"

"Just how naïve do you think I am?"

"Far more naïve than you are, apparently. It was nothing like that, I assure you. They were strictly there to dance."

"Yet you left?" I asked.

"I assumed that staying on would have offended your delicate sensibilities. Had you seen the dancers in question, I am certain you would agree."

I sighed. "I am not so judgmental, you know. I have never objected to you—"

"Emily!"

"It is just that Amity is so very . . . modern, I suppose one could say. She has made a concerted effort to persuade Jeremy that he will not have to abandon any of his bachelor ways after their wedding. I am half-convinced it is how she managed to catch him. I do hope you are not left regretting your own choice of wife. I never thought of myself as boring and conventional until now."

Colin laughed. "My dear, dear girl, you are anything but boring and conventional, and I must correct your mistakes. First, allowing one's husband to occasionally be entertained by cabaret dancers is hardly modern. In Paris, wives accompany their husbands to the Moulin Rouge. I have just never found the experience particularly enticing."

"You are quite certain?"

"Quite. Second, neither you nor Miss Wells has any sort of understanding of what, exactly, bachelors do. I am sure you would both be rather disappointed should you ever find out. The halls of debauchery are not nearly so wild as you expect. Do you really believe that most gentlemen . . ." He sighed. "How is it that I am discussing this with my wife?"

"How is it that you would be discussing it with anyone else?" I gave him a quick kiss, noticing that a very slight hint of color had crept onto his handsome visage. "I shall stop mortifying you, however, and will accept your assertion that you do not view the married state as one requiring enormous sacrifice."

"Quite the opposite, I would say." His eyes darkened with passion. "Perhaps we should retire—"

"I do hope, my dear, that you meant 'return,' not 'retire,' and, if so, you are quite right. We ought to return to the subject at hand." His countenance again colored ever so slightly as I spoke, and I could feel my own cheeks blushing in reply. I could not deny the appeal of retiring in the manner to which I knew he referred. "Jeremy left the casino early as well—although not so early as you. Do you know where he went?"

"It is of little consequence, Emily. The Prince of Wales has his yacht docked in Cannes. I should not be surprised if he joined the royal party."

"In the middle of the night?" I asked. He looked away from me.

"I know how close you are to Bainbridge, but you do not always understand him so well as you think."

"You are wrong on that point. Jeremy makes a show of profligacy, but when have you ever known him to actually follow through on something really outrageous? Does not my position on this point concur with what you were only just telling me about gentlemen and bachelors and marriage?"

"I think it would be best if we abandoned the topic altogether. I shall speak with Bainbridge and ascertain exactly what he was up to during the night. In the meantime, I must go see the Sûreté. They should have the autopsy results by now." He took me by the arm and steered me back toward the hotel before I could protest. His efforts would prove to be in vain eventually, as I had every intention of revisiting the subject later.

# Amity
# Six months earlier

How Jack managed to wrangle so much leave before being posted to Cairo was a mystery even to him. He half suspected Mr. Wells was behind it, although he could not determine how such a thing would be possible, even for the enterprising American. Not that he objected. Quite the contrary. He could not remember when he had enjoyed more pleasant company than that of Christabel and Amity. Some days he fancied himself in love with either or both of the girls, but he never could decide which he preferred, and he cringed at even making the comparison. Perhaps he could marry one of them and persuade his brother to take the other. After all, when one counted d'Artagnan, there had actually been four musketeers.

When he saw the amber light of the sunset reflected on Christabel's fair skin as they stood in the midst of Jaipur, the Pink City, her brow crinkled as she contemplated the best angle for a photograph, he was certain he should propose. Then, however, he noticed a deep longing in Amity's eyes as she stared across the reflecting pool at the Taj Majal, and he wondered how any gentleman could resist wanting to know everything about her. He adored them both, but the truth was, he had no reason to think either was in love with him, and perhaps that was just as well.

It was also just as well that he would soon be leaving India, for he could see that Mrs. Wells had grown tired of their endless excursions. She had come abroad with a purpose: to see her daughter well married. Jack knew she tolerated him only because he might eventually introduce Amity to his brother, the very eligible duke, and the more he considered the matter, the more he thought it a capital idea. Jeremy would gain an excellent, spirited wife. The dukedom (one hoped) would soon thereafter have a new heir. And he, Jack, would never again have to worry that he might be summoned permanently back to England. How could he finish exploring the Himalayas if he were forced by family obligation to live back home? He had begun a trek the previous year to see the great Peak XV—now called Everest after Sir George, who had identified it—but furious storms had prevented him reaching his goal. He was determined to set eyes on what the Great Trigonometrical Survey claimed to be the highest mountain on earth.

From that day on, he regaled the girls with stories of his brother, presenting him in the best possible light. As he told them, he realized that Amity was unequivocally the right girl for Jeremy. He need not edit his brother's history strategically, as he thought he might. Amity delighted in every scrape, every subterfuge, every debauch. She asked so many questions about him that Jack began to believe she was already falling for the duke.

During Jack's last week in India, they traveled to the Ajanta caves. Mrs. Wells had stayed behind. She had, she explained, seen the copies of their paintings displayed in the Crystal Palace in London before Amity had been born, and had no desire to make such a difficult trip to see the same thing again. Amity rolled her eyes, and complained that she ought to know the difference between a copy and an original, but her mother would not be persuaded, leaving Mr. Wells to organize and supervise the party. The journey was rough, along narrow roads and steep cliffs, but the destination was worth nearly any trouble. The caves were spectacular.

"I am a bit disappointed," Amity said, standing with Jack, inspecting the paintings by candlelight. "I had heard stories of tourist parties in this region being attacked by natives brandishing bows and arrows."

"You should have liked that?"

"Very much. I would have befriended them all and taken tea with them in their villages."

"You are an extraordinary lady, Miss Wells," Jack said.

"*Miss Wells?*" Amity crinkled her nose. "You are not going formal on me now, not after all this time, Jack."

"No, not really." He could hardly take his eyes off her beautiful face. "I am only teasing."

"I like it when you tease." She looked down, suddenly coy. "I am very pleased we will see you in Egypt."

For a moment, Jack wondered if maybe, just maybe, she was in love with him, instead of falling for the idea of his brother, and even though he knew her parents would never approve of the match, would forbid their marriage, he wished he could take her in his arms. Unable to think of anything suitable to say in reply, he took her hand and kissed it.

"Would you do something for me, Jack? Something I want desperately, but should never admit to anyone except you? Will you persuade your brother to visit you in Cairo?" She blushed slightly as she posed the question, and Jack thought she had never looked so beautiful. "I am told the society is second only to that in London, and there is nothing to do in England during the winter. Isn't that correct?"

Jack felt as if she had struck him and splintered his heart, but he recovered without hesitation. "It is indeed. Everyone retreats to country estates."

"Damp, horrible estates. Or so I am told." She took him by the shoulders and shook him playfully. "I am American, Jack. I am accustomed to central heating."

"I guarantee you would have not the slightest use for it in Cairo, Amity. And I will do my best to get my brother over just as soon as I can."

Her smile could have charmed anyone.

# 4

I did not accompany my husband to collect the autopsy results from the Sûreté. Experience had taught me that the police, no matter what the country, view ladies as nothing more than an encumbrance to any sort of investigation. Not that I am suggesting this was an investigation rather than a desperate search for something that might help us understand Mr. Neville's actions. Not yet, at least.

Cécile, Margaret, and I had retreated to the wide balcony of my suite to await Colin's return, knowing that any information he had to share would be better disseminated in private. The view our location afforded was magnificent. Palm trees lined La Croisette below us, their silvery green fronds dancing with every breeze that came off the Mediterranean while sunlight shimmered on the water, and the shades of blue, from cerulean to azure, were too numerous to count.

Cécile, who had ordered a salad of exotic fruits to be sent up to us, was searching through it with a fork and removing only chunks of mango, which she placed on a plate in front of herself. "You may rhapsodize about our natural surroundings as much as you like, Kallista, but to my mind the more interesting view is directly below us on the terrace. Look at the hat Madame Wells is wearing. What can she mean by owning such a thing, let alone displaying it in public? I count at least two mounted birds, and I have not the proper angle to make a thorough study of the odious object. I thought the fashion for such things had fallen out of favor."

"I like Birdie, even if she does allow her nickname to influence her fashion choices," Margaret said, popping a chunk of pineapple into her mouth and looking thoughtful as she chewed. "She did let Amity traipse all over India with very little regard to propriety. Would your mother have let you hunt tigers, Emily?"

"Never," I said. "I shouldn't have wanted to, however."

"My mother would have refused me India altogether." Margaret frowned. "I do despise her."

"Yet she let you have Oxford," Cécile said. "A fair enough trade for a make-believe broken heart, *oui*?"

"Yes, yes," Margaret said. "But it doesn't seem fair that I have the least noxious mother of all of us. Except perhaps you, Cécile. We never hear about your mother."

"She is no longer with us. If she were, you would find her deeply disappointing."

Margaret sighed. "Cigarette?" She held out an elaborately engraved golden case.

"I would prefer a cigar," I said.

"Ask and ye shall receive." Margaret produced three from her reticule. "I believe one ought to be prepared for every situation." Cécile begged off hers, but Margaret and I indulged, dissolving into laughter as Margaret tried—with a spectacular lack of success—to teach me how to blow rings with the smoke. She had attempted to do this countless times since we had first met, but I had never shown even the slightest sign of having the skills necessary to master the trick.

"You have, I believe, tormented Monsieur Hargreaves enough, *mes amies*," Cécile said. "He has been leaning against the door for some time now, tolerating this exhibition. I cannot tell if he is amused or suffering from acute despair."

"It is amusement, Cécile, I assure you," Colin said, lowering himself into a wrought-iron chair. "We have little enough of it in our current circumstances, so I would not ask them to restrain themselves."

"You have the autopsy results?" I asked.

"Yes. Neville died from strychnine poisoning." Colin's voice, low and rough, reflected the somber look on his face.

"Strychnine? I do not think that would be my first choice for suicide," I said. "Is it not an extremely unpleasant death?"

"It is," Colin said. "Convulsions and asphyxiation."

"Mr. Neville may have used it only because it was all he could find," Margaret said. "He also may not have had any knowledge of what sort of death it would bring."

"*Oui*, Margaret. I imagine he cared more about the end result than the process of getting there."

"Where does one find strychnine in Cannes?" Margaret asked.

"I am afraid it does not matter now," Colin said. "He had dosed the entire bottle. There can be no doubt that he meant to die."

"The entire bottle?" I asked, feeling my eyebrows knit together. "That strikes me as odd. Wouldn't he have put the poison in his glass—in whatever amount he felt necessary—and then poured in enough whisky to make the deadly concoction tolerable?"

"What difference does it make?" Margaret asked.

"What if Jeremy had returned, found the body, and poured himself a drink to steady his nerves in the face of seeing his friend in such a state?" I asked. "He would be dead as well. I do not think Mr. Neville would have been so careless."

"I do not think Neville would have given the possibility any thought, Emily," Colin said. "He did not so much as leave a note. He may have done this in a fit of despair, during which his mind was too clouded to consider anything other than his own death."

I stood up and started to pace. "Now that I think of it, I cannot remember ever seeing Mr. Neville take whisky. Can you, Colin?" I asked. "When we first arrived in Cannes, Mrs. Wells hosted us all for dinner. There were drinks before, and most of us had champagne—do you recall?—appropriate to celebrate an engagement. Jeremy insisted on whisky though, as he is wont to do, and you joined him."

"Yes, I did," Colin said.

"Mr. Fairchild did the same. Jack was content with champagne until his brother cajoled him into switching over, but Jeremy was unable to convince Mr. Neville. I remember it quite well."

"Not everyone wants whisky before dinner, Emily," Colin said.

"Mr. Neville stated that he would prefer rum, and Jack goaded him about it, saying it was only fit for lowly sailors."

"I do remember this, Kallista," Cécile said, nodding. "Monsieur Neville insisted that this was not the case, and that he had enjoyed it greatly when he visited the West Indies some years back."

"And he went on to say that he had never much cared for whisky, finding brandy far superior. Jeremy trounced him soundly over holding such a position," I said. "Is it reasonable to believe that a gentleman, bent on ending his own life, would choose as his final drink a libation he has admitted to not liking?"

"Suicides are not rational, Emily," Colin said. "Neville was most likely intoxicated when he returned from the casino. We do not know why he had sunk so low, but for whatever reason, he chose that moment to end his life. I doubt very much that a man who did not care to leave any sort of note of explanation gave much consideration to the mixer for his poison. He drank whisky because there was nothing else in Bainbridge's room."

"Why didn't he go to his own room?" I asked.

"I haven't the slightest idea. We have no way of knowing," Colin said. "We can only know the conclusion, and it is a tragic and unsatisfactory one."

"We always want there to be more, don't we?" Margaret asked, passing Colin the cigar Cécile had rejected. "You are right, of course. None of us can be satisfied by what happened, and I think we must accept that if one is in a state of mind that allows for suicide, one is by definition incapable of rational action."

"I cannot agree with this, Margaret," Cécile said. "There are many elaborate suicides, where the victim—or should I say perpetrator?—goes to great lengths to explain his actions."

"But not always," Colin said. "In this case, Neville may have acted rashly and with very little planning."

"I want to know more about what happened at the casino. What catalyzed this in him?" I asked. Colin put his hand over mine.

"My dear, sometimes we must accept that we cannot know everything. Uncovering every detail will not bring back Neville."

"It might reveal this to be something other than suicide," I said. "I will never believe that he would have poisoned the entire bottle. Not in Jeremy's room."

"It was a bloody waste of life, Emily," Colin said, standing and crossing his arms. "Accept it as that and nothing more."

"I fear your husband is right, Kallista. There is nothing further for us to do here. Seeking more information can do little but increase the pain Monsieur Neville's friends are already feeling. They miss him keenly and feel as if they let down a man who was always there when they needed support. To ask questions now—do you not think this would only cause Bainbridge to blame himself all the more?"

"Quite right, Cécile," Margaret said. "He is already miserable enough. He does not need his friends doing anything that would make him feel worse."

How could I object to such a sentiment?

# Amity
## Five months earlier

When at last the day came to leave India, Amity made a careful study of her every emotion, but could not identify so much as an ounce of regret or sadness. This came as a surprise, for she adored the subcontinent with a passion she had never before felt for a place. Egypt beckoned her, not so much the pyramids or the history or the sweeping desert, but because it brought with it the possibility of meeting the Duke of Bainbridge. Jeremy. Her lips curled into a smile whenever she thought of his name, and if she admitted this response to be foolish, which it was, given that she had not yet met the gentleman, she did not care. She knew, without question, she stood on the precipice of a great change in her life, a change that, at last, would bring her happiness.

No detail of the journey troubled her: stormy seas; dirty, hot train compartments; carriages traversing rough, dusty roads. None of these mattered. They were all leading her to joy. So long, that is, as she could convince Jack to lure his brother to Cairo.

# 5

Many visitors to Cannes, coming to escape the bleak English weather, take extended drives in the countryside every afternoon, rhapsodizing over the trees heavy with lemons and oranges, the scent of rosemary in the air, and the sweeping views of the Mediterranean afforded by the winding roads that climb the hills along the coast. Mrs. Wells had arranged many such excursions for us, but after Mr. Neville's death, none of us had the heart for them. We could not, however, remain holed up in the hotel, morose and despondent forever. To do so would have been decidedly un-English. Furthermore, Jeremy and Mr. Fairchild needed to have some relief from their state of melancholy. Mr. Fairchild had become so bleak, he had not even attempted to discuss cricket with anyone in days, and while I welcomed the absence of such conversation, I knew it signaled deep pain. In an effort to cheer them up, Amity organized an expedition. We were to walk all the way along La Croisette until we reached Le Suquet, the medieval part of Cannes, where we would turn away from the sea and meander up the steep, narrow streets that led to Notre Dame de l'Espérance, a church whose construction was begun in the twelfth century, and the remaining bits of the castle once occupied by the Lérins monks.

Amity's parents, along with Cécile, stayed behind. Cécile insisted she would find no solace in the adventure, and much preferred a quiet afternoon on the terrace. "The south," she had said, "is meant for re-laxation, not for an amateur Cook's tour." Augustus was nowhere to be found, so we set off without him, Jeremy and Amity leading the way. Jack was carrying Christabel's bulky camera for her, and she accepted the offer of his arm with a blush that betrayed her feelings for him. I wondered if before long we would be celebrating a second engage-ment. Margaret and Colin were arguing about the relative merits of Romanesque and Gothic architecture, so I walked with Mr. Fairchild.

Mr. Fairchild, the eldest son of a well-to-do banker, had met Jer-emy and Chauncey Neville at Harrow, where he had started two years later than most of the other boys, and, hence, was something of an odd man out. Mr. Neville, sensitive to anyone who felt out of place, quietly took him under his wing, and soon he was fast friends with the entire set, as well as the best batsman at Harrow. When it was time for university, Mr. Fairchild and Jeremy went up to Oxford to-gether, while Chauncey made his way to St. Andrew's. Their Oxford years sealed their brotherhood, and it was Mr. Fairchild who was to stand with Jeremy at his wedding.

I did not know any of Jeremy's school chums well. I had met them all at various times, when they had come home with their friend be-tween terms, but schoolboys have little use for girls younger than themselves, and by the time I was out in society and might have proved interesting, they had long since finished university. Mr. Fairchild had taken Mr. Neville's death with a quiet acceptance, but I could tell he had been profoundly affected by the loss. While Jeremy was wont to bury his emotions with an outward show of strength and humor, Mr. Fairchild's sensitivity was not so easily hidden. I had come upon him twice in the past days, staring at the ocean from the pier across from the hotel, his eyes misty. Naturally, he bucked up as soon as he saw me, but I could tell the effort took a toll on his spirit.

We set off along La Croisette, the wind stronger next to the water than it had felt directly outside the hotel, but the bright sun warmed the air, and we could not have asked for a more beautiful day. The weather changed with astonishing frequency, from hot, to perfect, to chilly, sometimes in the space of a single hour, but that only added to the charms of Cannes. While there, one never had to accept for the long term the monotony of that singular grey that plagues the skies of England. Even when it rained, the wind would soon blow away the clouds to reveal the cerulean sky.

"Amity is quite a force of nature, isn't she?" Mr. Fairchild asked as he escorted me along the pavement. "Just the sort of girl for Bainbridge. Until I met her, I never thought he would voluntarily agree to matrimony."

"He was quite set against it," I said.

"Yet now he is on the verge of being happily settled. She is a capital girl. I am immensely fond of her." He coughed. "Do you mind if I smoke?"

"Not at all," I replied. "Everyone is immensely fond of Amity. She is possessed of the sort of exuberance for life to which no one can object."

"No gentlemen, at least. I think she is less successful among the ladies."

"Her parents give her a wider berth than that to which we are accustomed in England," I said. "I believe we all envy her that."

"You are discretion itself, Lady Emily," Mr. Fairchild said. "Do not think me unaware of her . . . shortcomings, shall we say? I aim to be congenial and polite in most situations, a position that does not always afford one the pleasure of candor."

"You are not fond of her, despite your statement to the contrary?" I raised an eyebrow.

"I would not go so far as that. It is simply that—" He blew a silver stream of smoke toward the sky. "I ought not to be so uncharitable."

"I do not like to think of myself as relishing gossip, but I suspect you and I are closer on this subject than I would have anticipated."

"Amity acts more like a schoolmate than a fiancée," Mr. Fairchild said, taking a deep drag on his cigarette before looping my arm through his and starting to walk again. It seemed as if the guests of every hotel in Cannes had poured out onto La Croisette, eager to take advantage of the day. We stepped aside to avoid slamming into a small boy who was skillfully rolling a hoop along the pavement while a smaller girl chased after him. "She is the only lady I have ever met who asked if I would teach her how to bowl a cricket ball. Can you imagine? Christabel nearly fainted when she heard her friend ask, and told me in no uncertain terms that she could think of nothing more tedious than my favorite game." He smiled. "A point of view that does not trouble me in the least. Once Amity realized Bainbridge has no interest in the sport, she told me she no longer needed to learn. I half expected her to come with us to the casino that awful night, and that she would drink all of us under the table."

"Come now, Mr. Fairchild, you cannot think her capable of such a thing!"

"It is beneath me to say it, but I implore you not to judge me. I have always felt a bit protective of Bainbridge. There is so much bluster to him, with all his talk of being useless and vapid and bent on nothing but debauchery. Beneath all that, I think he is not so corrupt as he would like us to believe."

"I could not agree more."

"If only you had married him!" He finished his cigarette and flicked away the butt.

"That, Mr. Fairchild, would have been a disaster."

"Forgive me. I speak out of turn. I am a great admirer of your husband. He is a gentleman worthy of you. I suppose if I am critical of Miss Wells it is because so much in her behavior reminds me of one of the first questions Bainbridge posed in a letter he wrote to me soon after meeting her in Cairo. 'Can such a girl exist?'"

"You think her character false?"

"I should like very much to know if she was so fond of whisky and cards and gentlemen behaving badly before she decided she wanted to be a duchess."

"She has a fortune of her own and has no need for his."

"But you know these Americans, Lady Emily. They long for the satisfaction of a title. They are all scrambling to increase their fortunes and their influence. That is the trouble with a meritocracy. One always feels that one must prove oneself, over and over. Once in possession of a title, however, one may sit back, breathe deeply, and enjoy it."

"I don't see what difference it will make to her father," I said, "and he is the one scrambling to keep the fortune multiplying."

"The title secures their social rank, even with their fellow Americans, who are not supposed to care about such things. I have no doubt his business associates are not so immune to the luster of blue blood. After all, what they really want is to be admitted to the club. They cannot be born into it, but with a big enough fortune, they can buy their way in through marriage. Lord knows there are enough impoverished noble families in Britain to satisfy their needs."

"So you think Miss Wells is after nothing more than a title?"

"I do."

"I suppose it is difficult for me to understand the appeal."

"That, Lady Emily, is because you were born with the blood. An earl's daughter will always be an earl's daughter. You take it for granted, and have been afforded the privileges of rank all your life."

"Do you think she will make him happy?"

"For a while." Mr. Fairchild tossed his ivory-handled walking stick into the air and caught it without breaking his stride. "Bainbridge is unlikely to remain a devoted spouse when at last the time comes that whisky and cards are less interesting to his wife than they appear to be now. That is not much different than most marriages, so I ought not be concerned. Yet there is something about her . . ." His voice trailed. "We must speak no more on this subject. Bainbridge is happy, and the choice of wife is his alone."

"Did Mr. Neville approve of the match?"

"Wholeheartedly. I think he was half in love with Miss Wells himself. Not, mind you, that he would have ever acted on the emotion. Enough, though. Let us enjoy this fine day while we can. Why court trouble before its time has come? It is good to be outdoors and engaged in physical activity. Perhaps we could organize a game of croquet when we return to the hotel."

"I should have thought you would suggest cricket," I said.

"We would not have the correct number of players even if I could convince you ladies to play. Although, if I may be so bold, you would look quite fine in whites. Refashioned in an appropriate style, of course."

The steep streets of Le Suquet had slowed our progress considerably, and our pace was hardly half what it had been along La Croisette. Houses lined the narrow passages, their walls painted pale shades of yellow, ranging from the creamiest vanilla to the deepest gold. Their shutters, pastel green, blue, lavender, and lilac, were closed against the heat of the day—Amity should, perhaps, have had us make an earlier start—and flowers spilled from the window boxes beneath a handful of them. This section of Cannes felt a world removed from the seaside, with its grand hotels and wide promenade. Here no one had bothered to plant palms. The gardens were filled with citrus trees and redbuds and the evergreens imported by Napoleon's soldiers at the beginning of the century. Men in striped shirts populated the outdoor tables at quiet cafés, waiters bringing them cool glasses of the rosé wine produced in nearby Provence.

The number of tourists we encountered declined as we continued our climb up the increasingly steep hill. Most of them preferred to stay on La Croisette and the fashionable streets nearby or, if they proved slightly adventurous, took carriages to view the medieval church at the top. As we approached Notre Dame de l'Espérance, the pavement opened into a wide staircase that led to the old castle walls.

"None of you should ever forgive me for making us do this in the heat," Amity said. "It was much cooler down by the sea. I did not realize the sun up here would be quite so unforgiving."

"Not nearly so bad as Egypt," Jeremy said, exchanging a nauseating look with his fiancée. "I can think of several occasions on which we suffered more there."

"Correct as always, darling," she said, and kissed him.

"Ho!" A voice came from the walls above. "You are all pathetically slow. I have been here for ages." It was Augustus, standing on the ramparts, a large yellow carnation in his buttonhole and an umbrella shading his pale features.

"What a treat," Margaret said, dropping Colin's arm and looping hers through mine. "I do despise that boy."

"This is a topic that can do me no credit," Mr. Fairchild said, leaving us to it. "Deliver me, Hargreaves." They pulled ahead, leaving us to continue our discussion in private.

"I have not had much conversation with him," I said. Margaret slowed her pace so that we fell behind the rest of the group. "He scuttles away whenever I speak to him."

"I have talked to him enough to believe that he is the sort of person who might enjoy tormenting kittens," Margaret said. "There is cruelty in nearly all of his comments."

"Does he not collect butterflies?" I asked. "I recall Amity saying something to that effect."

"Yes, and I am convinced he does so only because he likes sticking pins through them. Lord, it's hot. Will we ever reach the top of these stairs?"

We did, although it took a considerable effort in the heat, but the view from the top of the old walls proved well worth the climb. The church stood immediately beneath us. Opposite it, to the north, the terra-cotta tiled rooftops of the city spread farther below us, but to the southeast they gave way to the Mediterranean, whose waters, now the color of lapis lazuli sprinkled with silver, had become rougher since we left the hotel. The wind felt stronger as well, but that was to be expected on the ramparts. I was surprised, however, to feel a shiver go through me. Colin came up behind me and draped a shawl over my shoulders.

"I knew you would feel chilled by the wind after the exertion of the climb."

"You are very good to me," I said. He wrapped his arms around me and I pressed against him. "Margaret has already gone down to the church and appears to be questioning an unsuspecting priest about something or other. She has got Mr. Fairchild in tow," I said. "Jack is helping Christabel with her camera near that olive tree—"

"I prefer the view of the sea," Colin said.

"Do allow me to finish, please. Amity and Jeremy are with her brother, still on the walls, but a fair distance from us. Which means, my dear husband, that we are very nearly alone."

He eyes sparkled. "Your powers of observation are enviable," he said. "I cannot believe I was foolish enough to allow the view to distract me when I ought to have been—"

I turned to him and kissed him. Had I allowed him to keep talking, the opportunity might have escaped us. "I think the monks would have approved, do you not? They would not have constructed their church and castle and walls in such a romantic spot otherwise."

"Surely the monks constructed these battlements with an eye to defense rather than—"

He stopped as a scream pierced the air. It was Amity. We moved as quickly as possible along the rough and uneven path through the ramparts until we reached her. Her face, drawn and pale, and her eyes, filled with tears, suggested some sort of injury, but it was Jeremy, not her, who appeared to be the worse for wear. He had fallen, face first, into the crenel between the solid parts of the battlement and appeared to be convulsing.

"Jeremy!" I pushed Augustus away and reached for my friend, stopping only when it became clear the convulsions were due to laughter. "What happened?"

"Oh, my dear, dear Amity." He ignored me altogether and reached for his fiancée. "You ought not shriek like that—it will make a man think something terrible has happened." He covered his mouth with his hand and shook his head, unable to control his mirth. "What will our friends think? If you were behaving like a lady, my dear, you would not want to draw attention to the fact that I tripped."

"Jeremy—"

Amity interrupted me, but Jeremy had not so much as taken notice of our arrival. "I tripped, my love," she said, brushing away her tears, "and I fell right against you. Thank heavens the force wasn't enough to send you . . ." She gulped and the tears started again.

"It would have been difficult to get him to really fly." Augustus's voice was flat. "The crenel is nearly three feet deep, I would say."

"Thank heavens for that," Colin said. "Are you hurt in any way, Bainbridge?"

Jeremy was brushing dust from his jacket. "I am not certain that my lapels shall ever truly recover, and my pride has, without doubt, taken a serious blow. Other than that, I am entirely unharmed."

"How did this happen?" I asked.

"As I said, Emily, I tripped." Amity's eyes were dry and clear again. "These cobbles or stones or whatever paves the walk are slippery—and we both know that ladies' shoes are not meant for vigorous expeditions. The smooth soles are a hazard on any surface. I reached out for Jeremy as I started to fall, but wound up pushing rather than grabbing him. You are quite certain I have not hurt you, my love?"

"Quite," Jeremy said, kissing his fiancée on the cheek. "Are we going to look at this wretched church or not? I can't say I have a mad desire to stay up here any longer."

We descended from the walls—all of us, that is, save Augustus, who remained perched above, looking down in our direction with an eel-like grin on his face. I cannot claim any strict knowledge of eels, but I am certain that should one ever have the occasion to grin, it would bear an uncanny resemblance to him. Even after I turned away I could feel him watching me, and I was happy to disappear into the cool darkness of Notre Dame de l'Espérance. Happier still that Colin had had the foresight to bring me a shawl.

It did not take long to tour the small but lovely church, and soon we were back outside and again in the sun. We crossed through a stone archway and into a yard next to the old castle keep. Margaret and Amity had already made their way inside, the rest of the group trailing behind them—all except Augustus, who was now sitting on a wall much lower than that of the ramparts we had crossed. I walked over to him, nodding to tell Colin to go with the others.

"It is much warmer again here," I said, sitting a few feet away from him. "The wind is not nearly so strong as it was above. I am struck as well by the difference in temperature when one is in the shade versus the sun."

"I feel neither heat nor cold," he said, not looking at me. His attention was focused below us. Flowering shrubs and trees planted along the wall were flourishing, and butterflies flitted from blossom to blossom before coming to rest on the fernlike leaves of a smallish mimosa tree.

"Do you know the name of that one?" I asked, pointing to one of the flying creatures whose wings were a striking shade of blue. "I cannot think when I have seen a butterfly quite that color."

"It is the *Iolana iolas*, in French *l'azuré du baguenaudier*. I am quite certain you have creatures of a similar shade of blue in England."

"I do not doubt you, but I cannot remember seeing one. It is such a lovely blue."

"The underside of its wings are grey, utterly unremarkable."

"Yet the tops almost shimmer," I said. "Such beauty."

"Beauty does not interest me," Augustus said.

"Why not?" I asked.

He shrugged. "I like things that are deeper, that have meaning and truth."

"That is a noble position, Mr. Wells. Many young men are easily distracted by exterior trappings."

"I am not so very young, Lady Emily. I am twenty-three years old."

I would have guessed he was no more than seventeen, but now, as I studied his face, I could see it was more mature than it appeared at a casual glance. "Not so very young, then," I said. "I understand you are something of an expert in the study of butterflies."

"I prefer burnets. They are a type of moth."

"What color are they?"

"They are a genus, *Zygaena*, so their members can be any number of colors." His tone felt like a reprimand. "I like the red and black ones the best." An *Iolana iolas* landed on the wall next to him. He flattened his hand, palm up, near it, as if coaxing the delicate creature to come to him. The butterfly, looking almost as if it were hopping, moved onto his palm, and slowly Augustus lifted it until it was nearly level with his eyes. "They are very fragile, you know."

"My nanny told me to never touch a butterfly's wings," I said. "That doing so rubs off the scales and leaves him unable to fly."

Augustus grunted. "Not quite true, but it is the wicked sort of tale people like to tell children." He lowered his hand and then, moving with deliberate care, reached out with a single finger from his other hand and gently stroked the butterfly's wings.

"I don't think you ought to—"

"Are you squeamish, Lady Emily?" He held up the finger to me, and I could see traces of powdery blue on it. "I shall keep going. Our friend will still be able to fly, he just won't be such a lovely shade of blue."

"Stop, Augustus!"

"Have you ever seen an old butterfly?" he asked. "Sometimes they have patches on their wings that are almost translucent where the scales have been rubbed away. It can happen over time." He was petting the wing again.

"Please stop. Why are you doing this?"

"Because I like to. I am giving him character, making him appear older and wiser than he is."

I clapped my hands loudly, startling the poor creature to fly away. "Butterflies are not meant to show signs of character and wisdom, Augustus. You might have harmed it."

"I believe, Lady Emily, that I am better acquainted with butterflies than you. You may have harmed it far more than I by scaring it. As you saw, it was still perfectly capable of flight. I caused it no substantial damage." He held out his hand flat again. "Here. Let us catch another."

"No, Augustus, I do not wish to do any such thing. Please leave them be."

"You do realize it is necessary to kill them if one wishes to study them, do you not? Science requires it. Is it not a beautiful thing, a discipline that requires darkness to reach the light?"

# Amity
## Four months earlier

Restlessness consumed Amity almost from the moment she arrived in Cairo. She might have told Jack she believed the society was second only to that in London, but in fact she would have preferred Paris, or some other cosmopolitan capital. Although she had come to adore India, she did not miss its humidity, yet she did not prefer the dusty heat of Egypt. Cairo was a filthy place, full of whining children, their hands outstretched, begging with thin, wheezing voices for money, no matter where she turned. Christabel, however, felt altogether differently about it. She had come with the intention of catching a glimpse of some distant sort of relation, an eccentric lady who had married an even more eccentric archaeologist. Unfortunately, the lady in question proved uninterested in family connections, and would not agree to a meeting. Christabel took the failure of her purpose in stride, and threw herself into exploring the region and enjoying its society.

She insisted that Amity accompany her when she shopped for trinkets in the Khan el-Khalili, rebuking her friend when Amity insisted there was nothing to be seen that she would wish to purchase.

"How can you not long for these little leather slippers?" Christabel asked. "The work on them is exquisite and you will never find their equal in New York, of that I am certain. I am taking three pairs, and I shall feel like an exotic princess every time I wear them."

"You are very easily amused, Christabel."

"I do not take your remark as a criticism. What has happened to you, Amity? You were unhappy when you arrived in India, but no sooner had we started exploring than you fell in love with the place. Will you not give Egypt the same chance?"

Amity curled her lip. "Were it possible to escape from the feeling of constantly having sand rubbing against my skin, I might."

"You will feel differently after we see the pyramids tonight."

Christabel's optimism proved incorrect. Amity appeared in all ways unimpressed by the Giza plateau, and refused to climb to the top of the Great Pyramid.

"There is no view to see in the dark," she said.

"Look at the stars above us, Amity," Christabel said. "Imagine being even closer to them, with the lights of Cairo stretched out before us."

"I thought we would have seen Jack by now," Amity said, not bothering to so much as glance at the stars. "We have been here for nearly three weeks."

"He is in the army, dear. It is no surprise that they would be keeping him busy."

A rowdy group of tourists on camels approached them, whooping hellos. Amity turned her back and ignored them. "I thought he was going to meet us at the station when we arrived."

"He telegrammed before we left India to say that would not be possible."

"I suppose there is little chance of us meeting his brother now."

Christabel placed a hand on her friend's arm. "Now I understand your melancholy. Is it possible that you have thoroughly fallen in love with this gentleman before even having met him?"

"Don't be ridiculous. Of course I am not in love with him. By all accounts he is a dreadful boor," she said, lines etching her normally smooth brow. "It is only that I had believed Jack would keep his word and introduce us. I am trying to keep my mother happy—you know why she has brought me here."

"You do not fool me, Amity," Christabel said. "You have set your heart on the Duke of Bainbridge. I hope the man himself does not prove a disappointment."

"He won't. I have never been more certain of anything in my life." She sighed. "From all that Jack has told me, he is perfect in every conceivable way."

"Jack will come to us eventually, and if he is able to persuade his brother to join him in Cairo, we will be the first to meet him. Until then, would you not prefer to distract yourself with the magnificent sights that surround us?"

Amity crossed her arms across her chest. "You are unlikely to relent until I agree to climb this wretched pyramid."

"Precisely. Come, your father has already hired guides to assist us."

Amity did not enjoy a single moment of the excursion. She objected to the rough manner in which the guides—three of them per lady—all but dragged her up the enormous stone blocks of the pyramid. It was a singularly unpleasant experience. The view from the top, as she suspected, was pedestrian. To suggest the lights of Cairo were of any interest was ludicrous, and as for the stars . . . Amity had never understood why people found them so noteworthy. The full moon, she allowed, was spectacular enough, but she could have seen that from her bedroom window in New York.

While the rest of the party exclaimed over the panoramas, Amity sat on a stone and tapped her foot, glaring at her parents.

"There is no need to pout, child," her mother said, poking her with a walking stick. "It is unbecoming."

"Is there someone here I ought to be trying to impress?" Amity asked, a scowl across her pretty face.

"There is plenty of society to be found here, and you know well why we couldn't have started in London. Your reputation may have preceded you there, so we were forced to make acquaintances in far-flung outposts of the empire before descending upon the capital. Get up and either enjoy yourself or pretend to. I don't care which." Mrs. Wells tugged on her sullen daughter's arm and brought her to her feet.

"Why do you bring up my reputation, Mother?" Amity asked. "No one aside from yourself and Daddy have the slightest inkling as to what happened in New York. I haven't ruined your chances of joining the aristocracy, although you ought to bear in mind that I will be the one with the title, not you."

Mrs. Wells raised her hand and slapped Amity soundly. The ensuing red splotch blossoming on her daughter's fair cheek was plainly visible in the moonlight. "That is quite enough from you."

# 6

The unsettling feeling that consumed me during my conversation with Augustus on the wall near the castle stayed with me for the remainder of the day. Everyone else enjoyed our outing, and when we arrived back at the hotel, Mr. and Mrs. Wells, along with Cécile, were waiting for us on the terrace, where they had caused three round tables to be pushed close together so that we might all converse with ease as the sunset painted the sky with colors of which our friend Renoir would have approved. Augustus did not acknowledge me when he appeared, taking a seat next to his mother and making no further attempt to speak to me that evening. If anything, he avoided me.

"I have had such a strange afternoon," I said to Cécile, pulling her aside so that I could speak to her quietly. I wanted a word with her away from the group.

"I heard all about Bainbridge's fall," she said. "It sounds like much ado about very little."

"I am not sure that I agree," I said.

"What are you suggesting?" she asked, and I recounted for her Augustus's treatment of the butterfly. "Do you think Augustus pushed him deliberately? Why would he do such a thing? He does not seem particularly attached to his sister."

I frowned. "I have observed the same. He does not seem particularly attached to anyone, yet he is the only of her brothers who is here, and that may in and of itself signify."

"Jeremy's mother is not here," Cécile said. "Does that signify something as well?"

"She declined the invitation because she is still recovering from la grippe. It would not have been wise for her to travel."

"The south of France is known for its recuperative powers," Cécile said. "If anything, it would have done her good to come."

"Only if the journey itself didn't cause a relapse."

Cécile shrugged. "I do not think she is delighted that her son is marrying an American. I have no basis for this, *bien sûr*, but my instinct tells me it is so."

"She may have objected to Mrs. Wells's party in principle—a fortnight-long fête to celebrate an engagement is not the sort of thing to which she would be accustomed."

"She would find it gauche, as do I," Cécile said. "But that is of no consequence. I never object to a holiday in the south."

"Be that as it may, Augustus unsettles me."

"I am certain that if he ever spoke to me, I would feel the same. A man who torments a butterfly—"

"Could be guilty of far worse."

"*Non, non, non*, Kallista. I agree his actions may indeed reflect extreme deficits in his character, but they do not necessarily correlate with—with what? Wanting to fling his sister's fiancé off a medieval parapet? Promise me you will not mention this to Monsieur Hargreaves."

"Why ever not? Have you not always counseled me that honesty is essential in marriage?"

"I have, Kallista, but I am afraid that this current manner of thinking would only make him—and others—believe you are in some way jealous of Mademoiselle Wells."

"I have never heard anything so absurd! We are speaking of her brother."

"*Oui*, but by extension, you criticize his family, including his sister. Given that you and Bainbridge have shared such a close friendship, anything that suggests you do not wholly approve of his betrothal makes you appear envious."

"That is absurd," I said. "I have no objections to Amity."

Cécile raised an eyebrow. "None?"

"Well, none of any significance. I only want Jeremy to be happy."

"Then let him be, Kallista. The marriage will be what it will be. It is for you to judge neither its merits nor its flaws. Tolerate the Wells family with equanimity for the rest of our holiday. When we are back in Paris, we can then express ourselves with more candor."

I took Cécile's words to heart, although I did not wholeheartedly agree with them. She was correct on one count: Jeremy's happiness mattered above everything, and if throwing myself into enjoying our time in Cannes would help secure his happiness, I would do so with abandon. The following afternoon, we embarked on a sailing expedition. Amity had planned a luncheon on the ship, and we were treated to all the delicacies of the region, served as a buffet: plump olives, tapenade, bouillabaisse, pissaladière, and raviolis niçois, which reminded me how recently the Riviera had been part of Italy. Waiters poured rosé wine as soon as we had stepped on board, and kept our glasses filled throughout the trip.

"If I consume any more wine my head will never stop spinning," I said to Colin, glancing around me to make sure no one would notice as I tipped the contents of my glass over the side. "Do you think you could play horrified husband and refuse to let anyone pour more for me?"

"Amity has a rather specific idea about what a raucous afternoon must include, doesn't she?" Colin took the glass from me. "Fear not, I shall protect you."

"Emily, do settle something for me, will you?"

I turned around to face Amity, who had Jeremy on her arm.

"Happily," I said. "What is it?"

"I have been told that your extremely handsome husband swam across the Bosphorus for you when you were in Constantinople. Is it true?"

"Indeed it is," I said. "Legend has it that Leander swam the Hellespont nightly to visit his love, Hero. The story has inspired countless others to follow suit as a means of proving their own love. A devoted lover chooses the Bosphorus as it is a more difficult swim. There is a tower called either the Maiden's or Leander's—"

"You were on your honeymoon, were you not?" Amity interrupted.

"Yes."

"This, Jeremy, is not the Bosphorus, and we are not yet on our honeymoon." Amity said, her words slightly slurred. The wine was having an even more profound effect on her than I. My mother would have been shocked at her indecorous appearance.

"That is true, but as you have not brought me to the Bosphorus, I will content myself with another feat," Jeremy said. "Lord Byron didn't swim the same direction as Leander when he made his trip, and I take that as precedence for allowing the task to be altered as necessary."

Colin scrutinized Jeremy. "Swimming now would not be a good idea. The sun may feel warm, but it is only April, and the water is cold. Byron, you may remember, Bainbridge, succumbed to a fever after his own swim."

"I have not the weakness of character exhibited by the poet, gifted though Lord Byron was."

"Character does not come into it," Colin said. "The water is too cold for a swim."

"Given that you pride yourself on weakness of character, I should think you would not dare to prove yourself more worthy on that count than Lord Byron," I said.

Jeremy did not so much as acknowledge that I spoke, but instead turned to his fiancée. "I shall tell the captain to navigate toward that small island, there, the one with the monastery on it. We aren't so very far from it now, are we? Certainly not farther away than I can swim, although I suspect the Bosphorus is wider."

"Colin, you must persuade him not to do this," Amity said. "You of all people know what a gentleman in love is prepared to do for his lady, and I cannot bear the thought of him putting himself at risk. He has had rather a lot of wine."

"This is a foolish idea, Bainbridge, far beneath your consideration."

Jeremy looked not altogether steady on his feet, and his eyes showed signs of the overconsumption of spirits. "That, my dear man, is precisely why I intend to do it." He strode off in the direction of the bridge, leaving Amity behind, wringing her hands.

"Is there nothing you can do to stop him?" she asked Colin. "Please."

"When a man is bent on something so rash he is unlikely to be dissuaded on any account."

"Someone at least ought to try," I said, and followed after him. The captain, good man, refused to take any part in the scheme, but that did not put off Jeremy. Instead, he stalked toward the prow, peeling off first his jacket and then his waistcoat, dropping them both onto the deck.

"Jeremy!"

"I suggest, Em, that you retreat at once, lest you be offended by the sight of me *en dishabille*." He unfastened his collar and flung it down.

"Jeremy, please! You must listen to reason."

Reason was not part of his plan, however, and when he began unbuttoning his shirt, I felt I had no option other than to retreat. A few moments later, with a cry of tallyho and a splash, Jeremy plunged into the water. Now his friends were all on his side, cheering him on as he swam in the direction of the island. I alone refused to take any pleasure in his ridiculous stunt and leaned my back against the railing, crossing my arms and pointedly looking away from the spectacle.

"Don't be a spoilsport," Margaret said, sidling up to me. "He's making quite an effort."

"He is behaving like a reckless child," I said. Mr. Fairchild and Jack were shouting accolades, and Amity was clapping and shrieking with delight. Irritation welled in me, but I did not turn to look. I did not want to be a spoilsport, but I could not escape the feeling that something sinister lay beneath everything that had occurred since our arrival in Cannes. Then, just as the sun slipped behind a cloud, throwing us into shadow, the tenor of Amity's voice changed. Panic replaced exuberance.

Turning back around and clinging to the rail, I saw Jeremy flailing, far away from the boat. He was waving both his arms in the air, as if to signal us. He was too far away for any cries to reach us, but I was convinced he was shouting for help. Colin must have believed the same, as he stripped off his jacket, kicked off his shoes, and dove off the side of the boat without the slightest hesitation. Jack ran for the captain, and within moments, they had launched a dinghy. Colin reached Jeremy before it, and held him afloat until he could remand him to his rescuers. When Mr. Fairchild and Mr. Wells helped them back on board, we wrapped them in heavy blankets and plied them with coffee to ward off the cold. The sun had not reappeared, and rain clouds threatened from above, bringing with them a stiff breeze.

"I admit, Em," Jeremy said, through chattering teeth, "that there was a certain amount of wisdom in your efforts to stop me, but you know me too well to have thought I would abandon my scheme."

"You had better hope Colin doesn't fall ill," I said. "I shall never forgive you." In the past, this would have been Jeremy's cue to tell me that his intention all along had been exactly that. That he wanted Colin finished off by some dreadful illness, so that, at last, we could be together. I would roll my eyes and make some sort of vaguely biting reply while Colin laughed. This time, however, Jeremy let the opportunity pass without so much as a word.

"I hardly think Colin is the one we need to be worried about," Amity said. "Jeremy was in the water far longer and is at much greater risk."

"No gentleman worth his mettle would fall ill after a little swim," Mr. Fairchild said, but his teasing tone did nothing to lighten Amity's mood. She glowered at me and made a point of not speaking to me for the duration of the voyage.

"I don't know what you did to so offend her," Margaret said later that evening, when we were all snug in the hotel, rain lashing against the windows. "It was a stupid stunt—of that there can be no doubt—but you can hardly be held accountable."

"Miss Wells feels that your attempt to stop Bainbridge after you followed him was a clever ruse to spur him on," Colin said. "She insists that because you know him so well, you were fully aware of the effect your pleas would have on him."

"No one heard what I said to him once we were away from you all, so she is basing her claims on nothing but speculation. I can assure you I did not spur him on. Why would I do such a thing?"

"Jealousy," Cécile said. "She means us all to believe that you are infatuated with Jeremy and that you do not want to see him happily married."

"I cannot think when I have heard anything quite so absurd," I said.

"It is true, though, that we should have known Bainbridge would react exactly as he did to our efforts to dissuade him," Colin said.

"Yes, all our efforts—yours and Amity's included," I said. "This is intolerable."

"Mr. Wells has asked that you and Colin dine separately from the others tonight," Margaret said. "He claims that Amity is almost insensible she is so upset. I told him Cécile and I would stay back with you, although I am inclined to say we ought to descend upon them like Valkyries in the dining room. Why should we let that wretched girl have her way?"

"It is not worth making a fuss," Colin said. "We shall have dinner sent up here, and spend a much more pleasant evening the four of us than we would by forcing ourselves where we are not wanted."

"Emily, I am so very sorry." Jack, who had been sitting quietly, listening, at last broke his silence.

"I assure you, Jack, you bear no responsibility for any of this," I said. "I think it would be best if we went home. Colin, can you book us on a train tomorrow?"

"So soon?" Cécile said. "Kallista, I know I have been hard on you about Mademoiselle Wells, but she is now not behaving in an acceptable manner. You should not let her drive you away."

"I am finding it increasingly difficult to appreciate any of the pleasures of Cannes," I said, angry at feeling tears smart in my eyes. "Whatever I do is criticized."

"You cannot think of leaving us," Jack said. "I will say what no one else will: All of these bad feelings stem from Neville's death. He put us on edge and made it impossible for this holiday to be anything but awkward. Mrs. Wells should never have insisted that we remain after the funeral, and when she did, my brother ought to have stopped her instead of persuading you all to stay. You shoulder none of the blame, Emily. If you go now, we should all go."

"Aptly said." Colin crossed to me and crouched in front of me, taking my hands. "We all stay or none of us stay."

"Then it is obvious," Cécile said. "We all stay. Fair or not, Kallista will be blamed if the party is abandoned. There is plenty of champagne to be had here, and we shall make our own society. If Mademoiselle Wells continues to be difficult, we will not bother to notice."

"Your suggestion is a reasonable one, Cécile," I said. I did not want to spoil Jeremy's holiday, but felt that whatever I did would prove wrong in the end. "I shall stay. But heaven help you all if Jeremy catches so much as a cold. Amity will persuade you all that it is a result of my having put a curse on him."

"Emily, if you were to curse Bainbridge, I should hope you would have the good sense to aim for a more crushing blow," Colin said. "What can a cold hope to accomplish? He is not, after all, Jane Bennett, and even she managed to recover after her ill-advised ride through the rain. You would have to do better than a cold."

# Amity

## Four months earlier

Birdie and her daughter did not speak for two days after the incident at the pyramids. Their silence might have continued for longer had Captain Sheffield not—at last—called on the party at Shepheard's Hotel, where the luxurious accommodations had failed to make even the slightest favorable impression on Amity. His arrival, and the subsequent adventures of the Three Musketeers, restored her good spirits. Now the Khan el-Khalili teemed with exotic treasures, the pyramids and the sphinx were magical, and the society at Shepheard's second to none. Better still, Jack had persuaded his brother to join him in Egypt.

"I almost wish the duke weren't coming," Amity said, as she and Christabel sat at a table on the crowded terrace at Shepheard's the afternoon of his much-anticipated arrival. "We are having such fun with Jack. What if his brother is not so affable?"

"Amity, you have been desperate to meet the duke for months. Can it be that your nerves are plaguing you now?"

"Almost certainly," Amity said, giggling and then pausing while a waiter delivered finger sandwiches and cakes to accompany their tea. "At any rate, even if he shows not the barest interest in me, he is bound to demand more of his brother's time. You in particular will dislike that."

Christabel blushed. "Am I so obvious?"

"Not at all," her friend said, stirring sugar into her steaming cup. "It is only because I know you so well that I can read your feelings."

"Do you think he knows?"

"Christabel, dear, you shall have to become much more forthright if you want him to guess what resides in your heart."

"I shall do nothing of the sort until I have a clearer picture of his own feelings on the subject."

"Your English reticence will do you no favors, my friend." Amity fidgeted, opened her parasol, and leaned back in her chair. "If I were you, I would be suggesting to Jack that he ought to have a capable photographer on hand to capture his myriad adventures."

"I could never be so forward." Christabel's eyes widened. "To imply that I would be willing to travel with him—"

"As his wife, my dear. That is not so shocking," Amity said, closing her parasol and sitting up straight. "Here they are now, so I suppose we ought not continue strategizing on the topic. We must make it look as if this is the most casual tea we have ever had." Two lanky gentlemen, one in uniform, the other in a light-colored linen suit, expertly tailored, mounted the stairs outside the hotel. "He is more handsome than I would have expected. I've always pictured dukes as pale, elderly, and infirm."

"I could have told you Jeremy is nothing of the sort," Christabel said. "I cannot claim to know him well, but we have met several times, and he is what most mothers consider dangerously charming. As you know, he quite refuses to marry, much to their chagrin."

"Jack only touched briefly on the subject. Why won't he marry?"

"His heart was broken by the dearest friend of his youth, Lady Emily Hargreaves, and he has never recovered. He is in possession of both fortune and title, so if you do want to catch him, you shall have to rely on more than your dowry. There is nothing Jeremy needs."

"Except, perhaps, love." Amity squinted as she studied the taller of the gentlemen approaching their table. She held up her hand for him to kiss even before his brother could make the introduction. Without the slightest sign of hesitation, Jeremy Sheffield, Duke of Bainbridge, took the little gloved hand and lingered over it.

"My brother warned me about you, Miss Wells, and, as you see, I am not waiting to be properly introduced. Whatever will your mother say?"

"Nothing, your grace, that could be repeated in public," Amity said. "Unless, of course, your intentions prove to be honorable."

"I do hate to disappoint a young lady's mother, but I cannot bear to be less than honest with you, Miss Wells. My intentions have never been honorable, and I am too old to change my habits now."

"Then, your grace, I must beg you to take a seat. Christabel and I are taking tea, but perhaps you would prefer whisky?"

"She is a pistol, Jack." The duke kissed Christabel on both cheeks before sitting next to Amity. "I like her already."

# 7

The rooms at the Hotel Britannia were all en suite, and the facilities left one nothing short of utterly satisfied. I took a long bath before dinner, luxuriating in the deep tub, whose waters Meg, my maid, had scented with rose oil. My ablutions leaving me feeling greatly refreshed, I vowed to befriend Amity Wells, and to do everything in my power to ensure that she and Jeremy enjoyed the rest of this dreadful holiday in their honor. Cécile may have been right in her observation that I was harder hit by Jeremy's engagement than I realized, for although I harbored no romantic feelings for him, the very act of him taking a wife would herald a necessary alteration in our friendship, and it was only natural that I would mourn the change to some degree. Perhaps this had caused me to be less generous with Amity than I ought to have been, and after the chaos of Jeremy's ill-fated swim, I thought it best that I do what I could to try again with her.

"I have let out the seams just a bit, madam," Meg said, as she lowered my favorite Worth gown over my head. "Babies do take a toll on the waist." There had been a time when I might have mourned the loss of my waistline, but I cared very little about it now.

"You need not remind me about my waist," I said, and smoothed the icy blue voile skirt. "I would rather have you letting out seams than pulling these stays tighter. I have always been fond of breathing."

"You're still awfully slim, madam," Meg said. "I shouldn't worry." While she wrestled with the tiny buttons that fastened the back of the bodice, I clasped a diamond and sapphire necklace around my neck. "Do you think this jewelry is too showy?"

"Too showy, madam? Not at all. If I owned it I would wear it every day without exception. It's stunning."

"I want to be careful not to do anything that might be interpreted as an attempt to upstage Miss Wells."

"Lady Emily, that necklace would upstage the queen herself. The sapphires make your eyes flash the same color as the stones. It's almost like you're more goddess than woman."

"You have been reading Homer, haven't you, Meg?"

"Yes, milady. You did give me the book. Can't say I like that Achilles bloke much. I find myself wishing I could give him a good slap and force him out of his tent."

"I could not be more pleased." I smiled and removed the necklace. "Bring me the lion chain instead." I had purchased this piece in Greece, although the dealer told me it had been found in Italy. It dated from the fourth century B.C., and from the front looked like a simple, heavy gold chain. The clasp featured two golden lions, their eyes enameled in blue. In antiquity, it would have been worn with matching earrings, but, alas, they had not survived the ravages of time, so I had careful reproductions made based on the clasp, and now snapped them into place.

"You look very exotic," Colin said, adjusting his cuff links as he came into the dressing room. "Going Greek tonight, are you?"

"I thought it more discreet than diamonds and sapphires."

"My dear, you are so perfectly exquisite your beauty could never be described as discreet, no matter what you choose as adornment."

Meg sighed. "Are you going to moon over her, Mr. Hargreaves, or are you going to let me finish dressing her? You're already nearly late."

Far from being late, we were the first of our party to arrive in the dining room. After consulting with the maître d' to ascertain that the Wellses had not made any specific arrangements to the contrary, I asked that everyone be served a special cocktail, made with champagne, as soon as they reached the table. I wanted to offer a festive toast to Jeremy and his bride. The barman concocted a gorgeous drink, combining my requested bubbles with raspberry liqueur. Even Cécile, who ordinarily objected to any deviation from champagne, agreed it was delightful. When we were all gathered, I rose from my seat.

"It is with great pleasure that I raise my glass to Miss Amity Wells, the only lady on earth charming and radiant enough to tempt the Duke of Bainbridge into the bonds of matrimony. I wish you much happiness together and am honored to have been included in your celebrations."

The others cried "Hear, Hear!" and drank with gusto. Amity's glass remained untouched, as proper etiquette demanded. One does not drink in honor of oneself. Colin stood next.

"Bainbridge and I have had our differences in the past, too numerous to count, let alone catalog, here tonight. He has publicly committed himself to the lofty goal of becoming the most useless man in England, and I must now state, for the record, that he shall never accomplish the feat. By persuading—using means I cannot begin to understand—Miss Amity Wells to agree to be his wife, he has given London society its brightest gem. No one could describe the architect of such a scheme as useless, in England or elsewhere. To Bainbridge!"

We all shouted "To Bainbridge!" and drank, yet still Amity did not touch her glass. She turned in her seat and waved for the waiter. "Could I please have something else? I cannot abide even the idea of this beverage."

"Champagne, mademoiselle?" the waiter asked.

"Yes, of course. What else would be appropriate for toasts?" She looked directly at me as she spoke.

Mr. Wells made a speech that brought tears to his wife's eyes. Jack followed with several ribald stories about his brother, including one from the Olympics. Jack had run a race organized for the occasion to re-create the famous journey from Marathon to Athens taken by a messenger in the fifth century B.C. to bring word to the Athenians that their army had defeated the invading Persians. That ancient runner had collapsed and died after completing the task, but his modern descendants fared better. The final bit of the race took the competitors into the newly restored stadium in Athens, where Jeremy sat in the stands to cheer on his brother. Rather than remain in his seat, he rushed down and ran next to Jack during his final lap. This caused a great deal of confusion and not a little outrage, but Jeremy, undaunted, argued that he ought to have a medal for his effort, despite the fact not even Jack's pace had been good enough to secure a place at the front of the pack.

Mr. Fairchild spoke next, doing his best to rehabilitate Jeremy's reputation, pointing out that his friend often argued that he deserved medals, and that the incident in Athens was little more than a tempest in a teapot, no matter what the Greek prince on hand had wanted to call it. By the time our food had arrived, the party had settled into comfortable conversation, each of us focusing on our dinner partners, turning to the opposite side at the start of each new course. When we were finished, the gentlemen retired to the smoking room for port and cigars—I refrained from making any criticisms of what I viewed as an antiquated custom—and we ladies waited for them in the lounge, just off the lobby of the hotel. I went so far as to accept the sherry Mrs. Wells offered me, although my dislike of the beverage and preference for port were well known.

When the gentlemen returned, we decided to take a turn along La Croisette. The rain had stopped, and the night turned clear, lit by a bright moon. Amity paired us all up, putting me with her father and Cécile with her fiancé. Once again, she walked with Colin.

"Your daughter is so lovely tonight," I said to Mr. Wells as we walked.

"Thank you, Lady Emily. It is good to see her happy. Her life, you know, has not always been so easy."

"I had no idea," I said. "I am very sorry."

"Nothing serious, mind you, only the difficulties that arise from coming of age in a family like ours."

"I am not certain I understand."

"That is just as well. She admires you very much, but I think finds you somewhat threatening."

"Threatening?" I asked, crinkling my brow. "Heavens, I have certainly never intended such a thing."

"My wife and I have heard many stories, Lady Emily, about the duke's past. We were not entirely comfortable when he insisted on including you and Mr. Hargreaves in this party, but Amity requires that her fiancé have whatever he wants. I will speak to you more plainly than you are likely accustomed. Stay away from him. I will not have my daughter disappointed in love."

My heart pounded with outrage. "Mr. Wells, I can assure you that Jeremy has never been more to me than a dear friend, and that friendship has never crossed any boundary of propriety. That you suggest otherwise offends me deeply. I am not the sort of lady—"

"It would be best, Lady Emily, if we pursued the topic no further."

One may surmise the remainder of our stroll to have been discomforting, an observation at once inadequate and perfectly correct. When we congregated at the end of the hotel's pier and released our partners, I breathed a sigh of relief.

"Miss Wells, your necklace is a work of art," I said. "Look how the diamonds sparkle in the moonlight. You are Artemis herself." My own choice of jewelry had been correct. Amity was decked out in a collar of stones that, while spectacular, could only be described as an exercise in excess. My own diamond necklace, delicate and understated, would have underlined the tawdry display of hers.

"I own to being more taken with yours, Lady Emily," Mr. Fairchild said. How I wished I could have stopped him right there! "Your chain looks as if it is nothing, but then you turn and one is graced with the site of those two regal lions. If anyone is a goddess, it is you, and you are Athena. Or perhaps Hera. Who should it be? I never was good at classics."

Amity glowered. "You are too generous, Mr. Fairchild," I said. "It is kind of you to sooth the vanity of an old married woman, but wholly unnecessary, I assure you."

"If you are old, Kallista, I am positively ancient," Cécile said. "Do you mean to insult me so?"

"You know me well enough to know that would never be the case."

"No one could claim that you are old, Lady Emily," Mr. Fairchild said. While I was grateful for the compliment, I did not want him to say anything more.

"You are very kind. What if we return to the hotel and have some music?" I asked, hoping to redirect the conversation. "Amity has a voice like an angel, and I should so very much like to hear her sing. There is a piano in our suite."

"Capital idea, Emily," Colin said, stepping toward Miss Wells. "Your fiancé raves about your singing, and I have not yet heard you. Will you do me the honor?"

The Wells parents made their excuses, as did Cécile, but the rest of us went upstairs, where Colin poured drinks while Jeremy and Jack arranged chairs so that we might all see the performance.

"Margaret, will you accompany her?" I asked.

"Heavens, you know I have no musical talent," she said. "Even less than you."

"I do not think it ought to be me," I said.

"Very well, but consider yourself warned." Margaret lowered her voice. "I do despise her. She's being perfectly awful to you."

"It is of no consequence," I said, "but I am most grateful for your support."

Margaret seated herself in front of the piano and exchanged hushed words with Amity. Soon she played the opening notes of a pleasant little song by Mozart, and from the moment Amity began to sing, we were all captivated. A mezzo-soprano, her voice was rich and evocative, with more power than her slim frame would have suggested she had. When she finished, we all sat, unable to move, profoundly affected by her performance. The spell broke, and we all began to applaud, but Amity nodded to Margaret, who began to play again, another aria from the great composer, this one taken from *La Clemenza di Tito*. At the end, when we had stopped cheering for her—for cheering was indeed required after such a display of talent—she gave me a weak and extremely pretty smile.

"That was for you, Emily. I know how you adore the ancients, and I do want to apologize for Daddy having been so dreadful to you." It was a thoughtful gesture, given that the story, set in ancient Rome, did fit with my interest in classics. It also showed the depth of Amity's knowledge of music. So far as I was aware, the opera had only been performed once in London during our century, and probably not at all in America, yet she clearly had studied it.

"Did you hear your father speaking to me?" I asked, wondering how she knew he had been so very dreadful.

"Jeremy overheard," she said, furrowing her brow. "The darling boy told me everything, and I am horrified. Do please forgive Daddy for me, will you? I can't bear that he has made you upset."

"Of course I shall forgive him, and you, Miss Wells, are an angel," I said, and stood to embrace her, not missing the calculating look she gave me as I crossed to her. I wondered why she was now trying to appear to be my friend, but forced all cynical thoughts from my head. I would be her friend, for Jeremy. He would have peace, even if it were an uneasy one, if I had anything to do with it.

"And you, Lady Emily, are simply too very." The lighthearted charm was back in her voice. "We have spent far too long at odds with each other. It is time for us to be friends."

# Amity

## Four months earlier

Jeremy's arrival in Cairo changed everything for Amity. She still despised the heat, but when she complained, he took her fan and waved it in front of her face. When she longed for a moonlight excursion, he was always on hand to escort her, and she, knowing his habits from the stories told to her by his brother, always carried a flask of his favorite whisky. These nighttime adventures—to the pyramids, through gardens, on short boat trips along the Nile—raised the hackles of many society mothers. Surely the Duke of Bainbridge would not now ally himself with an American? Such a thought was not to be borne.

When Jeremy and his mates at the Turf Club organized a shooting party, Amity insisted on accompanying them and then shot better than any of the gentlemen. When they wanted to camp in the desert, she organized the details for them, and saw them off with a spectacular breakfast to fortify them on their journey. Upon their return, she had arranged for them all to be pampered like sultans and hosted a fantasia the following night in their honor. When, after a long evening that included too much wine with two of his Oxford chums, Jeremy staggered into the lobby at Shepheard's, very nearly causing a scene, Amity did not rebuke him. Instead, she laughed—that irresistible, sultry laugh—and told him that if he were her husband she would insist that he promise never to change his debauched ways.

"I am not so very debauched," Jeremy said. They were strolling through the expansive Ezbekieh Gardens, just across from the hotel, on a warm, starry evening. "Just debauched enough."

"I do adore that about you," Amity said, no hint of irony in her voice. "Furthermore, I understand you, *your grace.*" Now he heard irony, as he always did when she addressed him formally. "So much is expected of you, and none of it amusing in the least. My family is much the same, even if we have no title. I am to be a good little wife and have good little children and lead a perfectly tedious life. It is abhorrent to me. When I see you, a gentleman who has managed to remain vivacious and true to himself in the face of so much pressure, I cannot help but . . . well . . . I suppose I ought to say I cannot help but admire you."

"Ought to say?" Jeremy asked. "What do you want to say instead?"

"Nothing that would do me credit."

"I like the sound of it better and better." He stopped walking and turned to face her. "Tell me."

"No." She met his eyes and held his gaze.

"Tell me," he said.

"Never." They were standing so close together she could feel his breath on her cheek. "You wouldn't want a sensible wife, would you?"

"Never," he said.

"I wouldn't want a sensible husband."

"Tell me more."

"We've both so much money we could never run through it even if we tried," she said. "Imagine the fun we could have, refusing to be sensible together. We could devote ourselves to the pursuit of decadence. From what I understand, that is already what you do."

"Who told you that? Jack?"

"Your brother is your greatest admirer."

"I am not sure about that. He worries that I won't do my duty when the time comes and, hence, ruin his plans for further adventures."

"Perhaps you are right. Perhaps he isn't your greatest admirer."

"No?"

"Perhaps I am." She moistened her lips while keeping her eyes focused on his. "It is wholly inappropriate to say, I know, but then, perhaps I am wholly inappropriate." And with that, she leaned forward and kissed him. He put his arms around her trim waist and pulled her close, forgetting himself, but only for an instant.

"I am so terribly sorry." He stepped away from her. "I should never have—"

"Never have what? Kissed me back? It would hardly have been gentlemanly to leave me the only one kissing." She pursed her lips and gave him what he could only describe as a very saucy look. No sooner had he thought it than he was ashamed of himself. "I see what you are doing, *your grace*. You are struggling with your upbringing. Nice young gentlemen don't trifle with nice young ladies, do they?"

"Of course not. You are not, I hope, suggesting that I would ever trifle—"

"With me?" Amity laughed. "No, I don't think you would."

"We ought to return to Shepheard's. Your mother will not be pleased that we came here without a chaperone."

"You English are so very adorable! Do you really think my dear mother cares about such things? She knows I am perfectly capable of looking after myself and my reputation. I would never have agreed to walk here with you if I were worried that news of our excursion would ruin my chances with any of the myriad sunburned and tedious gentlemen who call on me to pay court. I want something else entirely. Something they can never offer."

"What?" Jeremy asked.

She took two steps closer to him. Her scent was intoxicating, sweeter than the flowers in the garden. "You, *your grace*."

Jeremy stepped back.

"I have shocked you," she said. "Good. Come to me tomorrow and we shall see what happens next. I shall be in my rooms at two o'clock." She turned away, then looked back over her shoulder and smiled before starting down the path.

"Amity! Wait! You can't go alone. Allow me to—"

"I am quite good at taking care of myself, *your grace*. You never need worry about me. Do not even contemplate following." She waved and disappeared from sight.

Jeremy stood, flustered. He looked around, wondering how many people in the garden had watched their exchange. There would be gossip, that much was certain, but Amity truly seemed not to care. His heart raced. That kiss. That kiss. Could it be that, at last, he had found someone who could make him forget another kiss, on a cold day in Vienna? A kiss that ought never have happened, but that still consumed him, even after all these years? He pulled a cigarette from his silver case and lit it, then drew smoke deep into his lungs. He smiled. Amity. Amity Wells. Could such a girl really exist?

# 8

Amity's offer of friendship to me coincided with a new pattern of behavior. She made a constant and dramatic show of protecting Jeremy. No longer did she encourage his debauchery, and she explained this—in excruciating detail—to be a direct result of his aborted ocean swim, which, she insisted, had not resulted in him falling ill only by the grace of God. Had she not gone on at such length, I almost certainly would never have given the matter a second thought, but her near obsession with the topic struck me as the lady protesting too much, and it left me unsettled, which, in turn, reawakened my suspicions about Mr. Neville's death.

Not wanting to draw any attention to my activities, I begged off a countryside picnic planned by the Wells parents—evidently no one was feeling too morose for such a thing any longer—and stayed behind in town. I saw them off in front of the hotel, waving with great vigor until their carriages were out of sight and feeling a pang of guilt at abandoning Colin. I consoled myself with the knowledge that Cécile would spend the day praising his unearthly good looks while Margaret alternated between playing chess with him and badgering him about Latin poetry.

Once they were gone, I retreated inside, where I spent an extremely pleasant hour reading *Philoctetes* in the original Greek. I shall leave it to the astute reader to decide whether my choice of this particular work of Sophocles was appropriate to the situation. Confident enough time had passed that there was little chance of the picnickers returning for some forgot item, I set off on an errand of my own.

I started with visits to apothecaries, where I discretely inquired as to the availability of certain poisonous substances. My questions did not lead to anything of significance until I spoke with my fourth apothecary.

"We have occasional cause for such things, madame, especially for the elimination of pests," he said. "As for strychnine in particular, the taste is so very bitter it puts off even the rats. May I inquire as to your interest in the substance?"

"It is only that—" I stopped.

"Are you a friend of the English gentleman who took his own life at the Hotel Britannia by this very means?"

"I am."

"Then I am most heartily sorry for your loss," he said. "I am afraid it will offer no consolation, but your friend's choice of method tells me that he had planned this in advance. No one in Cannes sells it—we have no need to—so he must have brought it with him."

"You are quite certain?"

"There can be no question of this," he said. "Arsenic and belladonna I have on hand, as do my colleagues. But strychnine? Never. I am confident about this. The town is small enough that we all know each other and our stock well."

The notion that Mr. Neville had come to Cannes with the express intention of ending his life—and even had carried poison with him—made not the slightest bit of sense. Were he in such a morose state of mind, why would he have chosen an engagement celebration as the occasion on which he would commit such an act?

I thanked the apothecary and stepped into the street outside his shop, unsure of what I should do next. What exactly did this revelation mean? I walked for a while, considering the question. The fact that the entire bottle of whisky had been poisoned still tugged at me. Why would Mr. Neville have risked someone else drinking from it? Had he assumed its deadly nature would be immediately apparent to whoever found his body? Had he poisoned it before leaving London, knowing that none of his friends would balk at finding whisky in his luggage, particularly when he was traveling with Jeremy, but not wanting to risk carrying the poison separately, lest it be discovered? Or was his mind so full of despair that he had never considered what would become of the rest of the tainted whisky after his demise?

I wandered aimlessly, following side streets away from the water, up the hills, and then back down again. The second time I reached La Croisette, I changed direction, and walked parallel to the sea, going back and forth, street by street, until the sun hung directly overhead. The morning was behind me, but I felt I had not squandered it, even if I still wrestled with the questions that tormented me. As I crossed a narrow road in order to avoid a pile of rubbish on the pavement, I noticed a sign hanging above a doorway, indicating a physician's office. This was precisely what I needed.

Not, of course, to treat any ill of my own. My constitution is hearty, and I rarely succumb to the complaints that aggravate tourists. No, I wanted to speak with a doctor about Mr. Neville and suicides in general. Fortified with purpose, I pulled on the door handle, but it did not budge. All decent Frenchmen stopped work for a civilized lunch; my pursuit of knowledge would have to wait. I glanced at the watch pinned to my lapel and considered my options. It was unlikely the doctor would return to work for more than an hour at least—the French idea of a midday break is rather different from its English equivalent. I was not near the hotel, so I decided I would grant a respite of my own and walked until I settled upon an agreeable looking café, where I took a table and ordered lunch.

The waiter, a stout, personable man, treated me like an old friend rather than an inconvenience, an attitude quite unlike that of many of his Parisian counterparts. Noticing a flush from exertion on my cheeks, he suggested a glass of rosé, to which I did not object, and he brought it while I lingered over the menu. After a bit of lively discussion with him about the choices, I asked for ratatouille, and sat back, munching on the bread he had left for me.

My table, outside on the pavement, afforded me an excellent view of all the passersby in the street. A steady stream of tourists, identifiable by the red Baedeker's guides clutched in their hands, processed in seeming endless quantity, their line broken only on occasion by a Cannois, obvious by the bags they carried, full of fresh produce—and the occasional live chicken—from the local market. I sipped my wine. The rosé was lovely, crisp and cool, fruity and light, and somehow managed to diminish the burden I felt I was carrying whenever my thoughts returned to poor Mr. Neville.

The relief proved temporary. A prickling sensation on the back of my neck returned me to harsh reality. Someone was watching me, but considered analysis of the scene before me revealed nothing. Twice the gentlemen at a table near mine thought I was looking at them, and I blushed with embarrassment. Further study, however, revealed a slight figure standing in the shadows of a doorway on the far side of the street. His hat was lowered, obscuring much of his face, but the slim hands with their long fingers clasped over his walking stick were unmistakable. I recognized them at once as the fingers I had watched stroke the wings of that unfortunate butterfly, back at the castle wall.

Augustus had followed me.

Augustus, whom I had seen with my own eyes that morning enter the carriage occupied by his parents. Surely the picnic had not been abandoned. Rather than pretend I had not noticed him, I decided to take decisive action. I waved and shouted.

"Mr. Wells! Have you lunched? Do please join me!"

He started at the sound of my voice, but had few options other than to respond. He crossed the street and stood next to me. "I am not hungry, Lady Emily."

"What happened to the picnic?" I asked. "You may not be hungry, but that is no cause to refuse all refreshment. Take a seat and I shall order you a glass of rosé. It is lovely."

He frowned, but did not object. "The picnic . . . the very idea was tiresome. I thought I ought to join them, but we had gone no further than a mile down the road before I felt the inane conversation would drive me out of my mind. I ordered the carriage to stop so that I might alight from it. I walked back to town, and have been . . ." He paused here, his voice hanging in the air. "I have been having a bit of a wander. As have you, Lady Emily."

My heartbeat quickened. Had he seen me visiting apothecary after apothecary? "My husband suffers from the occasional headache, and while peppermint oil offers him substantial relief, I have read that a concoction of neroil, sweet marjoram, and rosewood oil can prevent them from occurring altogether. It seems that the marjoram and rosewood are easy enough to come by, but I have yet to locate any neroil."

"Where have you looked?" he asked.

"Several apothecaries." I gulped the rest of my wine.

"I should try the Marché Forville, the local market. Do you know where it is, on the rue Louis Blanc?"

"I believe I do," I said, shocked that he was offering what appeared to be a useful suggestion.

"There is a woman there who sells herbs and has a selection of oils. If she does not have that which you seek, she may know someone who does."

"Thank you, Mr. Wells. I am much obliged. You are quite knowledgeable for someone who has never before been in Cannes. I am impressed."

"I make it my business to know useful things. One never knows when they will come in handy."

The waiter appeared with my ratatouille. Augustus looked at it with disdain and asked if he might have some tapenade. The waiter obliged quickly, bringing with it more fresh bread.

"Why did you wish to avoid the picnic?" Augustus asked as soon as the waiter had disappeared.

"I own the idea did not appeal to me," I said, debating how candid I should be with him. "I am still upset by Mr. Neville's death and am finding it difficult to dedicate myself to the pursuit of pleasure. I do hope my inability to do so with abandon has not impinged upon your sister's high spirits."

"Amity has never let anything impinge on her high spirits, as you so charmingly call them." He covered a slice of bread with a thick layer of tapenade. "It is one of the many qualities in her that I admire and wish I could emulate. As it is, I am left to feel slights more deeply than she ever would."

"Are you often slighted?"

"I am well aware that my manner appears odd to many people," he said. "I pretend not to care and react by armoring myself with further eccentricities."

"I am sorry if you feel misunderstood."

"I have never been misunderstood, merely disliked. Amity is the only one who has ever taken pleasure in my company, and now I am to lose her."

"You shan't lose her, Mr. Wells. She will always be your sister, but I do understand that her living in England after her marriage will change your relationship significantly."

"Oh, she won't live in England, Lady Emily. She would despise that."

"I am afraid she won't have any choice in the matter. Her husband-to-be sits in the House of Lords and has an estate to manage." Granted, Jeremy had not voluntarily seen the inside of the Lords on any day but that of the State Opening of Parliament since he had inherited his title, and even then, he insisted he only went because he liked the figure he cut in his ducal robes.

"I think she would prefer to be even farther away from our parents," he said.

This took me aback. It was a shocking confidence, blunt even for an American. I wanted to ask him to expound on his statement, but I did not wish to draw attention to it in case it scared him off. "I have always felt that England is not large enough to put adequate distance between myself and my mother."

"Perhaps I have spoken out of turn," he said. "I do not mean to leave you with the impression that my dear pater and mater are in any way unsatisfactory."

"I would have thought no such thing. Your parents seem perfectly amiable."

"I shouldn't think you would hold that opinion after the way Pater spoke to you on the pier."

I coughed. "I was not aware anyone other than myself had heard his comments."

"That is not quite true, is it, Lady Emily? My sister told you Bainbridge overheard the conversation, and I hear everything. I make that my business, too." He popped the last bite of bread into his mouth. "Are you planning to finish your ratatouille? It did not appeal when I first saw it, but tempts me now and I should very much like a taste. You don't mind, do you?"

After lunching with Augustus, I felt more off balance than ever. He had proven simultaneously more congenial and more strange than I could have ever expected; I hardly knew what to make of him. When our table was clear and our check paid—by my companion—I excused myself, explaining that I intended to see a physician. I hoped he would not make further inquiries into the reasons for my plan, but, alas, Augustus Wells knew no social bounds.

"Are you ill? You seem fit as a fiddle."

"What a charming expression," I said. "I am not ill, but there are some matters . . . it is best that I do not explain."

He stared at me, without blinking, until I started to wonder if he was having some sort of a fit.

"You will excuse me?" I waited for his response, but none came. "Mr. Wells?"

He turned on his heel and dashed away from me. Once he was out of sight, I started for the physician's office, keeping vigilant watch to be certain Augustus was not following me. The door was unlocked now, and a surly older woman told me that her son, the doctor—a man called Roche—would soon be at liberty to speak with me.

"I am most grateful for your time," I said, taking the seat he offered me in his wood-paneled office. "You have no doubt heard of the suicide that recently occurred?"

"Yes, the Englishman. He was a friend of yours?"

"He was."

"Then do accept my condolences."

"Thank you," I said. "I was hoping you could help me to better understand what happened, because the details of the incident strike me as unusual." I gave him as thorough an accounting as possible of what had happened.

"Your concern, shall we say, over the issue of the entire bottle being poisoned is a valid one. Generally speaking, most suicides are careful to harm no one but themselves. However, Lady Emily, the state of mind in which an individual must be to take such action is by definition so unhinged that we cannot draw conclusions from what we view as irrational behavior. The very act goes against all of human nature. There is not much stronger in us than the instinct to survive."

"I also believe that the fact he did this in his friend's room rather than his own may be significant."

"Again, there is no way for us to know." He removed his spectacles and polished them with a scrap of silk that had been sitting on top of his desk. "I apologize for not being able to better help you. He may have gone to his friend's room because he believed that his friend was capable of dealing with the fallout from finding him. He may not have wanted that burden to fall on an unsuspecting young hotel maid."

"What about the fact that he left no note?"

"Romantic as the notion of suicide notes is, most people do not leave them."

"Do you have any idea where he might have got ahold of strychnine in Cannes?" I asked. His response confirmed what the apothecary had already told me. "Why would he have come here, carrying the poison, and do such a thing now?"

"Are you quite certain he was as close as you think to this friend whose room he used? Perhaps his choice of location was deliberate. Perhaps he blamed this friend for ruining his life? Was there any resentment or jealously between them?"

"Not so far as I know," I said, "but, as you have already said, we cannot know precisely what he was thinking."

"I am sorry not to be of more help," Dr. Roche replied. "Even someone who specializes in psychology could offer you little more, unless he had treated your friend."

I thanked him for his time and exited the office, my eyes straining against the bright sunlight as I stepped outside. Much as I wanted to know more about what had happened, I questioned the wisdom of continuing my pursuit. What good could come of uncovering strains of tension—or an all-out feud—between Jeremy and Mr. Neville? I would have stopped then and there, were I not still convinced that, even in a suicidal rage, even if he were angry with his friend, Mr. Neville would not have left a poisoned bottle of whisky next to Jeremy's bed.

Unless Jeremy had been the intended victim all along.

# Amity
## Four months earlier

"You are late," Amity said, opening the door to the large suite of rooms at Shepheard's Hotel her parents had got for her and Christabel to share. There was a useless sort of native servant outside, but Amity did not much like him, and ignored him as best she could. She ushered the Duke of Bainbridge inside.

"It is only half two," Jeremy said, a sly grin on his face.

"I told you two o'clock." She closed the door, leaned against it with deliberate and studied elegance, and looked up at him through her long, dark lashes. "You are late."

"I assumed that, like all fashionable ladies, you would not be ready on time."

"What makes you think I am a lady, fashionable or otherwise?"

"Are you going to offer me a seat?" he asked. "Not that you are anything but extremely fetching in your current posture, but I suppose you know that already. I should not be surprised to learn that you have practiced leaning with such grace."

"You may as well have a chair," she said. He followed her into a sitting room that opened onto a balcony overlooking the botanical gardens across the street, where only last night she had kissed him, and took a chair across from the one onto which she draped herself.

"Where is your mother?" he asked.

"Shopping with Daddy. We most likely have only an hour of peace before they return."

"And Christabel?"

"She went with them. Unfortunately, I found that a headache prevented me from joining them," Amity said. "Is that color I see rushing to your cheeks? Are you horrified at finding me here alone?"

"A bit, yes." He tugged at his collar.

"I haven't summoned you under these circumstances to trick you into marrying me, if that is why you are concerned. I do like you, though. I liked kissing you. Liked it enough, in fact, to want to know you better. So you stay just where you are, *your grace*, a safe and respectable distance from me, and we shall sit here and talk, so that I might determine just how interesting you are."

"I have never met anyone quite like you, Miss Wells."

"I should hope not. I like to think of myself as an original."

Jeremy wished he could loosen his cravat. This girl was intoxicating. This girl might just be worth relinquishing his freedom. After all, he could not hold off marriage forever. His brother would never forgive him if he did, even if he regularly insisted that should Jeremy die without an heir, he would turn the whole estate over to their cousin. "Do you like cards, Miss Wells?"

"If by cards you mean poker."

"Teach me."

She smiled. "I shall return in two minutes, with everything we need."

"There are cards and markers on the table." Jeremy gestured toward the window.

"But there is no bourbon, *your grace*. Poker—and I—require bourbon."

"She is too good to believe, Jack! I think I shall have to propose," Jeremy said that evening, when he met his brother for dinner at the Turf

Club that night. The dining room was full of Englishmen; the only Egyptians were those serving them. At the table to Jeremy's left were two gentlemen arguing over the merits of that afternoon's polo match. To his right, an elderly ex-Army officer was doing his best to convince his son that investing in racehorses was not a sound financial strategy. "Imagine the best chap you know—the one with whom you can trust all your secrets. The one who knows what you need almost before you do. The one who makes sure there's always whisky on hand. That's what Amity is like."

"I am well aware of it," Jack said. "I did meet her first, if you recall. I suspected you would take to her."

"You suspected right. I mean to speak to her father tomorrow."

"I can't imagine you'll find any trouble there. They brought her here with the intention of finding a suitable husband."

"She has told me as much. Can you imagine?" Jeremy asked. "There is nothing we cannot discuss. It is so very refreshing. She will be more than diverted when I describe for her the conversations I am overhearing here tonight. That chap is going to buy his racehorses no matter what his father says." He lowered his voice as he spoke and motioned to his right.

"Racehorses aside, Cousin Randolph will be most despondent," Jack said. "I always promised I would hand things over to him if you died without an heir. You know full well I have no intention of playing lord of the manor. My plans run in another direction altogether."

"They always did. It has never ceased to infuriate Mother."

"I do not believe she has ever given enough consideration to my plans to formulate a reaction to them. But what will she think of your future wife?"

"She will not like that Amity's American, but she will fall in love with her the second she lays eyes on her. Who could do otherwise?"

"Your optimism is impressive," Jack said.

"At any rate, it is not her decision. There are some perks to being duke, old boy. You might regret not having the chance."

"Impossible, I assure you." Jack motioned for the waiter. "I think this calls for champagne. My brother, ready to marry. I feared I would never see the day."

"Can we have whisky instead, Jack? You know I prefer it."

Two weeks later, the engagement was official, and the Wells family, along with the Duke of Bainbridge, returned to England with the express intention of introducing the future duchess to her mother-in-law. Jack remained in Egypt, preferring to save his leave for the wedding festivities—including, as Mrs. Wells insisted, the party she was planning in Cannes. As predicted, the duchess (who would not be referred to as the dowager until her son married) balked at the idea of an American taking her place, but after half an hour spent alone with Amity, she was as smitten as her son. Soon thereafter, the best of society had the opportunity to agree with them both, when Amity was introduced at a ball at her fiancé's estate.

Amity had never dreamed she would be so close to clutching all the happiness she had ever wanted. Her worries were limited to one small thing. A trifle, really, something she was certain she could take care of if she only could manufacture the right occasion. She had not exchanged many words with Lady Emily Hargreaves at the ball, but a few had been enough for her to long to be closer to her. Whatever she did, she had to win Emily as a friend.

# 9

I was sitting on our balcony, delighting in the view and the soft scent of flowers in the air, when the picnickers returned. They looked merry, if a bit exhausted, as they climbed down from the carriages. Amity beamed at Colin, who offered a gloved hand to assist her as she alighted and led everyone to the terrace for a spot of refreshment. Colin looked up to find me, waving and calling for me to join them. I nodded in agreement, smiling and waving back.

"Do hurry, Emily," Margaret shouted. "I've a capital scheme all planned out, but it shall never work without you."

"I am on my way," I said, but then stopped and leaned over the railing. Augustus was descending from his parents' carriage. He saw me staring at him—aghast, as I could not reconcile his rejoining the party with him having lunched with me in Cannes—and gave me a jaunty little salute, full of arrogance and devoid of respect.

On my way down, I passed Mr. and Mrs. Wells in the lobby. The exertion of the day had left them tired and they had refused the invitation to join the others on the terrace.

"It is best that we leave the young people to their raucous amuse-ment, don't you think, Lady Emily?" Mrs. Wells's question, as she waited for the lift—her girth suggested she had little tolerance for stairs—seemed to imply, by its tone, that I, too, ought to leave the young people to their raucous amusement. Never mind that *the young people* included my own husband, not to mention Cécile.

"I am not sure what Madame du Lac would think of your saying that," I replied, smiling sweetly. "But you must be exhausted. I do hope we will see you at dinner."

"Not tonight, I am afraid," Mr. Wells said. "We are having it sent up to us. My wife needs rest."

When I reached the terrace, Margaret was holding court, having taken a seat in the center of a group of tables that had been pushed together so that they might hold our entire party. "Tomorrow. It must be tomorrow," she was saying. "I cannot bear to wait any longer. None of you will regret joining me. It will be simply the most fantastic excursion!"

I did not interrupt her. Having come from behind, I knew she had not seen my arrival. "I am quite serious," she continued. "Tomorrow. The concierge has given me the ferry schedule, and we will—I shall brook no argument—we will be on the first boat. If we had not already had one aborted aquatic incident, I should swim to the island myself at this very moment."

"I wondered when you were going to insist on the Îles de Lérins," I said. "You disappointed me when you did not mention it the day of Jeremy's misguided dive into the water. I assume you were too distracted by the subsequent furore to make the connection to the Man in the Iron Mask."

"You made the connection, Emily?" Margaret rose from her chair, took me by the shoulders, and shook me, only half playfully. "You knew all this time that we were a mere stone's throw from that pitiable man's sad prison cell, and you didn't tell me? I shall never forgive you. You know how I adore that book."

"It never occurred to me that you were not already fully aware of it," I said. "I assumed you were planning some spectacular sort of attack on the island."

"I am ashamed, so thoroughly ashamed." She hung her head down to emphasize the point. "This is what comes from my refusing to read Baedeker's until today. This is the low level to which Latin poetry has brought me."

"You read Baedeker's today?" I asked, thrusting my friend back into her seat and accepting the one next to her, from which Mr. Fairchild had leapt to offer me a place. "For one day I leave you to your own devices and you are reading travel guides?"

"Mock me all you wish, Emily, but I am despondent. You, my dearest friend in the world, knew all about the Île Sainte-Marguerite and did not mention it once to me."

"I believe we have already covered this ground," I said. "You have, I gather, planned an expedition for tomorrow?"

"Yes, but you have ruined at least two-thirds of my pleasure by denying me the right to having been the one to discover the prison."

"My dear, even Baedeker was hardly the first. It is a well-known stop for tourists," I said. "If you would like, I shall pretend to have no idea where we are going until you reveal it to me as you stand on the prow of the ferry, sweeping views of the old fort in front of us. Perhaps, for dramatic verisimilitude, you could turn away, and, without us seeing, don a mask of iron, and then spin around, your face covered, and announce our destination as we shriek in horror."

"That was, more or less, what I had been hoping to do," she said, drawing her eyebrows close together. "The concierge promised he could procure for me a mask before the morning, although he could not guarantee it would actually be fashioned from iron."

"Alas, poor Margaret," Colin said. "All your plans dashed."

"My spirits shall rally; they always do. Give me a cigarette, Hargreaves, and order me a drink."

"How was the picnic?" I asked.

"Perfect," Amity said. "Although Mr. Fairchild tried to make us all play cricket. We did miss you terribly, Emily. Augustus says he lunched with you."

"Yes, he did." He was now sitting at the far end of the group, his arms crossed and his back to the table. "Yet he managed to catch up with the lot of you?"

"Only as they returned to town," Augustus said, without turning to face us. "I knew the road on which they would arrive and thought I might as well walk there as anywhere else."

"Daddy made the carriage driver stop to collect him. And you, Emily, I understand you went to see a doctor? I do hope you are not unwell?"

"No, Amity, I am not. Thank you for your kind concern." I hid my shock at her having asked so indiscreet a question.

"Do you have joyful news to share with us?" Amity asked. "Will you be able to stomach a boat ride tomorrow morning? Do you"—she stopped and laughed—"find yourself in a delicate condition?"

"*Mon dieu*, Mademoiselle Wells," Cécile said. "That is not a question that ought to be asked." I was grateful to my friend for balking at Amity's impertinence.

"I thought Emily to be a great flaunter of conventions," Amity said. "It is one of the things I most admire about her. I do apologize if I have made her more radical than you should like."

"I am not in a delicate condition, or any other sort of condition," I said. "I merely wanted to better understand Mr. Neville's actions."

Amity slouched elegantly in her chair and threw her hands in the air. "There is a capital way to bring a party to a crashing end."

"Amity." Jeremy took her hand. His eyes were pained. "Please—"

"I will not apologize, my love," she said, pulling her hand away. "I am tired of tiptoeing around the very idea of Mr. Neville. He proved himself nothing more than a selfish coward who did everything in his power to take away our happiness. I am sorry for all of you who grieve his loss, but we ought to remember that he chose his course of action with deliberate calculation.

"Mr. Neville may have had no choice at all," I said, aghast. "His—"

"I am afraid, Emily, that I am going to have to insist that this be the end of the matter," Amity said. "Enough death, enough jealousy, enough of every negative thing. We are here to celebrate, and if you find yourself unable to do so, then I am heartily sorry. Do not think me cruel, but I cannot bear to see Jeremy suffer any more than he already has."

"I understand," I said, doing my best to convince myself that she had not intended to be rude. Her enthusiasm was not always appropriate, but that did not render it deliberately malicious. "Do please forgive me."

"I do not mean to scold, Emily," she said. "Only to drag us all—even if it should require kicking and screaming—out of these morose shadows and back into the sunshine." The sentiment was a noble one, worthy of an Englishman, and I could hardly fault her for voicing it.

A waiter, who now appeared bearing a heavy tray of drinks, could not have better timed his arrival. Margaret made a rousing toast to Mr. Neville, saying that from this moment onward, we would remember only happy things about him, and the mood was restored to its earlier jubilation. After she spoke, Augustus turned slowly and watched me with the same unblinking stare he had unleashed on me that afternoon. I was not the only once to notice.

"He knows something, doesn't he?" Mr. Fairchild asked, pulling me aside when I had got up from my seat to move so that I might better talk to my husband.

"Whatever do you mean?"

"Augustus," he said, frowning. "He knows more about Neville's death than he is letting on. Did you speak of it with him today?"

"No. The subject only rose when we broached it just now," I said.

"I am surprised by Amity's words. I thought her fondness for Neville ran rather deeper than it appears it did," he said.

"I do not believe she meant to disparage him, only to remind us that we ought to live in the present and focus on positive things."

"Perhaps all the sobbing she did at the funeral cleansed her of her grief." Mr. Fairchild's lips were drawn in a tight line. "It may not be so easy for the rest of us."

Margaret could never be accused of failing to follow through on her ideas. The next morning, she sent members of the hotel staff to bang on all of our doors before the sun had risen. In order to cushion the blow, she asked them also to bring breakfast, a gesture that we all appreciated, but that did not eliminate yawns and sleepy faces when we met in the hotel lobby. There were carriages just outside, waiting to take us to the Quai Laubeuf, from whence the ferries to the nearby Îles de Lérins departed. On Saint-Honorat stood a medieval monastery, and it was this island to which Jeremy had attempted to swim. Our destination, however, was Saint-Honorat's sister island, Sainte-Marguerite, home of Fort Royal.

Only twenty minutes from Cannes, Sainte-Marguerite had for centuries served as the favored location for ships to dock when their passengers and crew planned to go to the mainland. The Romans had used it as a military installation, taking advantage of the natural defenses formed by its steep, rocky cliffs, and I ached to see what archaeologists might discover should they ever excavate the site. In the seventeenth century, the infamous Cardinal Richelieu decided to construct a fort on the island. By the end of that century, part of that fort was being used as a prison, and it was here that the mysterious Man in the Iron Mask, made famous by Alexandre Dumas's novel of the same name, was incarcerated.

The Man in the Iron Mask was not the only notorious prisoner held in the fort. Twenty-odd years ago, Marshal Bazaine, former commander of the French army, escaped from his own cell after being sentenced to death for treason. Margaret assured us we would face no criminals during our visit, violent or otherwise. The prison was little used now, and those convicts it did hold were in a separate section of the building from the Man in the Iron Mask's cell.

We stepped off the boat onto the island's small dock and followed a narrow path along the coast, gradually making our way uphill as we passed the stone houses of the few civilians who lived on the island. Many of them operated businesses that catered to the fort's soldiers, and we saw more than one welcoming café. I was particularly taken with the almost medieval scene of a group of women washing their laundry at a public well, where the water had been directed to flow through multiple stone troughs worn smooth by years of repeated use. The women sang and gossiped as they scrubbed their coarse clothing against the sides of the rock; I could easily imagine the scene having been repeated with little change over many previous centuries.

Lush vegetation lined both sides of the cobbled path once we had gone beyond the little village, and its incline increased. Colin offered his arm to Cécile, whose face had grown red with exertion. Amity and Margaret were skipping, arm in arm, as if they were schoolgirls.

"Don't you adore her?" Jeremy asked, slipping his arm through mine. "She has such a passion for life."

"She does indeed."

"I do so want the two of you to be friends," he said.

"How could I not befriend the only girl who has ever managed to capture your heart?" I asked.

"Other than yourself," he said, winking. The gesture warmed my heart, as it had been so long since he had acted that way, but even as I relished the feeling, it reminded me that I must be careful not to flirt back lest Amity read more into our behavior than the well-worn habits of old friends.

As we walked past spots where the plants lining the path thinned,

I could see bits of old brick, Roman from the look of them, narrow and long. It was as if the island had swallowed up abandoned buildings, revealing their crumbling remains to remind us that we, too, were only temporary guests. This was my first inkling that there was something sinister about the island. In any other setting, the path would have made for a pleasant garden stroll, but here, history and war and violence and crime converged. I increased my pace and soon realized I was all but dragging Jeremy alongside me.

When the tall, grey walls of the fort were nearly in front of us, the path opened to become wide stairs, its incline too steep to be managed efficiently in any other way. After we passed the ravelin, separate from the main part of the fort, and often the first line of defense, we approached the Royal Gate, where a smartly uniformed guard snapped to attention and nodded to us as we walked through. He was used to tourists.

Inside the walls stood what looked, for all practical purposes, like a town. There was a church with a large clock on its tower, and rows of stone buildings that in other circumstances would have housed shops and living quarters. Here they were barracks, and despite the cheerful green hue of their shutters, I found them ominous. In a way, the fort was charming, but at the same time a desolate sense of isolation permeated it, chilling me to the bone. Even the sounds of soldiers marching and the barked commands of their officers got lost in the sound of the wind whipping off the ocean below.

"Madame Michaels, I have been expecting you," a young officer said, greeting Margaret with a bow. "I am eager to give you a tour of this fascinating place. Do please come with me." We followed him, first to the chapel, which was typical of its sort, a simple, functional space that would amply serve its purpose. From there, we continued up the stairs that went past its door, and onto a grassy hill that led directly to the top of the parapets. The view was incomparable, and if one directed one's focus strictly to the Mediterranean and the coast of the

Riviera stretching far to the east and the west, one would be swept away by sublime beauty. The water sparkled and the buildings looked as if they were stacked like children's blocks up steep cliffs. But if one were to turn, even slightly, so that the battlements and the barracks and the prison came into view, the earth seemed to split between the gentle and the evil.

Most likely, these feelings consumed me because I knew too well the legend of the prisoner in the Iron Mask, but my soul grew uneasy on Sainte-Marguerite. For thirty-four years, that anonymous man languished here in his cell, with his guards ordered to shoot him dead should he dare remove his mask. No wonder, then, that he inspired so many stories, so many theories as to his identity, none of which ever could be proved true.

"The building just below us is used to store explosives," our young guide explained. "You see it is built lower than where we stand, almost dug into the hill, so that should there be any sort of unfortunate accident, the damage would be minimized."

"Happy thought," Amity whispered to me. "Are you enjoying yourself?"

"I am, thank you," I said, "although I must confess that there is . . . something terrifying about this place."

"I could not agree more," she said. "I feel as if evil lurks here. Do not laugh at me, Emily, I forbid it."

"I shouldn't dream of laughing," I said. "The same thought occurred to me."

"If the two of us came to it separately, it must have some merit to it," Amity said, slipping her arm through mine. "Do you think the Romans sacrificed virgins here?"

"The Romans did not sacrifice virgins," I said. "Animals, however were a different matter."

"Either way, it is deliciously creepy, but at the same time truly frightening," Amity said. "I am disappointed about the virgins, though."

"If you will continue this way, please," the officer said, waving us down from the walls, back around the chapel, and into the midst of the barracks. "This, as is obvious, is where my fellow soldiers and I live while we serve here. Not of any interest, I assure you. Barracks do not provide much beyond the most basic of comforts, and although they are fitting for soldiers, they would be shocking to ladies. Through here, you can just see the terrace on which Marshal Bazaine paced while he was a prisoner. I shall delay no longer in bringing you to what you came for. Onward to the prison."

We crossed through a large, dusty parade ground, on the far side of which an imposing building stood, its back abutting the fort's wall. A round tower faced inward, and I wondered if it was within its confines that the Man in the Iron Mask had languished. The officer led us into the building, chatting congenially with the guards at the entrance, and motioned for us to follow him into a wide, dimly lit corridor.

"This is the cell in question," he said, pointing to one in a row of heavy wooden doors studded with metal. "You may visit at your leisure. I shall wait for you without."

Christabel and Jack reached the door first. She poked her head in, squealed, and pulled it out. "I have no interest in going in all the way," she said. "It is entirely too awful for my tastes. I shall not photograph it." Jack, gallant gentleman that he is, accompanied her back outside, though not before he took a quick look into the cell. Augustus, whose expression communicated nothing but boredom and disdain, followed soon thereafter. Mr. Fairchild and Margaret were thick as thieves, pacing the room in an attempt to measure it.

"It is much bigger than I would have expected," Margaret said. "It must be at least fourteen feet across. And a window! Did you expect such a window?"

There was a quite large window on one side of the fireplace—yes, the cell contained a fireplace—but three sets of sturdy metal bars, one flush with the cell's wall, one another foot beyond the first, and the last on the far end of the deep windowsill, a good four feet from the wall, ensured that its presence would offer no hope for escape. A toilet was installed on the other side of the fireplace, sunk into the wall by a foot or more. Square terra-cotta tiles covered the floor, and I wondered if the fire would be adequate for keeping away the chill in the damp winter.

Not that comfort was the goal of such a room. The prisoners here were allowed basic furnishings, and the officer, who had peeked back in to see how we were getting along, told us that the Man in the Iron Mask had tapestries and rugs. On the wall opposite the fireplace, someone had painted an elaborate mural, that, despite its state of disrepair, seemed to me an attempt at the sort of decoration one might have found in a Roman villa. Urns and garlands and figures that were now too decayed to recognize filled the space above the door. I wondered if a prisoner had painted them, but our guide did not know.

"Much more pleasant than a townhouse in London at the height of the season," Jeremy said. "I think I shall inquire as to the possibility of taking up temporary residence here."

"I can assure you your future wife would object in the most strenuous terms," I said.

"Emily is too right," Amity said. "I do believe I am going to rely on you as an ally, Emily. Between the two of us, we might be able to civilize him."

"Only if you use an extremely liberal definition of the word civilize," I said, sending Amity into a gale of lovely laughter. As the sound echoed in the chamber which, though large for a prison, was still, to my mind, claustrophobic, I began to feel once again that sense of evil that permeated Sainte-Marguerite.

Cécile appeared to share my feeling. "I do not like it," she said. "To hold a man here, for all those years, keeping his identity secret. I cannot stand to spend another moment in the confines of these walls." Colin looked to Mr. Fairchild, I suppose hoping that he would offer to escort her out, but his friend was so taken with looking out the window that he showed no sign of having heard Cécile, so my husband ushered her from the space. Jeremy and Margaret followed them.

"It is so horrible," I said, "I can hardly bear to remain, but at the same time, I cannot tear myself away."

Mr. Fairchild turned back into the room. "I know just what you mean. Thirty-four years. Do you think he really never removed the mask?"

"Surely to wash his face," I said.

"But if the guards were ordered to shoot on sight, would he have taken the risk, even for a moment. How does one sleep in a mask of iron?"

"Very badly, I imagine, although given the length of time—all those years—a person would adapt, somehow." I stood in the center of the room and looked up at the tall, arched ceiling. Wind rattled in the chimney and Mr. Fairchild and I both froze, staring at each other.

"That is quite enough for me," he said, and took me by the arm. "I cannot think when I have better appreciated my freedom."

The others were waiting for us outside, where the officer and the guards who stood at the entrance of the prison were regaling them with tales from the fort's past. Cécile, tired of the enterprise, voiced the loud opinion that it was time we return to Cannes. In response, Margaret threatened to spend the night in the cell. This sent the guards into peals of laughter. I was about to interject my own thoughts when I felt a tug on my sleeve.

"Did you see my reticule in the cell after I left?" Amity asked. "It's gone. The strap must have broken."

"I don't remember seeing it," I said.

"I'll go back and look," she said. She walked approximately six feet in the direction of the prison entrance, then stopped and turned back to me. "Do you know, I feel quite incapable of entering that space alone. How ridiculous."

"It is not ridiculous. I'll fetch Jeremy."

"I don't want him to know. He likes my strength, and I fear it is too early to show him my weaknesses."

"What about your brother?" I asked, looking for Augustus. "Where has he gone?" I did not see him anywhere in the courtyard.

"I do hope he hasn't managed to get lost," Amity said. "Finding him is probably more important than going after my reticule. There was nothing of import in it."

"I shall go after your reticule," I said. "You look for Augustus." I slipped back into the prison—although calling it that seemed almost silly given the current lack of guards. It was, at this point, more of a prison in theory than in actuality, at least that was what I told myself as I returned to the corridor lined with cells. The door to the Man in the Iron Mask's cell was partially closed, so I pulled it open, feeling the weight of the door working against me. Amity's reticule was on the floor, near the fireplace, the satin ribbon loop that would have held it on her wrist torn at the seam. I crouched down to retrieve it.

As I returned to standing, two wretched sounds accosted me: the creak of metal scraping against metal and the thud of a solid mass of wood. I could not move, knowing all too well what I would find when I turned around to face the door. It would be closed.

Worse still was what followed, the click of a lock.

# Amity
## Two months earlier

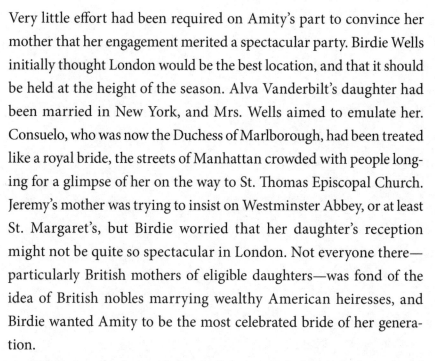

Very little effort had been required on Amity's part to convince her mother that her engagement merited a spectacular party. Birdie Wells initially thought London would be the best location, and that it should be held at the height of the season. Alva Vanderbilt's daughter had been married in New York, and Mrs. Wells aimed to emulate her. Consuelo, who was now the Duchess of Marlborough, had been treated like a royal bride, the streets of Manhattan crowded with people longing for a glimpse of her on the way to St. Thomas Episcopal Church. Jeremy's mother was trying to insist on Westminster Abbey, or at least St. Margaret's, but Birdie worried that her daughter's reception might not be quite so spectacular in London. Not everyone there—particularly British mothers of eligible daughters—was fond of the idea of British nobles marrying wealthy American heiresses, and Birdie wanted Amity to be the most celebrated bride of her generation.

While her mother and the duchess argued about the location of the wedding, Amity suggested Cannes as an alternative to London for the engagement festivities. Would it not, she asked, seem like a half-hearted compromise to tell her future mother-in-law the engagement party would be in London rather than the wedding? And didn't the French know better than anyone how to celebrate?

Birdie, exhausted from arguing about the wedding, capitulated to her daughter's demands, and no sooner had she started planning the party in earnest than she realized the brilliance of Amity's idea. Cannes was refined and elegant, not crass like Monte Carlo, and would establish Birdie and her daughter as the sort of ladies who ought to be at the center of London society. When Amity became the Duchess of Bainbridge, she would render Mrs. Astor and her Four Hundred irrelevant. No one in New York would care about invitations to that once famous ballroom; instead they would long to be included in the parties hosted by the Wells family, so that they might one day make the list for those thrown by the duchess.

Amity did not care about any of this. She was in love, and all she wanted was to be with her prince. Of course, he was not actually a prince, but she happily ignored that detail, and set about planning her party in Cannes so that it would solidify all of her hopes and dreams. Jeremy had invited the Hargreaveses, and this would prove the perfect occasion for her to get to know Emily; given the closeness of her fiancé to that lady, it seemed imperative to Amity that the friendship extend to her. She would do everything she could to ensure it, and they would leave the Riviera as dear to each other as sisters; of this, there could be no doubt. Amity would accept nothing less.

# 10

Mustering my courage and burying my nerves, I flung myself in a single movement at the sturdy door to the Man in the Iron Mask's cell. As I expected, it was immovable. There was no handle on the inside, and I could not get it to budge even by throwing all my weight against it. I began to beat on it, crying out for help, but the wood was dotted with metal studs that tore at my hands, leaving them bloody and bruised. I screamed until my throat was raw, but to no avail. The guards assigned to this little-used section of the building must still be outside, cavorting with my friends.

I crossed to the window and rallied myself. Obviously, I would not be left here for long. No one was going to leave me on the island, and surely in a few minutes someone would come looking for me. Amity knew where I was. The only potential delay in my rescue could come from it taking her longer than she had hoped for her to find Augustus. Surely at any moment, Colin would burst through the door and free me.

Despite my attempts to focus on these comforting thoughts, panic began to bubble inside me, due largely, I believe, to the history contained within the walls of the cell—walls that seemed to grow closer with every passing moment. I pride myself on the ability to think rationally, and I did my best to treat the situation as an investigation of sorts. How many people had been graced with the opportunity to experience what life really had been like for the Man in the Iron Mask? Here I stood, locked in his cell, trapped, scared, cold, hungry—well, I was not hungry. The day was warm, and the cool stone of the cell no imposition on my comfort. But I was trapped, and I was scared.

I had heard the lock. Someone had deliberately incarcerated me here, if I may take the liberty of using the term. Was Margaret playing some sort of prank? I could not believe she would do such a thing. I checked my watch; it had been only a little more than a quarter of an hour. Surely they would not keep me waiting much longer.

At last, the lock clicked again, and relief washed over me. I waited for the door to open, but it did not.

"Hello?" I called out. "Is someone there?" There was no response. I pushed against the door, but it did not budge. Then, leaning against it with my entire weight while pressing my feet hard into the floor, I pushed again, and this time the door moved, only a few inches. I could not understand what was impeding my progress. The wood was not dragging on the floor—there was a gap between the bottom of the door and the tiles. With a third push, expending all the effort I could muster, I managed to move it enough so that I could slip through the opening and back into the corridor.

Once free, I saw that there now stood in the corridor a large rain barrel blocking the door. It had kept it from swinging freely on its hinges. Without pausing, I rushed out of the building—the guards had not returned to their posts—and out to the parade ground, where, so far as I could tell, my friends had not taken note of my absence.

"I do so very much appreciate you all coming to my rescue," I said.

"Your rescue?" Jeremy asked. "Em, I was wholly unaware that you allow yourself to be rescued."

"Sometimes, Jeremy, it is necessary." I turned to Amity. "Did you find Augustus?"

"No, but the guard at the Royal Gate told me that he had already left and started for the dock, so I imagine we will see him on the boat. You look terrible, Emily. I do hope locating my reticule didn't do this to you."

"I did find it," I said, and handed it to her.

"Your hands!" Margaret exclaimed. "What happened?"

"I went to retrieve Amity's reticule from the Man in the Iron Mask's cell," I said. "While I was collecting it, someone closed the door and locked me in. I screamed for help, but no one was close enough to hear me. As you can see, my attempts to beat open the door took a greater toll on my hands than on the door."

"Someone trapped you?" Colin asked.

"I heard the lock click after the door shut."

"Did you hear anything else?" he asked.

"No. Eventually, I heard the lock again, but I still could not open the door." I told him about the rain barrel, and he ran off, back into the prison. Amity insisted on bandaging my injured hands with handkerchiefs and fussed over me like I were a wounded child.

"It is quite all right," I said. "No lasting harm done."

"It is most unacceptable," Cécile said. "I want to know the identity of the miscreant who played this trick on you."

"If it was a trick," Amity said. "What if he had left her longer? What if she had fainted in terror and struck her head as she fell? This is no lighthearted prank."

Colin returned. "I saw no rain barrel, Emily."

"It was there and so heavy I could barely move it."

"It is not there any longer. I searched the other cells and the rest of the corridor as well, but found nothing."

"How strange."

"Were you playing a trick on us, Emily?" Amity asked, a smile spreading across her face. "You are so very! I was actually worried that

some maniac was after you! And your hands—what were you thinking, injuring yourself? Did you think we would not believe you if you
had no physical proof?"

"That is not what happened at all," I said, shock racking my body.
"I told you—someone locked the door. I heard it click." The tenor of
the group around me changed almost imperceptibly, but I could feel
that no one believed my story to be credible. Neither Jack nor Mr. Fairchild would make eye contact with me, and Christabel had turned
away from me altogether. Cécile and Margaret, upon whom I thought
I could rely, remained silent. Only Colin offered support, standing
close and squeezing my wrist, not wanting to further bruise my hands.

"Badly done, Em," Jeremy said. "I was ready to go complain to the
commander of the fort and insist that he interrogate all his soldiers
until someone confessed."

"You assume I have invented the story?" I asked.

"Someone could have moved the barrel," Margaret said, but her
tone was not convincing.

"So quickly?" Mr. Fairchild asked. "And without any of us noticing?"

"We were all focused on Emily," Colin said. "Her story along with
the injuries to her hands could have served as a ready distraction. It
is possible that there are places in the prison I did not know to look."
With a few words, he persuaded the guards to search with him, but
when they returned, he was shaking his head. "Nothing, I am afraid."

"It is time we return to the mainland," Cécile said. "I do not think
we shall find any satisfactory answers here."

The boat ride back to Cannes took only twenty minutes, but I feared
this trip would feel like an eternity. Tension hung over us all, and I
overheard Mr. Fairchild and Jack saying that they understood Cécile's
comment about satisfactory answers to directly imply that she believed
I had orchestrated the incident. Outraged by this, I went to her, confident that they had misinterpreted her words.

"I do believe you, Kallista," she said, "and I will tell the gentlemen as much. But it is very strange, do you not think?"

"Of course I do," I snapped. "After all, I was the one trapped in that awful cell."

Margaret joined us. "Do not listen to any of this rubbish," she said. "I think we were all swept up by the mood of the island. It is a foreboding place, and our imaginations have run away with us."

"My imagination has not been called into action," I said.

"I was not suggesting anything of the sort," she said. "But the rest—they are inventing stories for their own entertainment."

"I confess I thought neither of you believed me," I said.

"I am wounded," Cécile said, striking her breast. "How could you think us capable of such disloyalty?"

"It is beneath me," I said, lowering my head and tugging at the makeshift bandages on my hands.

"We should have spoken up on your behalf," Margaret said.

"I am terribly sorry," I said. "I should have had better faith in you both."

"It does not merit further thought," Margaret said.

I nodded. "You are right, of course, but it does trouble me that we have not the slightest idea of who did this. I hate to even ask the question, but did either of you actually see Augustus leave the fort?"

"Excellent question," Margaret said. "He would have thought this a capital joke."

"Yes," I said, "but he was at the boat before us, and the guards did confirm his departure through the gate. Would he have had time to do it?"

"He could have arranged it in advance," Margaret said.

"I think, Kallista, it is best that we put the incident behind us. No harm would have come to you—despite Mademoiselle Wells's extremely dramatic cries of horror. Anyone who knows you is well aware of the fact that you would never have fainted in the circumstances. The soldiers, perhaps, did it to amuse themselves. These military men are not always so civilized as one would hope."

"You are quite right, and there was no lasting harm done. My hands are not badly hurt—I did not need them bandaged—and it shall make for an excellent story." The ferry had left the island far behind, parting the choppy lapis waters of the Mediterranean before us. Other vessels crisscrossed the Rade de Cannes around us, their passengers lining up on the decks to take in the spectacular views of sea, coast, hills, and distant mountains. Before long, we could start to make out the Hotel Britannia on the shore, and I knew that we would soon be back at the Quai Laubeuf. I did not entirely regret the end of this particular adventure.

Before we arrived, Cécile soundly scolded Jack and Mr. Fairchild for their unkind interpretation of her words, and told them that they each owed her a bottle of champagne by way of apology. They agreed without argument, and Jack suggested that I should receive the same bounty. Soon we were all laughing again, the mood restored.

"I do not like that island," Mr. Fairchild said, leaning next to me on the railing as the boat approached the dock at Cannes. "No one is going to convince me that you would have staged that stunt, Lady Emily. I am heartily sorry about what you overheard—please believe me. I was only shocked at the idea that Cécile had so little faith in you. Of course it had to be a misunderstanding. I ought never to have given the notion even the slightest credit."

"Thank you, Mr. Fairchild."

"And what could you have meant to accomplish by doing such a thing?" he continued. "Would it not have been more dramatic to wait for someone to come looking for you than to rescue yourself? The whole thing is very odd. It is as if the goal of the instigator was to make you look bad."

"It doesn't matter now," I said. "Cécile is right—some soldiers may have done it, thinking it would be amusing."

Jack, standing on my other side, frowned. "No. A soldier would not find that amusing. Take it from one who would know."

Colin and I retired to our room shortly after dinner that night, neither of us in the mood for prolonged social interaction. My husband undid his tie, letting it fall loose on his white shirt, and tugged at his collar. "I am concerned about what happened on the island," he said. "I cannot make the slightest sense of it."

"I think it was Augustus," I said, and detailed for him all my encounters with him.

"There is no question that he is strange," Colin said, "malicious, even, but I do not see why he would attempt to harm you." He opened the doors to our balcony and stepped outside. Below us, candles danced on the terrace, their light catching on the myriad diamond necklaces adorning the ladies sitting there. Lights from boats dotted the harbor, gliding along as if by magic, the vessels themselves hidden in darkness.

"A stroll through town wasn't my only purpose the day you were all picnicking," I said, pulling a wrought-iron chair away from the matching table and turning it so that it faced the water. I confessed to him my visits to the apothecaries.

"Are you suggesting that Augustus Wells objects to you asking questions about Neville's suicide?" Colin asked.

"What if it wasn't a simple suicide?"

"Neville killed himself, Emily, there is nothing more to it." The silver smoke from his cigar gracefully snaked up to the deep navy sky. "And if there were, it would be down to the Sûreté to deal with the investigation. We are not here in any sort of official capacity, and Neville's death is not likely to draw the palace's attention."

"We have chosen to pursue cases on our own before, and we could now," I said. "Amity sobbed through the funeral. What if she considered him more than just her fiancé's friend? And what if Mr. Neville poisoned the entire bottle because he expected Jeremy would find his body and then steel his nerves with a fortifying drink? What if he intentionally left the rest of the whisky where he knew Jeremy would drink it, ensuring that neither of them would have the woman they both loved?"

"We have exactly no evidence to support this theory," Colin said. "Suppose it is true—Neville failed to do anything but take his own life. Would you have his reputation so slandered? And for what?"

"It is important to know the truth."

"If Neville fancied himself in love with Amity and we expose that now, it will only serve to make Amity feel culpable for his death."

"Maybe she was culpable," I said. "She might have encouraged—"

"Stop." He rose from his seat and stood behind me, putting his hands firmly on my shoulders. "Even if she begged him to elope with her and then changed her mind and refused to ever see him again, she is not responsible for his death. No one bears that blame but the man himself."

"You are right." I sighed, removed the cigar from his hand, took a long drag before returning it to him, and went back inside, where I flopped onto the bed. "I do not know why I am having such difficulties accepting what happened."

"Let us analyze what is troubling you," Colin said, lying next to me. "First, we have an entire bottle of poisoned whisky rather than a glass."

"Second, we have the use of strychnine, a poison not readily available in Cannes, which suggests it was purchased before the start of this holiday."

"And you believe Neville would not have deliberately planned his suicide to coincide with an engagement celebration?" Colin asked.

I stared at the ceiling. "Not necessarily. Let us imagine that he and Jeremy had some sort of spectacular falling out, and that it left Mr. Neville furious. Jeremy, with his carefree attitudes, did not so much as notice how deeply his friend took their argument, and invited him to this party."

"Neville, outraged, decides to show Bainbridge once and for all that his disregard for everyone around him is unacceptable," Colin said. "He decides to take his own life, not only because of the argument, but because of other things in his life that may have been catalyzed by it—the inability to pay debts, that sort of thing—and to do so in his friend's room, by poisoning his friend's favorite whisky."

"No one who has spent more than half an hour with Jeremy would ever believe him capable of understanding the meaning of such a gesture unless it were accompanied by a very detailed explanation," I said, rolling onto my side to face my husband.

"What if Neville did leave a note?" Colin asked. "And someone removed it from the room before the maid found him."

"A moment. A maid found him?" I asked, sitting up.

"Yes. She had been sent up with extra pillows."

"At five o'clock in the morning?" I asked.

"Not by Neville. He had already been dead for at least an hour."

"Who requested the pillows?"

"The desk clerk said Bainbridge did, on his way into the hotel."

"Jeremy didn't arrive until we were down for breakfast," I said. "Are we to believe that he returned to the hotel, requested pillows, and went out straightaway?"

"Evidently he did," Colin said. "I asked him about it."

"Why would he do that?"

"He said that he was planning to walk along the beach and was afraid that Augustus might be lurking about somewhere—he does have a way of popping up at the most inconvenient times—and he wanted to see if he was in the hotel. He inquired at the desk, where he was told that the younger Mr. Wells had already retired to his room, and threw in the request for pillows as an attempt to make his question less memorable."

This differed from the account of the evening he had given me. He had not mentioned pillows. "Why would he care if Augustus saw him on the beach?"

"That, my dear girl, is a question I am not at liberty to answer."

"So he was with someone—presumably one of the dancers—and did not want to be discovered. The maid would have known that the duke was not in his room, and would have been instructed to go in and leave the pillows. If Jeremy had not asked for them, he would have found Mr. Neville upon his return."

"Precisely."

"Pillows? Really?" I looked at him in disbelief.

"I agree. It is inane, and wholly superfluous. The desk clerk would never have thought it odd for him to inquire after another guest."

"Yet by acting as he did, Jeremy may have saved his own life. Had he found Mr. Neville, he almost certainly would have poured a glass of the tainted whisky for himself," I said. "Our friend is most fortunate."

# Amity
## Cannes, present

Chauncey Neville. Amity hated the man. Despised him. Wished she could shake him until his teeth chattered. That, of course, was not possible now that he was dead, and it was not—not at all—that Amity did not feel deeply sorry that the man had ended his own life. That was a horrible, unspeakable tragedy. She had, after all, liked Chauncey. He was handsome and sweet, always ready with a witty, though quiet, observation if one was able to coax him past his shyness. He even, on occasion, had ribbed Emily about her love of ancient Greece. Kindly, of course. He had been so downright kind it was nothing short of irritating.

It did boggle the mind that a lady—no matter how beautiful and how well-dressed—who spent most of her time buried in the study of ancient texts could attract the attention and admiration of so many gentlemen. Amity credited Earl Bromley for that—his rank ensured that everyone would adore his daughter, no matter what awkward interests she chose to pursue. Still, Jeremy? Amity would never understand their friendship—they seemed to have very little in common—but she accepted it, and although it was proving somewhat more difficult than she had anticipated, she was confident she would soon count Emily among her own closest friends. She only hoped she could do so without being forced to read *The Iliad* or some other wretched poem.

Now all that mattered was doing everything necessary to keep Jeremy's spirits up in the wake of his friend's death. The funeral had been a poky little affair, with no outward signs of grief from Chauncey's friends. Stiff upper lip and all that. Amity was the only one who had cried, and she was ashamed to admit, even to herself, she was crying more because her party had been spoiled than because Chauncey was dead.

It sounded cold; she knew that. But no one had forced him to drink that whisky. It was a wholly selfish act, spoiling all of their fun. Jeremy had balked at the idea of staying in Cannes after the burial, but she had insisted, and called on his English sensibilities. Surely the weakness of one man should not destroy those who remain? He had acquiesced, of course, and had convinced the others to stay. Jeremy would never deny her anything; it was his most attractive quality.

# 11

Colin, having learned that Mr. Neville's luggage had not yet been sent to his brother, employed all of his skills in the art of persuasion to convince the hotel manager that we needed to search it. It proved no small feat, as Monsieur Fortier showed admirable dedication to respecting the privacy of his guests. In the end my husband convinced him (it would take the strength of a demigod at least to resist his dizzying logic), but the manager asked that we keep our actions quiet. We agreed and followed him to a storage room in the basement of the hotel.

"I would never allow this if Monsieur Neville were still alive," Monsieur Fortier said.

"Of course not," Colin replied. "This is an unusual situation, and I very much appreciate your discretion."

"I should perhaps tell you . . ." The man hesitated, and rubbed his hands together. "You are not the first to have asked to inspect Monsieur Neville's luggage."

"Who else did?" I asked.

"Another member of your party. Monsieur Fairchild."

"Did you allow him to do so?"

"I most certainly did not," Monsieur Fortier said. "Unlike you, he had no sort of official identification. As I have already told you, even with that I would have hesitated were Monsieur Neville still alive. I take the privacy of my guests seriously."

"You are a good man," Colin said.

Mr. Neville's luggage consisted of a single trunk and a small suitcase. We had the keys to them both—they had been in his room and Monsieur Fortier had kept them in a separate envelope to send to his brother, along with the bags. We started by opening the suitcase. Its contents were unremarkable: toiletry items, a shaving kit, several books, a pair of binoculars, and various other personal items. I flipped through the books while Colin applied himself to inspecting the trunk.

"Clothes, boots, hats. Surprisingly, some pieces of local pottery. I suppose he bought them as souvenirs."

"That is quite sad," I said.

"It is. Anything between the pages of the books?"

"Nothing yet. There is a packet of writing paper and envelopes, but it does not look as if any of them have been used. I wonder to whom he had planned to write?"

"You are picturing him as lonely only because he has no family of which to speak—evidenced by the decision to bury him here," Colin said. "That does not mean he did not have a life full of friends."

"Did he have a sweetheart, do you know?" I asked.

"I do not. Bainbridge would be a better source of information than I," Colin said. "I did not know him well."

"Here's something," I said. "A pressed carnation at the bottom of the case." I held it up. "Yellow, just like those Augustus always wears in his buttonhole. It was protected by a folded piece of tissue paper."

"In a book?"

"No. Under the box that held his shaving kit. I imagine whoever packed the case either did not know what to do with it or didn't notice it. I wonder if Mr. Neville had a particular interest in botany?"

"Seems unlikely," Colin said. "I believe him to have been nearly as dedicated as Bainbridge to the pursuit of useless behavior."

"Do you think we should ask Jeremy about any of this? Would it be useful or merely serve to upset him further?"

"I am at a loss, Emily. I agree this suicide has many odd facets to it, but I am not convinced we are dealing with something more sinister. It is one thing to search for answers when it causes no further harm or leads to justice, but in this case, we may be accomplishing very little while reopening still raw wounds."

"I wish I knew where he got the strychnine."

"Would it really make any difference?"

"It might." I sighed. "Seeing any evidence of melancholy or despair would matter more."

"I do not want you to feel uneasy about this," Colin said, stroking my cheek with his hand. "I shall ring my colleagues at Scotland Yard and ask them to question Neville's servants in London. I may not agree with you that there is anything of note to be discovered, but over the years I have come to respect your instincts, Emily."

When we had completed our study of Mr. Neville's belongings, we retired to the lounge, rather than the terrace, hoping for a bit of a respite from the rest of our party. I was in dire need of the fortification of tea, but Colin ordered a whisky. We had collected our mail and messages from the desk, and I was sorting through them. Mrs. Wells had sent word that she had booked a table at a restaurant in the old part of town for half nine, and Colin and I decided we would stroll over on our own rather than join the others in the planned parade of carriages. After dealing with the rest of the mail—nothing of consequence save a letter from Nanny telling us that the boys were thriving, but that Richard had knocked over and broken a Ming vase (the perils of having toddlers in a house)—I left a note for Mrs. Wells informing her that we would meet them there.

The lateness of the reservation gave us time to retreat to our room for a considerable—and extremely pleasant—interval. When the hour came to dress for dinner, I relinquished myself into Meg's hands with little enthusiasm. Because we were planning to walk, I thought it best to wear something more practical than a dinner dress, particularly as the fashion of the moment called for long, trailing skirts, and I chose a rose-colored walking costume with a skirt that just skimmed the toes of my comfortable American boots, which were all the rage in London. The matching jacket, neatly tailored, had three-quarter-length sleeves cut perfectly to reveal the profusion of lace on the cuffs of my blouse. I preferred to wear a smart straw hat, trimmed with roses, with the ensemble, but felt it was too casual for the evening, and instead selected a dashing little toque, made from taffeta and decorated with ostrich feathers.

Colin studied my appearance when he saw me. "Do you think that is quite appropriate?"

"It is a bit unusual, but practical as we are walking, and I do not think Amity or her mother would object to my appearing less fashionable and elegant than either of them."

Our stroll to the restaurant was an extremely pleasant one, as the night was fine, the stars bright in the sky above us, and the air still warm. When we arrived at the restaurant, it was a quarter of an hour before our table was due to be ready—we had wanted to give ourselves plenty of time—so we asked the proprietor of the establishment, who greeted us at the door, if we might take a seat near the entrance while we waited.

"You are here with the Wells party, *oui*?" The man asked. "They are expecting you."

Rather than being early, we were last to arrive. Not only was everyone else already seated, they were midway through their meat course. "Oh, at last, the Hargreaveses grace us with their presence!" Mrs. Wells exclaimed. "I do hope we have not inconvenienced you by inviting you to dinner."

"We were not to start at half nine?" Colin asked.

"Half eight," Mr. Wells said. "Never mind the confusion. Do take a seat."

Mrs. Wells looked me up and down, clearly displeased with my attire. "I am sorry if our humble gathering does not meet with your ideas of a fashionable dinner."

"Please don't think anything of the sort, Mrs. Wells," I said, sitting at the chair a waiter had pulled out for me. "I truly believed our table was booked for nine thirty."

"Your mode of dress suggests a complete lack of respect for your hostess," she said. "Did we force you to abandon some sort of sporting pursuit by asking you to dinner?"

"Em is lovely even in a walking suit," Jeremy said. "If anything, her understated elegance puts to shame all the finery in Paris." Mrs. Wells scowled at him.

"Mother, do not be so critical," Amity said. "Are you quite certain that you wrote the correct time on the Hargreaveses' card?"

"Of course I did. The rest of us managed to arrive on time and I am hardly new to writing invitations."

"Please accept my deepest apologies," Colin said, as the waiter brought us the soup the others would have started with.

"I shouldn't be surprised if you were behind this, Hargreaves," Mr. Wells said, his voice all good-natured congeniality. "You have had enough of these formal gatherings, as have I. It's high time we gentlemen have an excursion of our own. Who will join me on a trip to Monte Carlo tomorrow? The ladies can shop or gossip or whatever strikes their fancy. I am overdue for a spot of gambling."

"Can't I come, Daddy?" Amity asked. "You know how I love roulette!"

"Not this time, sugar," Mr. Wells said. "Gentlemen only."

"Very well," Amity said, her lips forming a perfect little pout. "I expect you back no later than eleven o'clock for a moonlight stroll and a surprise."

"What surprise?" Mrs. Wells asked, squaring her broad shoulders and pinching her lips together in a manner that reminded me of a fish.

"I have not yet decided that, Mother," Amity said.

It seemed that our lack of punctuality was no longer of much interest, so I applied myself to my soup. Jeremy, who was seated next to me, apologized for his in-laws-to-be.

"You must understand," he said, "that Mrs. Wells views you as a threat to her daughter's happiness. She railed against you for a good half hour before you arrived."

"That is not very civilized."

"She is American, Em, not civilized."

"Amity doesn't agree with her, does she?"

"Not at all," he said. "She was your staunchest defender. I am afraid I had to remain rather silent."

"Of course," I said.

"It was a bore, but I consoled myself by remembering that once I am a respectable married man, you can take me as a lover."

"Jeremy! What if someone else heard you say such a thing?"

"Yes, right, must remember: be more discreet."

For the first time since I had arrived in Cannes, I started to relax. Jeremy was back to his old self, Amity and I were becoming friendly acquaintances and I hoped that our belated arrival at this dinner would mark the last uncomfortable incident on our trip. On this last point, I could not have been more wrong.

Colin received a message from Scotland Yard the next morning before he was to depart for Monte Carlo. Their questioning of Mr. Neville's servants and an assortment of his friends revealed nothing to suggest that he was suffering from melancholy or any sort of disorder that would have led to suicide. Furthermore, his finances were solid and his bills all paid. Nothing suggested he was a man on the brink of self-destruction. I was explaining all this, and my theories about the case, to Margaret over breakfast. There were hydrangeas on the tables in the dining room that morning, blue and pink, and the air coming in from the terrace blew hot. We were the only two of the ladies yet down, and I wanted to take advantage of our solitude.

"You had better not let Colin hear you call it a case," she said, sprinkling fleur de sel over her eggs.

"We have no evidence solid enough for him to think this merits investigation," I said.

"To be fair, we don't."

"Correct. But do you agree that something is amiss?" I asked.

"I do and I am wounded that you did not bring me with you to question the apothecaries."

"I will more than make up for that today. The gentlemen have already left for Monte Carlo," I said, pouring myself a third cup of tea, "so we can set my plan into motion. Mr. Wells hired dancers to perform at his party. Amity believed they had come from Paris, but after making a discreet inquiry, I have learned they are local girls. I have arranged for us to speak to them this morning and, later, we must find and interview everyone else who assisted with the festivities that evening."

"We cannot let Amity or Mrs. Wells know we are doing this," Margaret said.

"No. I have left a note for Cécile, asking that she keep them occupied. We will owe her a great debt after this."

"I thought you had started to like Amity," Margaret said, poking at her eggs. "Although I couldn't quite understand why. She is awful to you."

"Jeremy said she defended me against her mother last night."

"That is true in every fundamental way, but I still do not trust her."

"I am doing my best to befriend her, but it has proven more difficult than I expected," I said, spreading ginger marmalade on a piece of toast.

"That, my dear girl, is because she is, at heart, vapid." Margaret patted her lips with her napkin and folded it neatly before placing it on the table. "When do the dancers expect us?"

"We will have to leave almost at once if we are to avoid running into Amity and Mrs. Wells. The girls will meet us at a café that is nowhere near the casino. I thought it would be preferable to speak to them away from their place of employment." I finished the last of my tea.

"This, Emily, is the only real fun we have had on this dreadful trip."

"You didn't enjoy Fort Royal and the prison?" I asked.

"I did, until that nonsense with you getting trapped in the cell." She furrowed her brow. "I am convinced there are extremely strange things afoot here, but I can pinpoint neither their source nor their intended goal."

"Let us hope the dancers provide illumination," I said. "If nothing else, I am certain they will be amusing."

# *Amity*

Amity had begun to think breakfast would never end. The day was already unbearably hot, and Birdie even more insufferable than the temperature in the hotel dining room. Emily and Margaret had abandoned them, rushing off even before the others had made it downstairs.

"They left, just like that, only leaving a note? And didn't even invite us to join them?" Birdie's face was all puffed up and red. Moments like these reminded Amity that her mother had never really left behind her childhood days spent on a ranch in Montana; she would have quite happily roped Emily like an unruly steer if she were here now, and, somehow, would insist to Amity that there was nothing inappropriate in the act. There was no use in answering her mother's inane question. It was the third time she had posed it. The first time, Amity had replied. The second time, Madame du Lac had made an attempt. Now, so far as Amity was concerned, it was Christabel's turn, and she knew her sweet friend would not let her down. She scooped up the last bite of kippers from her plate and rose from the table as Christabel spoke.

"Oh, Mrs. Wells, I believe they have done us a favor," Christabel said. "Are you really of a mind to visit Roman ruins on such a warm day? I had so very much hoped we could stroll through town and peruse the shops, perhaps find a quiet spot for tea. How would we have begged off joining them if we had been here when they set off?"

"It was impolite of them not to include us in their excursion," Birdie said, pulling on her gloves and adjusting her enormous hat. "The fact that we are fortunate not to be out with them is irrelevant."

"I do not quite understand Emily," Amity said. "I like her so very much, but I am afraid she is not much fond of me, and that brings me great sadness. I should never want to come between her and Jeremy. I know how much he values their friendship, and I am doing everything possible to grow close to her myself."

"That is very generous of you, Mademoiselle Wells," Madame du Lac said, casting a crushing glance at Birdie's hat before adjusting her own and picking up her parasol. "Shall we depart?"

As they passed the front desk, the clerk called out, saying that he had a package for Amity. "Lady Emily Hargreaves left it for you."

"How lovely!" Amity said, and then turned to her companions. "You won't mind if I delay us just a moment so that I can open it?" There were no objections. Amity tore at the strings around the box and then lifted the lid. Her face went pale and she swayed.

"What is it?" Madame du Lac asked, putting an arm around the girl and steadying her.

"I was talking about this hat just yesterday morning," Amity said. "I had seen it in a shop window and had thought to buy it today." She showed the others the sad contents of the box: a beautiful hat smashed almost beyond recognition.

"Why would she do that?" Christabel asked.

"I do not know." Amity's voice trembled. "Have I offended her in some way? I have done nothing but try to befriend her."

Madame du Lac marched back to the desk and demanded to know who had delivered the box. "Did Lady Emily leave it personally?"

"She was standing right in front of me," he said, "with the box just to the side."

"And she asked you to give it to Mademoiselle Wells?"

"It was clearly labeled, as you can see. I was in the midst of helping several other guests—morning is a busy time and we had several parties checking out."

"So Lady Emily did not speak to you directly about the box?" Madame du Lac asked.

"No, I cannot remember that she did, but it was evident that the box was hers. It was right next to her."

"Was she handing in her key, perhaps?" Madame du Lac asked.

"She did leave her key," the clerk said. "And the box."

"The label is not written in Kallista's hand," Madame du Lac said, turning back to the ladies.

"I do not see how that matters," Birdie said, puffing up her chest. "She is insulting my daughter. I feel that we should ask her to leave Cannes at once. If this engagement is not something she is capable of celebrating—"

"That is quite enough, Madame Wells," Madame du Lac said. "Kallista would never have done this. Someone left the box on the desk—"

"Just when your friend happened to be standing there?" Birdie asked. The two ladies could not have looked more different, Madame du Lac slender and elegant, Birdie built like a battle-axe.

"I have no doubt the timing was deliberate."

"As hard as I find it to believe that Emily would do such a thing, are we to believe there is someone else bent on hurting both Emily and Amity?" Christabel's voice almost trembled. "I cannot give that theory any credence."

"I am afraid, my friends, that I have lost the heart for shopping," Amity said. "Would any of you object if I stayed behind? I should like to lie down."

"We will all stay with you," Christabel said.

"No, I could not bear to know that I had kept you all from any fun. Go, please. Perhaps I could meet you later for tea?"

After consulting with the concierge, who recommended a tea shop, they agreed on a time, but no one felt right leaving Amity alone. She insisted however, asking only one thing: that they remove the destroyed hat.

"I do not think I could stand to see it again."

Madame du Lac picked up the box and took it back to the desk, speaking quietly to the clerk before she returned to Amity's side. "We ought not allow it to go out with the rubbish, Mademoiselle Wells. Someone is trying to torment you, and this is our only clue to the person's identity."

Tears flooded Amity's eyes. "A clue? Is it not obvious what happened? You cannot believe your friend would do such a thing, even when the proof is in front of you? Have I done something to offend you, Madame du Lac? To make you think I do not merit even basic kindness?"

"Do not be foolish, Mademoiselle Wells," Madame du Lac said. "I find you a quite delightful sort of young lady. Even if I did not, I should object strongly to anyone harassing you in such a despicable way. My experience has taught me, though, that in these cases the obvious solution is not always the correct one. Monsieur Hargreaves will be able—"

"Her husband?" Birdie balked. "Of course he will take the side of his wife."

"You do not know Monsieur Hargreaves, Madame Wells. If you did, you would be fully aware that should he find anyone—even his wife—guilty of a crime, he would let nothing stand in the way of his bringing her to justice."

"I cannot believe he would believe his wife guilty of even the smallest crime, no matter what the truth," Birdie said. "He dotes on her in a most sickening fashion."

"You could not be more wrong," Madame du Lac said, her tone sharp. "Monsieur Hargreaves would never shield the guilty. Truth and honor matter to him more than anything. Do not, I beg you, make such slanderous accusations about him again." She turned on her heel and marched out of the lobby, back to the lounge, without so much as giving Birdie another glance.

# 12

Margaret and I had quickly changed into walking costumes and sturdy boots, knowing we ought to look as if we were actually off to visit Roman ruins. Margaret had insisted on a pith helmet, but I refused to follow her example. After a quick consultation with the concierge, who recommended a carriage for our journey, we told him we much preferred the idea of taking the train to Fréjus, and that we could easily reach the ruins on foot from the station there. He warned us off the scheme, saying it would be much more pleasant in a carriage, but in the end realized he would not be able to persuade us and called for one of the bellmen to hail a cab to take us to the train. I dropped my room key at the front desk across from the concierge's station, left my note for Cécile, and off we set.

"I feel almost as if we are criminals on the run," Margaret said when we exited the cab at the station.

"Remember your Euripides: *The day is for honest men, the night for thieves,*" I said. "We are not harming anyone by our actions, but I do think it is important that we make sure our story is credible should anyone look into it."

"It is most exciting," Margaret said. "Far better than spending another day with that awful Mrs. Wells."

"She is not so very bad," I said, consulting my map. "If it is all the same to you, I should prefer for us to walk the rest of the way. The café I have chosen for our rendezvous is some distance from here, but if we were to take another cab, we would arrive far too early. We may as well pass the time with a stroll."

"Is there any risk of the others stumbling upon us on our way?"

"Not if we plan our route with care. Most likely, we have at least an hour before they could conceivably be ready to leave the hotel, and that will give us plenty of time to make our way beyond La Croisette and its environs. Our meeting place is in a residential neighborhood to the northwest of the station. There is no reason to believe Amity and the rest would venture anywhere near there, however they decide to spend their day."

It did not take long for us to have left the fashionable set far behind. The houses looked similar to those we had seen in Le Suquet, but their condition was not quite so good. The paint on many of their shutters was peeling, but their gardens were well tended and the streets were wider in this part of town. Stern-looking women swept their front stoops while children played in the streets. Trees heavy with tangerines peeked over walls, and I was tempted to pick the fruit as we made our way uphill. The effort was not inconsiderable.

"Ah, at last," Margaret said as we rounded a bend and came upon a small park. "I always feel that I am not really in France until I have seen old men playing boules. I far prefer it to Mr. Fairchild's attempts to make us see the virtues of cricket." We paused to watch the game—and to catch our breath—sitting on a bench underneath a tree. The park was rather more dusty than green, but it was pleasant enough, and we were happy for the rest. The sun was higher in the sky now, and the heat had increased accordingly.

"I do not think I could ever soak up enough sun to compensate for the damp winters I've spent in England. The Côte d'Azur is far more agreeable," Margaret said, tipping back her head and holding her arms out wide. "I might not have agreed to marry Mr. Michaels if

I had been better aware of just how relentlessly awful the weather was going to be."

"Nonsense," I said. "You would have followed him to the ends of the earth."

"I only wish he would suggest the trip," Margaret said. "The ends of the earth cannot possibly be so grey. Amity speaks highly of India. Perhaps he should take me there. I should like very much to see it."

"As would I. Her stories did bring it alive, didn't they? There are many things about her that grate on my nerves, but I must admit that she has a wonderful ability to appreciate exotic places. I should try better to get on with her."

"We both should," Margaret said. "She does not always make it easy. There is something—oh, it doesn't matter, does it? Jeremy adores her and we will suffer quietly alongside him."

"Come, we should start walking again," I said. "There is not much farther to go." In another quarter of an hour, we had reached the café. The dancers had not yet arrived, so we selected a table outside—I am sorry to report that the interior of the establishment left rather a lot to be desired—and debated what we should order. Margaret insisted on rosé, while I had suggested tea.

"It is authentic," she said, "and if we are to keep up our disguise—"

"We are not in disguise," I said. "The girls we are meeting are aware of our identities, and the only people we have meant to deceive are nowhere near here." Margaret crossed her arms and rolled her eyes. I ignored this and continued. "Nonetheless, we are in the south of France, it is past eleven o'clock, and local tradition does appear to dictate rosé at this time of day. I have always thought that when traveling, one ought to adopt as many local ways as possible."

"I should like to see the Roman ruins at some point," Margaret said. "It would be a shame to miss them."

"We could plan an outing. There are spectacular ones at Cimiez in Nice." I was not able to expand on the subject, as our three dancers arrived. They were all fresh-faced, young, and pretty, but their eyes betrayed world-weariness, and before too many years went by I feared that their faces would begin to reflect their hard lives, robbing them of their beauty far too soon. Despite what Colin had suggested about their appearance, they did not look like wanton women, but, to be fair, they were not dressed—or made up—for work. They were turned out well, each of them wearing extremely fashionable clothing that, though not made from expensive fabrics, was exquisitely sewn.

"Do you like our gowns?" Marie, the tallest of the three asked. "I see you admiring them and, perhaps, wondering how we can afford such finery. I will let you in on a secret. Violette is an excellent seamstress. There is no fashion plate she cannot copy. We give her the fabric and show her what we want and—voilà!—she works magic."

"You have quite a talent," I said. Violette, a petite girl with a voluptuous figure, blushed. "The House of Worth would be fortunate to have you."

"*Merci.*" Violette nodded.

"Rose does not speak much English," Marie said. "May we continue in French?"

"So long as you can tolerate my abominable accent," Margaret said, pouring wine for them all. "I speak Latin better than French." This, of course, was true, but only in the most technical sense. Margaret's French was excellent, although her accent did leave something to be desired, but her command of Latin was truly impressive.

"We so much appreciate your agreeing to meet us," I began, in French. "You entertained a group of gentlemen on the night in question—"

"There was no improper behavior, *mesdames*," Violette said, folding her hand in her lap. "We are dancers, nothing more."

"I did not mean to suggest anything of the sort," I said. "One of the members of the party took his own life that night, and we are trying to understand what happened." Fear flashed in Rose's eyes and she looked to Marie.

"None of us knows anything about that," Marie said.

"There is no question of blame," I said. "No one is suggesting that any of you catalyzed the tragic event. We have reason to suspect, however, that something may have happened between the gentlemen. Did any of them argue?"

"No," Marie said. "They were a congenial group. We performed in a private room after they had been playing baccarat for some time. Afterwards, we joined them at their tables. It is not unusual."

"I am sure it is not," I said. "Was anyone else with you?"

"Just Hélène," Violette said. "She has gone to visit her mother in Marseille."

"If I may ask, which of the gentlemen was it who . . ." Marie's voice trailed.

"Chauncey Neville," Margaret said. "Do you recall him?"

"*Non*, this must not be correct," Marie said. "He was the most kind of them all and appeared in every way happy to be with his friends. A bit quiet, perhaps, but a man very capable of enjoying himself."

"You are quite certain he was in good spirits?" I asked.

"*Absolument*. I spent much of the evening sitting with him," Marie said and smiled. "He was quite delightful."

"Did he show any signs of melancholy?" Margaret asked.

"None."

"Did he leave earlier than the others?" I asked.

"There was one gentleman who left immediately after our performance," Marie said. "I cannot recall his name, but he was extraordinarily handsome. To own the truth, we all rather regretted his absence. Another gentleman—the one who is to soon be married—stayed only for a while."

"Jeremy?" Margaret asked. "The duke?"

"*Oui*, the duke," Rose said, blushing, her voice soft.

"Did he leave by himself?" I asked.

"All of the others stayed with us until very late," Violette said, pulling apart a piece of the bread our waiter had brought for the table. "I could not tell you the precise time we parted—there were rather copious amounts of champagne consumed."

"But you ladies—you were all there until the end?" I asked.

"Hélène left a few moments after the duke," Marie said, "but she did not leave with him."

"It is quite all right if she did," I said. "We are not looking to pass judgment on anything that happened."

"I understand your point," Marie said. "Hélène had talked to the duke a great deal, and thought him most charming. Mr. Neville also took quite a fancy to her. He told me as much."

"Did Hélène find him as charming as the duke?" I asked.

"Not quite so charming," Violette said. "Not quite so likely to become a patron, if you will. Not for the evening, I mean, but . . . many gentlemen find it is convenient to set up a girl with an apartment and an allowance. This may shock you, but—"

"I am not shocked by any woman doing what she believes is necessary in order for her to survive," I said. "If anything, I blame the men and the society that refuse these women other ways to earn their livings."

"The duke is a duke. We all assumed him to have a fortune to match his title." Marie stifled a giggle. "Do forgive me."

"Is it possible that Mr. Neville was jealous of the attention given to the duke by Hélène?"

"I am most skilled at noticing such things," Marie said, "and saw no sign of it. After Hélène left, Mr. Neville ordered more champagne and sat with me for the rest of the night. Nothing about him suggested disappointment."

"What time did the party break up?" I asked.

"Around two in the morning," Violette said.

I nodded. "I should have asked if any of you care for luncheon. The food here—"

"Is not worth eating," Marie said. "The wine, however, is more than satisfactory. And the bread is not half bad." She picked up a piece from the basket and spread butter on it.

"Do you know when Hélène will return from her mother's?" I asked.

"She was supposed to be back the day before yesterday," Violette said.

"Is it usual for her to stay away longer than she had planned?" Margaret asked.

"Not at all. She was set to dance last night, and she knows that she will have to beg for her job when she does come back. We have to be dependable or we are let go. She needs the work, so something must have happened to keep her in Marseille."

"Do you know how we might contact her there?" I asked.

"I have her mother's details, but not much else," Marie said.

I wrote down the name and address she told me. "Do you know if anyone has heard from her since she went away?"

"No," Marie said.

"Was the trip planned?" I asked.

"Yes, of course, we all knew she was going. It was her mother's birthday."

"Are we offering you anything that helps?" Rose asked. "I do feel so awful about that poor man."

"You are being most helpful," I assured her. "I should like very much to talk to Hélène as well. Could you contact me at my hotel when she returns?"

"Of course," Rose said.

Margaret ordered a second bottle of rosé. "Does anything else about that evening stand out in your mind?" she asked. "Anything at all?"

"The gentleman in charge—Monsieur Wells, I believe?—he insisted in pretending that we were all from Paris," Violette said. "As if there are no talented dancers anywhere else in France. He is an insecure man, is he not? To worry so much about impressing his friends."

"And his son!" Marie looked to the sky and the others moaned in unison. "He is a real oddity."

"What did he do?" I asked.

"He sat in a corner table by himself and wouldn't speak to any of us," Violette said. "Now that I think of it, he left early as well, at least I think he must have, because I do not remember seeing him when we all parted."

"I don't either," Marie said. "Rose?"

"I never spoke to him." Rose said. "Didn't like the look of him. Something in his eyes put me off."

"Did Hélène speak with him at all?" I asked.

"She did," Marie said. "She is more patient that most of us."

So Jeremy had abandoned the party before the rest, as had Augustus. Hélène could have left with either of them, but I was inclined to believe it more likely that she went with Jeremy, not only because Augustus was so odious, but also because Colin had reported that Jeremy had been with someone when he stopped at the hotel desk to request more pillows—or at least someone had been waiting for him outside.

We sat with the girls for a little while longer, then thanked them for their time and tried to press some francs into their hands before we departed, but they refused to take them.

"If you need help, we are here for you," Marie said. "It is important that none of us feel we offer assistance in the hopes of compensation. Not from other girls."

"I feel very sad," Margaret said, as we walked away from the café. "It is so desperately unfair that they must live the way they do."

"I wholeheartedly agree."

"Do you think the House of Worth—" Margaret started.

"It is unlikely," I said. "There are too many prejudices about such things. Perhaps we can find a way to better help them when this wretched business is finished."

"Do you think Jeremy was with Hélène?" Margaret asked.

"I do, although—oh, I don't know. I cannot believe that he would—"

"That he would behave like most gentlemen of his class and rank?"

"He adores Amity."

"How does that factor into the equation?" Margaret asked. "Jeremy makes no effort to hide his debauchery."

"Yet have you ever heard of him doing something truly awful?"

Margaret hesitated. "No, I have not. However, leaving with Hélène, even if nothing came of it, would have given the appearance of debauchery."

"In front of Mr. Wells?"

"They did not leave together," Margaret said. "Hélène followed sometime after. That might have been a deliberate attempt at discretion. They could have met up outside, giving Jeremy the opportunity to make his friends think whatever he wanted them to."

"It would be naïve of us to assume nothing transpired between them, although I find it difficult to believe. We ought to speak to Hélène as soon as we can."

"Emily." Margaret stopped walking. "I do not believe that Mr. Neville took his own life. It makes no sense—and that is what makes me believe his death to be a perfect crime, because suicide in and of itself makes no sense. The irrationality of it makes it impossible to expect a thorough explanation. We are meant to accept that we can't have all the answers."

"And, as a result, we are told not to ask questions," I said.

"Who would have wanted Mr. Neville dead?"

"I am not sure anyone did. The poisoned whisky was not in his room, after all," I said. "Perhaps the question we need to answer is who wanted Jeremy dead?"

# *Amity*

Amity felt relief at having been able to persuade her friends—and her mother—to leave her alone at the hotel so that they might enjoy an afternoon of shopping. Perhaps it was selfish, as she knew they, too, were concerned about the ruined hat and the effect it was having on her, but she wanted to be alone. She retired to her room and paced, feeling greatly agitated. She tried lying down, but could not bear to keep still. Eventually, she decided a walk by the sea might calm her, and by the time she had descended to the lobby, she had decided she would also send a telegram to Jeremy in Monte Carlo.

"It was a foolish extravagance," she said, some hours later when the gentlemen, who had received her message as soon as they had arrived at the casino, returned to the hotel. "And I am most heartily sorry for having ruined your day, but I felt so vulnerable and exposed. I do hope you will all forgive me." She had summoned them to her room, where they had found her curled up on a divan, her face damp with tears.

"You did the right thing," Jeremy said, placing a protective arm around his fiancée's shoulder. "I do think, though, that we ought to open the curtains. It's dire here in the dark, and the day is fine. Sunshine will lift your spirits, my poor love." Mr. Fairchild did as Jeremy suggested, and also flung open the French doors that led to Amity's balcony.

Amity pushed Jeremy's arm away and rose from her seat. "I am so dreadfully sorry to have spoiled your fun. I ought never to have sent that wire."

"You should have thought to telephone, Amity dear," Mr. Wells said. "It would have been half the cost and even quicker."

"This is not the time to pinch pennies," Birdie said, her voice firm. She would brook no argument. "Amity has suffered a terrible thing."

"Where is the hat now?" Colin asked.

"The hat doesn't matter!" Amity said.

"I am afraid the hat does matter, very much," Mr. Hargreaves said. His handsome face was serious, and there was no hint of humor in his dark eyes. Amity preferred him less grim. This version of Colin Hargreaves was almost frightening in its intensity.

"Madame du Lac did something with it," Birdie said. "Amity wanted it thrown away, but the woman refused to satisfy her on that count."

"Jack, may I have a word?" Colin asked. Amity watched as they stepped into the corridor and wished she could follow and listen to what they were saying.

"Do you trust Colin?" she asked Jeremy, taking his hand in hers.

"Hargreaves?" he asked. "With my life. There's not a more honest bloke alive."

"I do hope you are right. It seems impossible that Emily would have done this—I cannot believe she would hurt you in any way, even through me—but I am afraid we must consider every possibility." Amity bit her bottom lip. "I hope you do not despise me for saying that."

"I could never despise you, my love."

"I have tried so very hard to befriend her." A small sob escaped from her lips. The door opened and Madame du Lac entered, followed by Mr. Hargreaves and Jack.

"Cécile has anticipated our desire to speak with her," Mr. Hargreaves said.

"You, as always, Monsieur Hargreaves, are too kind. I am merely responding to a note sent from Mademoiselle Wells, requesting that I meet you all here. Do forgive me if it pains you, Mademoiselle, but I have brought the hat with me."

"Thank you, Cécile." Colin took the box from her.

"I would ask you to remove the odious thing from my daughter's presence at once," Mrs. Wells said. "She has suffered enough already."

"Of course," Mr. Hargreaves said. "Will you accompany me, Cécile?" They quitted the room before Amity could think of a good way to stop them. She appreciated her mother's concern, and she dreaded seeing the hat again, but curiosity about Mr. Hargreaves's reaction to it consumed her.

"Why did you have to drive them away, Mother? I wanted to hear what they had to say. Why do you think I asked Madame du Lac to come here?" Amity balled her hands into fists and stormed toward the door. "I am going after them."

# 13

Margaret and I did not hurry when making our way back to the train station, where, for verisimilitude, we would hire a cab to take us to the hotel. We thought it best not to return too early in the afternoon, as no one would believe that we had found any Roman ruins less than thoroughly satisfactory and worthy of at least a full day's study. We stopped again at the park where we had earlier paused to watch the game of boules and sat on the same bench. I pulled out my Baedeker's and consulted it for what was, I am sorry to say, a somewhat meager description of the ruins at Fréjus.

"I am fairly certain there is an aqueduct there," Margaret said, shielding her eyes with her hands. The angle of the sun proved most inconvenient. "Mr. Michaels gave me a lecture on everything I ought to see while in the south of France, and I do recall an aqueduct. Yes. Yes. That was definitely in Fréjus. There may be an arena as well, but very badly preserved. Or perhaps it was a theater. I'm hopeless."

"I think it unlikely the others will know anything about the ruins," I said. "Furthermore, they are even less likely to be interested in hearing much about them."

"How can you be so unfair to your own dear husband?"

"Colin will take whatever we say as necessary, even if he knows it to be incorrect. We can trust him absolutely."

"He hasn't the slightest idea what we have been doing?" Margaret asked.

"He doesn't need to. He will recognize that there is more to our story the moment he spots a factual error in it."

Margaret took off her gloves, bent over, rubbed her hands in the dirt on the ground, and then smeared it, first down my left cheek and then across her nose. "No one will believe we have been climbing on ruins if we look so well put together. We should be dusty and perspiring."

"Truly, Margaret, you ought to abandon classics and pursue the theater. We do not need to be covered with dirt." I wiped my face with my handkerchief.

"That is perfect," Margaret said. "Now it looks as if you have tried to clean yourself up, which is exactly what you would have done after a day in the field. I shall leave mine untouched. No one who knows me thinks I would bother to make the effort, particularly when Mr. Michaels is not here."

"Anyone who knows Mr. Michaels would be well aware that he prefers you covered in ancient dust."

"Quite right, Emily. Could I have married anyone who thought differently?"

We sat in the park for two hours before starting the walk back to the station. We paused in the telegram office there to send a message to Hélène at her mother's house, asking that she contact me immediately. That done, we climbed into a cab and returned to the hotel, looking much the worse for wear.

"I am surprised to see none of our friends on the terrace," Margaret said as we walked past it. "I thought they had more or less taken up residence there."

"I am glad," I said. "This gives us the opportunity to speak with Colin in private before having to face everyone." We went up to my suite, where my husband and Cécile were standing by a corner table, their heads bent over a hatbox.

"What ho?" Margaret flopped onto the divan that faced the windows. "You must have met with success on your shopping expedition if hats have been purchased. Cécile, I do hope it wasn't *too very* of us to have left you alone with them—"

"*Too very* is a compliment, Margaret," I said, ribbing my friend with my elbow as I sat next to her. "At least so far as I can tell." We both dissolved into laughter, stopping only when I noticed the stern look on Colin's face.

"I am afraid things took a rather unexpected turn here today," he said. "Someone—the desk clerk says it was you, Emily—left a parcel for Amity this morning." I crossed to him, peered into the box on the table, and stared, rueful, at the sad remains of what had once been a lovely little hat.

"I recognize that," I said. "Amity had admired it in a store window."

"Yes," Colin said. "And now she believes you bought it, destroyed it, and gave it to her."

"I would never do that. You must know—"

"*Bien sûr*, Kallista," Cécile said. "No one of intelligence could give credence to the idea."

"Were you at the desk this morning?" Colin asked.

"Only to turn in my room key," I said. "The concierge summoned a cab to take us to the train station."

"Didn't he call to the bellman?" Margaret asked.

"Yes, I think that is right," I said. "The lobby was crowded when we were leaving. The desk clerk had a queue of people waiting to check out, so I stood at the desk for a while, but in the end left the key on it without speaking to anyone. I may have crossed back over to the concierge's desk after that, but I can't be sure."

"Do you remember seeing this box on the counter next to you?" Colin asked.

"I don't, but I am not certain that I would have noticed it." I inspected the container. "I did not write this label."

"No, it is not your handwriting," Colin said. "I have already visited the shop from whence the hat came, and the girl there told me that a fashionable lady of medium height and slim build purchased it. She could not remember eye color, but thought her hair was fair, although it was covered with a hat and a veil."

"That could be nearly anyone," Margaret said. "My hair is dark as midnight on a moonless night, but with the right hat and veil I could probably appear fair."

"Possibly," Colin said. "Please do not try." Margaret pursed her lips and refrained from replying, but I could see her mind working. No doubt, before long, we would see her attempt at passing as fair-haired.

"Did the shop girl recall writing the label?" I asked.

"She did not. She wrapped the hat in tissue, and placed it in the box, which she tied up with string, but she said the shop does not use that sort of label."

The label—more of a tag, really—was of a thick rectangle of cardstock with a reinforced hole punched in one corner, through which a bit of red ribbon had been threaded so that it might be tied to the string fastening the box. "I do wish there were something about it that seemed out of the ordinary, but I am afraid it is the sort of thing that could be purchased nearly anywhere," I said.

"We could hardly hope that whoever did this would have used monogrammed stationery," Colin said. His dark hair tumbled over his forehead as he leaned down toward the table, and his eyes flashed. He never was more handsome than when his mind was fixed on an investigation. "I wonder if there is a connection between this and the incident on Sainte-Marguerite?"

"And your invitation to Mrs. Wells's dinner," Margaret said. "I do not believe that she accidentally wrote the wrong time."

"Are you suggesting someone did it deliberately?" Cécile asked. "I am not sure what Amity—or her mother—could have thought to accomplish by such an act."

"Whoever did it made us—me—look rude and inconsiderate in front of our friends," I said.

"No one cared," Margaret said. "If anything, Mrs. Wells made herself look bad by reacting so strongly when you did arrive.

"It is as if someone wants your friends to turn against you," Colin said. "First, by making it appear that you played a silly trick on us in the prison to get attention, then by ruining a dinner party, and finally by sending a nasty gift to Amity."

"The hat was a misstep," I said, pressing both of my palms against the table. "For even if you all decided I was lying about the prison cell and the time on the invitation, why on earth would I ever sign my name to this poor hat?"

"Perhaps, Kallista, we are meant to think exactly that," Cécile said, shaking her head and sitting down in a chair near the window. "You would not do it—it would be foolish—and, hence, you do not look guilty, unless one believes you planned this episode carefully, to make it appear that someone else is trying to hurt your reputation."

"I see your point, Cécile, but it is causing my head to throb violently," Margaret said, following her and flinging open the doors to the balcony. The air was still heavy with heat.

"Amity doesn't believe I am behind this, does she?" I asked. "And what about Jeremy?"

"Amity is shaken and not thinking clearly," Colin said. "Jeremy is only looking to protect her." I could tell from his tone that he had very little faith in Jeremy's opinion on the matter.

"I must go to her without delay," I said. "I cannot let her think I am skulking around avoiding her."

"First perhaps you could tell us how it went with the dancers?" Cécile said. "I am most disappointed not to have met them myself."

"Margaret can tell you," I said, feeling extremely agitated. "I must see Amity now."

Margaret had begun to warm to the topic even before I made my way out of the room and looked as if she were about to perform the cancan as a method of getting her audience into the proper mood. When I reached Amity's suite, Jeremy opened the door to me, grave concern etched on his face. "What is going on, Em?"

"You cannot think I did this," I said, keeping my voice low. He stepped into the corridor and pulled the door closed behind him. "Why would I ever have signed my name to such a thing?"

"I don't know," he said, his voice tense. He focused his gaze, so far as I could tell, somewhere beyond my shoulder. "Mrs. Wells insists you did it just so that you could say that it was so ridiculous it proves it wasn't you."

"Cécile postulated that someone might come up with that theory," I said. "Why would I want to torment Amity like this?"

"I do not think you would, and neither does she." He shifted his weight awkwardly and blew out a long sigh before finally looking directly at me. "The others, though, are having a more difficult time agreeing with us."

"May I please speak with her?"

"She is sulking because I did not let her follow Hargreaves and Cécile when they took the hat."

He reached around to open the door, but it had locked when he pulled it shut. We knocked, and Jack opened it, his mouth a hard line when he saw me.

"Lady Emily," he said. He had never before in his life addressed me by my title. I walked past him without comment and went straight to Amity, who was sitting next to Christabel on a divan identical to the one in my own room.

"Amity, I cannot express my dismay at your having received such a cruel present, and I want to assure you that I had nothing to do with it."

Christabel looked away, but Amity met my eyes and smiled. "I knew you would never do such a thing. You've far too sophisticated a sense of the aesthetic to destroy a hat that lovely." Christabel glared at her. "Oh come now, Christabel, stop being so sour. Emily has never been anything but kind and gracious to me."

"Then who did it?" Christabel all but spat the words. I crouched in front of them.

"I understand your feelings, your anger, Christabel," I said. "I share them, and I promise that I shall do everything I can to find out who is tormenting our friend."

It was evident, both from the strained look in her eyes, and her little clenched fists, that Christabel was employing all of her will to keep from replying.

"You will help me, won't you?" Amity asked. "Colin said he would as well. He and Emily stop murderers, Christabel. Do you really think they will have the slightest bit of trouble finding whoever played this prank?"

"Can you prove you didn't do it?" Jack asked, standing up very tall and very straight, every inch the soldier. "Forgive me, Emily, but I must ask."

"It is all but impossible to prove a negative," I said.

"You were standing at the desk next to the box," he said. "The clerk insists he remembers that."

"That does not mean I put the box there," I said. "Can I prove that I did not? No."

"But we cannot prove that you did," Amity said. "He admitted that he did not see her carrying the box or placing it on the desk. It means so much to me that you came to me directly, Emily. I knew you had nothing to hide. Now distract me with something more pleasant. Tell me about your day. Were the ruins spectacular? I would so have liked to see them. Next time, you must include me in your plans."

A pang of guilt stabbed at me, and for a moment even I believed I had been to the ruins and that I ought to have invited Amity. I shook myself back to reality. "There was not much to see, I am afraid. We only went because Margaret had a telegram from her husband asking her to check an inscription he thought was there—he needed a quick answer for a monograph he is writing. We didn't want to disturb any of you so early, when there would have been so little to be gained by it."

"It would have been exciting," Amity said, "even if they were only small ruins. I've never seen someone search for an inscription with an actual academic purpose. And we could have brought a picnic on the train."

"I shall plan an excursion to Nice, specially for you," I said. "There are wonderful ruins there."

"You are simply too very! I will hold you to it and cannot wait to make the trip," Amity said. "Thank you again for coming to me, Emily. It does mean the world to me, as does your promise to help me uncover the truth of this hideous day. Now, you must have a bath without delay. You look a fright and we are to have cocktails on the terrace in only just an hour. I do not think Birdie can survive you being late again."

# Amity

Christabel and Jack rose and opened their mouths almost in unison to speak the minute Emily had left the room.

"You cannot believe her!" Christabel said.

"I want to believe her, but I have very grave doubts—" Jack began.

"That is quite enough from you both," Amity said, a sweet smile on her face. She tugged at the Venetian lace spilling from the cuffs of her emerald green gown. "Jeremy, my darling love, would never be friends with someone who could be so cruel, especially to me. I will hear not another word on the subject."

"Amity is right," Jeremy said. "Jack, you know Emily far too well to—"

"To what?" Jack asked, glowering. "To not have noticed the obvious thing no one is willing to mention."

"Captain Sheffield," Christabel's voice was small. "I think it is best—"

"Best that we keep pretending there is nothing else at stake here?" he asked. "I cannot remain silent, Miss Peabody."

"Why have you two regressed to such formality?" Amity asked, crossing first to Jack and then to Christabel, standing in front of each and studying their countenances. "It is decidedly odd, given not only our proximity these past months, but the nature of our friendship going back to our first days in India. Are the two of you trying to hide something?"

"What could we possibly have to hide?" Christabel asked, her face scarlet.

"What about you, Jack?" Jeremy asked, tilting his head and crossing his legs on the table in front of him. "I thought you could no longer remain silent? Or is candor necessary only when it pertains to personal matters that do not affect you?"

"You know that is not the case, Jeremy," Jack said. "I only mean to—"

"Think carefully before you speak, my dear brother," Jeremy said. "Words can cause irrevocable harm, even when they are not true, and I have had quite enough of this nonsense. Amity, we are not going to meet the others for cocktails. I am taking you to the casino, where we are going to spend the evening playing baccarat. I cannot bear a moment longer in the company of anyone save you."

"What a perfect idea," Amity said. "May we dine out as well?"

"Whatever you desire, my love." Jeremy beamed at her.

"I am so fortunate to have found you," Amity said. "What should I have done if my parents had forced some other duke on me? Do you know that before we met I worried that you would be old and grey, despite your brother's reassurances to the contrary? He made you out to be the handsomest man alive."

"I always thought Jack noble and honest, but I am most grateful that brotherly affection trumped the truth when it came to telling you about me," Jeremy said. "I owe you, Captain." He raised a glass to his brother and drank. "Now. Baccarat."

# 14

Back in my room, I applied myself to my ablutions with a focus on speed, not wanting to further irritate Mrs. Wells by being late again. Colin, looking extremely dapper in his evening kit—white tie suited him so very well—escorted me to the terrace. I had dressed without an eye to restraint, deciding that as Amity now seemed to be an ally, I no longer had to concern myself with upstaging her. Her mother, on the other hand, I thought might respond better to me if I presented myself to her in a blaze of fashion. My strategy proved correct.

That Mrs. Wells was unhappy with me was evident the moment that my husband and I stepped onto the terrace. She pulled her shoulders back and scowled, but then noticed my diamonds and rubies and the way they enhanced the silver threads shot through the pale shell pink silk of my gown. I had been so thrilled to discover, on my last trip to the House of Worth, that the balloonlike sleeves that had been popular for far longer than I should have liked had at last fallen completely out of fashion that I ordered three times the number of dresses I had intended. The Messieurs Worth were delighted, Colin amused, and I outfitted like an empress. Styles were softer now, meant to accentuate the hips and graceful movement. My enthusiasm had dampened slightly when I realized this meant that skirts had become so narrow as to restrict movement, but I no longer felt obliged to be an absolute slave to fashion, and I ordered my gowns cut wide enough so that I might move freely without destroying the overall effect.

The bodice of my gown, with its square neckline and long, chiffon sleeves that clung to my arms, laced up the back. An overskirt of chiffon covered the silk, trailing behind me like a little sea of pale foam. Margaret, recognizing immediately that I was no longer playing Mrs. Wells's game, grinned, and raised her glass to me as I greeted our hostess.

"What a lovely evening, Mrs. Wells," I said, kissing her on both cheeks. "It is as if the weather itself bends to your will. I cannot remember a finer night."

Mrs. Wells narrowed her eyes as she looked at me. "I must speak with you, Emily—"

"Lady Emily, please, if we are not going to be friends." I snapped my fan open and waved it in front of my face. "I can only assume that you mean to be stern with me for the sake of appearances, because no rational woman—and I do believe you to be rational, Mrs. Wells—could consider the notion that I would do anything to harm your darling little girl. I feel as if Amity is like a sister to me."

This rendered Mrs. Wells speechless. She had expected to be able to bully me, disparage me in front of my friends, and that I would cower before her, desperate to defend myself. A show of strength on my part was the last thing she had anticipated. Mr. Wells stepped forward and took my hand.

"I do not doubt you, Emily—and I shall use your given name rather than your title as I do consider you a friend. Apologies for having reacted badly all around to this situation. What does your husband make of this dreadful business?"

"I shall leave you to discuss it with him. I see a waiter with champagne and am feeling dreadfully parched." Margaret intercepted me before I had taken six steps away from Mr. Wells.

"Well done, Emily," she said. "They do tremble before the titled, don't they?"

"It is appalling, isn't it?" I asked. "Particularly given that I have nothing more than a courtesy title."

"I think you ought to have worn a tiara. That would have slayed Mrs. Wells."

"I am afraid it did not occur to me to bring one," I said. "Where are Amity and Jeremy?"

"They are not coming," Margaret said. Jack crossed to us and stood a few paces behind her. "They have abandoned us for the casino."

"Have they? How singular and how very like Jeremy," I said. "Why are you hovering, Jack? Are you attempting to hide behind a palm? That is very bad form, you know."

"I am told I must apologize," he said, sounding like a chastened little boy, "and am more mortified than you can imagine. I know you did not crush that hat and send it to Amity."

"Why did you ever suspect I would have done such a thing?"

"May I speak freely?" he asked, glancing around at the tables around us, now nearly all full.

"I do wish you would," I said.

He looked at Margaret. "In private?" She huffed, but left me to him. We walked to the edge of the terrace, where we would neither be in the way of any of the servers nor close enough to the other guests to be overheard. "Emily, my brother's feelings for you are no secret. They never have been. I know how much his friendship means to you, and I have noticed that in these weeks here in Cannes, the two of you have not been quite so easy with each other as you were before."

"A friendship between a lady and a gentleman is bound to change when one of them is getting married."

"You are already married."

"Yes, but do not think there was no period of awkwardness

between the time that I accepted my husband's proposal and now. This, too, will smooth over, but it will require a bit of adjustment from all involved parties."

"You are—do forgive me; I know I ought not ask, but I must—you are not in love with my brother?"

Laughter burst forth from me with such force that I fear I quite astonished the poor boy. A nearby waiter almost dropped his tray. "In love with Jeremy?" I covered my mouth with a gloved hand, but could not stop my mirth. "Jack Sheffield, whatever can you be thinking?"

"I only thought—I see now it was quite absurd."

"Oh, my dear boy, you have amused me like no other," I said. "Did you really think I was jealous of Amity and attempting to sabotage her engagement? To what end?"

"I suppose I had not thought much about that."

"Had I ever been in love with your brother I would have married him years ago, but I can assure you that neither of us would have been happy with the outcome."

"Can you forgive me?"

"I have known you since you were a baby. What choice do I have?" I could tell he was looking over my shoulder, and turned to see Christabel watching us. I waved her over. "All of this nonsense is behind us now."

"How can it be behind us when we still don't know who is bent on tormenting Amity?" Christabel asked. She was still careful not to meet my eyes.

"Rely on Colin and me to figure that out, but in the meantime, there is nothing to be done except to ensure that our friends are enjoying this celebration of their engagement. Look what we have done as a result of all this nonsense—driven them off to the casino because they are tired of the tension that has plagued our party. It stops now."

"I am heartily ashamed of myself," Jack said.

"Fetch some champagne for Miss Peabody," I said. "She looks as if she could use some." I excused myself and went in search of Mr. Fairchild, whom I found lurking on the pavement beneath the terrace, where he was leaning against a palm tree and smoking.

"You need not scold me for abandoning you all," he said.

"That was never my intention," I said. "What are you doing here all alone?"

"Wells exhausts me. If I hear one more word about copper mining I shall scream. I have never better appreciated how essential it is for gentlemen to remain gentlemen and not work."

"*All paid work degrades the mind,*" I said. "Aristotle. Do I need to convince you that it is not I who is tormenting Amity?"

He blew a thin stream of silver smoke from between his smiling lips. "No. I admit I took the note attached to the box at face value initially, but as soon as I gave the matter further thought I saw the inanity of it."

"I am glad, because I, too, find myself exhausted. Although not as a result of prolonged discussion of copper mining."

"Lady Emily Hargreaves?" A bellman approached us. "A telegram for you, madame." I took it from him, thanked him, and opened the envelope, frowning as I read the words.

"Is something wrong?" Mr. Fairchild asked.

"I am afraid something is very wrong. Would you please fetch my husband and ask him to come to me at once?"

"Of course." He vanished, leaving me to read the message again. It was from Hélène's mother. Her daughter, whom she had expected to see on her birthday, had never arrived in Marseille.

"What is it?" Colin asked, fairly flying down the steps to me. I handed him the telegram. He frowned, grasping the deeper meaning at once, and took me by the hand, leading me to the front of the hotel, where he waved for a cab.

Casinos had never held much appeal to me. I had only once been inside such an establishment, in Venice, and then only briefly. If planning to part with a tidy sum of money, I much preferred the idea of buying art or funding a worthwhile enterprise or ordering more frocks than I ought at the House of Worth to losing it gaming. Knowing the Cercle Nautique in Cannes to be a favorite haunt of the Prince of Wales, I expected it to be grand, with decorations that veered on the obnoxious side of rococo. On this point, I was mistaken. Colin and I marched up the steps to the main entrance and were ushered inside a singularly pleasant space. One could not say that it was discreet or restrained, but to my view, it was better decorated than Buckingham Palace, and considerably more comfortable. The lobby, all smooth marble and gilt trim, was wide and cool, with views to the ocean. Colin asked to see the manager, and within moments a tall, proud-looking man stood in front of us.

"I am afraid the girl may have come to some harm," Colin said, after having explained our search for Hélène.

The manager smiled broadly. "You are too worried, my good man. Girls like that disappear all the time, and for no nefarious reasons. Most likely she either grew tired of her work or she found herself a gentleman prepared to take care of her. You may inquire with the other girls if you would like, but I can assure you there is nothing about this that raises even the slightest alarm bells in me."

We did want to speak with the girls, and he led us through a maze of corridors, down to the dressing rooms near the casino's small theater. Marie spotted me at once, and waved.

"You are so beautiful," she said. "Violette! This gown! Can you make it for me?" Violette, who was leaning close to the mirror that ran the length of the wall made no move until she had finished carefully applying kohl around her eyes. Once done, she took a slim notebook from a case sitting on the counter below the mirror, and came to us.

"May I sketch, Lady Emily?"

"I do not think now—"

Marie did not hesitate to interrupt Colin. "You may tell us why you are here while she works." Their costumes, garish and bright, exceedingly low cut, and with skirts shorter than that allowed for evening wear, along with the generous application of rouge, made them look rather different from the girls Margaret and I had met at the café. I could now understand why my husband had initially told me I would be shocked by their appearance. This is not to suggest that I felt even the slightest shock—I am not so easily taken aback—but gentlemen, even enlightened ones, often think ladies are far less worldly than we are.

"You have met my husband?" I asked.

"Not formally." She extended her hand to him. "It is a pleasure of the highest order."

"We are here because we are concerned about Hélène," I said. "She did not go to her mother in Marseille."

"Where else would she have gone?" Marie asked. "She certainly hasn't been here."

"I went to see her yesterday," Violette said. "Her landlord's wife told me she was not there, and that she hasn't had a glimpse of her since she left for Marseille."

"Where does she live?" Colin asked, taking no notice of the bustle of activity surrounding us. Chorus girls were rushing by in colorful costumes, while others touched up their rouge or fixed their hair. A burly man standing at the door barked at them if he thought they would be late for their performances, but his remarks revealed a greater fondness for them than he perhaps intended. He was more friend than boss.

"We've a show in half an hour, or I would take you myself," Marie said, "but we can give you the address." Without having to be asked, Violette tore a page from her book and wrote down the directions as well as the landlord's name.

"You don't think that something has happened to her, do you?" Rose had come up so quietly I had hardly noticed her.

"I very much hope not," Colin said. "None of you has had a word from her since she was supposed to have gone to Marseille?"

"Not a single one," Marie said.

"Think carefully. Are there any gentlemen to whom she might be attached?" Colin asked.

"No, there hasn't been anyone particular for a long while," Marie said.

"You are certain?" I asked.

"Absolutely," Violette said.

"And is there anyone you thought she might be trying to culti-vate?" Colin asked.

"No," Marie said. "Hélène never wanted that sort of thing. Did her best to avoid it. Of course, her mother had a bit of money, so she was only supporting herself and her salary here is enough for that."

"Has anyone troubled you recently?" Colin asked. "I am aware there are men who are more forceful than they ought to be."

"Not recently, no," Violette said. "This is not a brothel, Monsieur Hargreaves."

"I apologize for the question," Colin said, "but at this time, I must pursue every possible angle." We thanked them and returned to our cab, ordering the driver to take us to Hélène's modest abode. She lived far from the center of town, above a butcher's shop, in a worn but neat building. Colin banged on the door with the head of his stick until we heard footsteps approaching.

"There's no cause for such excitement!" came a voice from behind the door. Keys jangled, locks clicked, and the door swung open. Behind it stood a man who could only have been the butcher. His face was red and jolly, his hands broad and strong, but it was the blood-stained apron tied around his ample waist that gave away his profession. "Can I help you?" he asked, a look of astonishment on his face.

"Most sorry for having disturbed you, Monsieur Soucy," Colin said, and introduced us. "We have come to inquire after your tenant, Hélène Mignon."

"She is away, visiting her mother," the man said.

"May we take a look at her rooms?" I asked. "We are quite concerned about her. Her mother has informed us that Hélène never made it to Marseille, and we are hoping to find something—anything—that can explain her change of plans, if indeed it was she who changed them."

"Never reached Marseille? That is rather alarming," he said, and ushered us inside. "The stairs are narrow and steep. Do be careful. I apologize for my appearance. I am working late tonight to prepare an order for a wedding feast tomorrow."

"There is no need to apologize," Colin said. "It is we who have interrupted you."

We followed him up four flights of stairs to a battered door in the attic. He fumbled with the keys on a large ring, trying several before settling on the one that fit in the lock. "I never have been able to keep track of these well, but then I rarely have cause to come up here." When at last the door swung open, a vile, overwhelming odor seemed to blast from the room. The stairway had been illuminated by gas lights, but Hélène's apartment did not have any, so her landlord struck a match and lit an oil lamp that stood on a small table next to the door.

Colin picked up the lamp, and we began to inspect the space. There was only one small room, furnished with a bed and two tables, one with a chair near the gabled window, the other by the door. A dresser was placed on the wall next to the bed, and on top of it was a pitcher and basin set. On the larger table was a package, wrapped in butcher's paper.

"I gave her a beef roast to take to her mother," the butcher said. "She must have forgot it and now it's a rotting mess." The smell was so strong I nearly retched. "I had better open the window." He tugged at the sash until it lifted, but the small amount of air it let in did little to dissipate the aroma clinging to everything in the room.

A scrap of pale green muslin peeking out from under the bed had caught my eye and I reached to pull it out, a sinking feeling coming over me as I tugged and found it weighted down. I tugged harder and felt something hit my arm and looked down to see a cold, bluish hand. "Colin, could you please bring the lamp over here?"

# *Amity*

Baccarat proved not quite so entertaining as Amity had expected it to be. The casino was beautiful—she loved the crowded rooms, the plush carpets, the glistening chandeliers, and the overwhelming sense of excitement—but the games themselves? Amity much preferred poker. Yet Jeremy was taken with baccarat, and bet again and again.

"If you always bet on the banker, you shall come out ahead in the end," Amity said, after more than an hour of watching him.

"It is not that simple, my love." He hardly even looked at her.

"I am going to try a different game. You don't mind, do you?" Now she had his attention.

"Have I bored you? I am a cad, I know. I get too caught up in it. Just when I think I have it all figured out, I lose everything."

"Perhaps, then, this is a good time to stop," Amity said. "I quite fancy roulette." He pressed a stack of chips into her hand.

"Let us see if your luck is better than mine."

Roulette was straightforward; there was no pretense of heavy thinking or strategy, no numbers to add up and consider, despite what the portly gentleman to Amity's left insisted as he narrated his plans in a gratingly loud voice. She lost as often as she won and found she enjoyed both sensations equally. Losing felt so rough and real, she could not help but welcome it.

"You are up a shocking amount," Jeremy said. This was not true, Amity knew, but she had amassed a large stack of markers—no larger than what he had given her to start—so he assumed, like any gentleman to whom money is meaningless, that she must be winning. "Let's have some champagne and sit for a while. I am so enjoying having you all to myself."

"I do hope Daddy hasn't been tiring you out with all his talk of business. He does go on." As they crossed the gaming floor and came out into the bright atrium, Amity caught a glimpse of two familiar figures. "Heavens! Is that the Hargreaveses?"

"It is," Jeremy replied, immediately stepping forward to flag them down.

Amity gripped his arm. "Wouldn't you rather we stayed alone? Have our champagne and then, perhaps, go for a stroll on the beach?"

Jeremy laughed. "You would risk your reputation by allowing me to take you for a wholly unsupervised turn on the beach? At night? Have you no sense of decorum?"

"None at all." Amity lifted herself up onto her tiptoes and kissed him. "I am wild and wanton."

"You ought not do that here."

"Are you blushing?" Amity asked.

"Of course not." Jeremy pulled a face and brushed off the front of his jacket. "I merely have no desire to create a scene."

"We are to be married, my love. I do not think one brief kiss shall brand us as immoral, and even if it did, I should think that would appeal to your desire for debauchery."

"Quite right," Jeremy said, tugging at his shirt cuffs. "Apologies." He took her by the hand. "Why don't we bring the champagne onto the beach?" He found a barman willing to give them a bottle, but not glasses, to remove from the premises.

"I don't understand why he cares where we drink it," Amity said, "but I suppose he is right to be protective with his crystal. We probably would have dropped something before the night was over."

They fairly flew down the steps outside the main entrance, danced along the street, and crossed to the other side. "Should we go all the way down to the hotel?" Jeremy asked.

"Not our hotel," Amity said. "We don't want to see anyone we know." She started off in the opposite direction of the hotel.

"It is too cold for anyone to be out, really, so I doubt very much that we would run any danger of—"

"Come." Now she took his hand and pulled him behind her. The air had turned chill, and she wished she had a warmer wrap with her, but Amity was not about to let the temperature dampen her spirits. They walked along La Croisette until they reached the quai with the ferry dock. "I saw a very pleasant little beach along here from the boat the other day." She hiked up her skirts so that she could climb over the large boulders that separated the sand from the pavement. Jeremy rushed to get ahead of her so that he might offer her assistance, but she refused, nimbly navigating the rocks on her own. Before she stepped off the last one, she paused. "I have never been able to abide the feeling of sand in my shoes."

"I can carry you."

"No." She sat down on a rock and pulled off her shoes. "Now you must look away. No cheating." He could hear the rustle of silk. "All clear," she said. He turned back to her and she was waving her stockings and laughing. This prompted him to remove his own shoes and socks, and they tramped across the beach in high spirits. Jeremy popped open the champagne and they guzzled it, straight from the bottle.

"I never thought, my love, that there could be a girl like you." He passed her the bottle. "You are a marvel."

"And you are a dear, sweet man," she said, and then took another swig of champagne. "That's the bottle, all but gone. Now will you let me kiss you?"

# 15

The sight of that poor, cold—and obviously dead—hand stunned me. I could barely control my voice, and my limbs were shaking so hard that I sat on the floor, uncertain whether I would be able to keep my balance. I did my best to steady myself and again asked Colin to bring the lamp.

"I am afraid that I have found Hélène," I said. Colin handed the lamp to the landlord, who held it above while my husband gently reached under the bed and pulled out the sad little body from beneath it. The butcher gasped and the light swayed. His wobble focused my own nerves, and I rose to my feet and stood next to him. "Is it she?" I asked. He nodded. I took the lamp.

Despite the discoloration and bloating of her body, one could still see a delicate beauty in her fine features. Her dark eyes were open, with that hideous blank look that marks the dead and leaves no doubt that the soul has fled from the flesh.

"She has been dead for some time," Colin said. "The back of her skull is badly fractured."

"I should have known," the butcher said. "I should have noticed the smell. I—"

"None of us noticed the smell until you opened the door," Colin said. "Be a good fellow and summon the police for us."

"I don't understand. She was to visit her mother. She must have fallen. If only—"

Colin took him by the shoulders. "Right now, we must get the police, as quickly as possible. Can you do that for us?"

"Yes. I should tell my wife—"

"First, the police."

"All these days and she was here—"

"I'll go," I said quietly to Colin. "Get him to sit down and do your best to calm him. He is in shock." I pulled the blanket off the top of the bed and wrapped it around the man's shoulders.

"You are far better at this sort of thing than I," Colin said. "I can get the police—"

"I cannot bear to be in here with her for a single moment longer," I said, the words tumbling out in a rush. He gripped my hand and let me go. I was in such a rush to get away from the hideous smell of death and the awful look on Hélène's once beautiful face that I nearly fell down the stairs. When I reached the bottom, I pushed the door open and ran straight into the quiet street, gulping in the fresh air. Our cab was waiting for us at the curb, and once I had collected myself enough to speak coherently to the driver, I ordered him to take me to the police.

I was moving through a haze and have no memory of speaking to anyone at the station, but must have done, because now I was back in the cab, a gendarme next to me. "The coroner will follow us shortly," he said. "You say she has been dead for some time?"

When we reached Monsieur Soucy's building, I did not accompany the officer up the stairs. I could not bear to face again the horror of what that smell meant. The coroner arrived with his van and three more gendarmes followed shortly thereafter. The commotion had, not surprisingly, aroused the curiosity of the butcher's wife, who had marched upstairs to see what was happening, only to turn on her heels and flee. She stood next to me.

"I did not see her," Madame Soucy said. "They would not let me in the room." She was a sturdy, strong woman, thickly built, with kind eyes and greying hair pulled back in a tight knot at the nape of her neck. "I only kept renting to her because I thought she was a good girl, no matter what the implications of that job of hers. She did not run around with unsavory gentlemen. Never made a spectacle of herself."

"Can you think of anyone who would have wanted to hurt her?" I asked.

"Hélène was a sweet girl." Her voice broke. "Always had a kind word for everyone. She had wanted to join the ballet in Paris, but her mother forbad it, and she came here. Worked for a while as a maid at one of the fancy hotels, but that's awful labor, waiting on the ungrateful rich." She looked away from me. "Apologies."

"There is no need," I said.

"When they started doing performances at the casino, she auditioned. I warned her off it, but she wouldn't hear me. The money was better, that much is certain, but I was never convinced it came on anything but very hard terms."

"Did she have many friends?" I asked.

"The other girls she worked with adored her. One of them came round looking for her the other day. I gave her a piece of cake and some coffee and tried to convince her to look for other work. Sickens me to think that all the while poor Hélène was upstairs—" She stifled a sob. I put my arm around her.

"I think we could all use some very strong coffee. May I help you make it?"

In the aftermath of violent death, it often helps to give survivors a task on which they can focus. While Madame Soucy made the coffee, I took cups from a shelf in her pantry and put them on the kitchen table. "Hélène ate with us," Madame Soucy said. "She paid for room and board. There is no kitchen in her room."

"You must have known her fairly well, then," I said. Madame Soucy handed me a creamer and asked me to fill it. I looked around, and she pointed me to a deep windowsill where she stored her milk. The glass bottle was cool from the night air.

"Not well enough, apparently." She filled the cups and sat at the table. "You say she was murdered?"

"I am afraid so."

"But it was her head, was it not? Couldn't she have fallen?"

"Even if she had, it would have been unlikely to have resulted in such an extreme wound. Furthermore, she was tucked under the bed. A blow strong enough to kill her would have rendered her unconscious, and she would not have been able to move."

"If only I had heard something or seen someone."

"Are you here most of the time?" I asked.

"Yes."

"Did Hélène have many callers?"

"Callers? Lady Emily, I do not think you understand our circumstances here. Hélène did not have callers. Her friends—the other girls from the casino—came occasionally to collect her. Other than that, no one ever came looking for her."

"Do you remember the day she was to go to Marseille?" I asked.

"*Oui*, my husband prepared for her an excellent piece of meat to take to her mother."

"That is a generous gift."

"Hélène was careful with her money. We knew she could not afford to bring something for her mother, so we thought we would offer something."

"I imagine she would have got it from you just before she planned to leave for Marseille?"

"*Oui*. She would not have wanted the meat to spoil."

"Yet she brought it back up to her room. I noticed no portmanteau there. Had she carried her luggage down with her when she came to get the meat?"

"This I do not recall."

"Did you give her the roast?"

"*Non*, we left it for her in the back so that she could fetch it whenever she wanted without disturbing us. Mornings are busy in our shop."

"Had you planned that?" I asked.

"We left a note on her door the evening before so that she would see it when she returned home from work."

A clatter on the stairs signaled that the men had finished in Hélène's room. All the color drained from Madame Soucy's face. "Are they bringing her down?"

I nodded. Only after I had heard the sound of the coroner's van doors closing did I step back outside. Colin clasped my hand in his as we watched it drive away. We exchanged a few more words with the gendarmes before returning to our cab.

"There was no valise in her room," I said.

"I noticed the same thing," Colin said.

"What a dreadful thing. I shall never forget her face." I fought to control my nerves. "She was to take the eleven o'clock train the morning after Mr. Wells's party at the casino."

"And we know that she did return home," Colin said. "The gendarmes are going to question the neighbors to see if anyone saw her come in, and whether she was alone."

"Is that Augustus?" I pressed my face to the dingy window of the cab. Colin rapped on the wall to signal the driver to stop. A thin figure in evening kit stood in the distance, leaning against a streetlight, but before I could see his face, he turned around and disappeared into the darkness. In a swift move, Colin followed, but he returned soon after, shaking his head.

"I could not find him," he said. "Too many winding streets and too little light."

It was before midnight when we returned to the hotel, and the lobby was teeming with activity. There were several lively groups in the lounge, and a party of gentlemen, whom I supposed were returning from the casino, made a loud entrance. Behind them, I saw Jeremy and Amity.

"You ought to speak to him," I said to Colin. "If he was with Hélène . . ."

"Of course."

"Should I say anything to Amity?"

"Not now, I don't think," he said. "There is no point in troubling her." He gave me a quick kiss and headed for Jeremy. "Bainbridge, you are just the gentleman I require. Join me in the smoking room? I have some particularly fine cigars and I have never known you to object to whisky."

Amity did not look pleased to see her fiancé pried off her arm. "We ought to insist on going with them," she said. "What are we left to do if they are so ready to abandon us?"

"Ladies are not allowed in the smoking room." I frowned. "I approve no more than you do of this slight. Did you enjoy the casino?"

"It was everything I hoped," she said. "Did you?"

"Me?"

"We saw you and Colin but couldn't get your attention. We had wanted you to join us for champagne. Did my mother do something to make you flee her little fête?"

"Not at all," I said.

"Then you have smoothed over the incident of the hat?"

"Only so far as keeping her from insisting on placing the blame on me. Tomorrow I hope to start gathering answers as to who might have purchased it."

"I do not doubt you shall succeed." Her eyes were bright and her hair was escaping from its pins. "Are you as taken with baccarat as Jeremy? I found it tedious, but promise me you will never tell him so."

"I would not dream of it. We were at the casino only briefly. Colin had to consult on a matter of business. Of course he would tell me nothing about it." I hoped that lie would stop her questions.

"What would the gentlemen say if we insisted on as many secrets as they have?" Amity asked. "I promised Christabel I would go to her the moment I returned. Will you excuse me?" We bade each other good night, and I watched her go. Her hair was in a state of some disarray, as was her gown. The hem was damp, and sand clung to it. Obviously she had not spent the evening in the casino any more than I had. I waited until she had entered the lift to go upstairs myself, and then took the stairs to Cécile's room, where, as I had hoped, I found both her and Margaret. Margaret, who was standing on a chair, was reading aloud from Virgil.

"*Flectere si nequeo superos, Acheronta movebo.*"

"Cécile does not speak Latin, Margaret," I said. "*If I cannot move heaven, I will raise hell.*"

"*Merci*, Kallista," Cécile said.

"I am afraid I bear sad tidings," I said, as Margaret leapt down from the chair. My face must have betrayed the serious nature of my news. "Hélène is dead. Murdered."

"*Mon dieu*," Cécile said, shaking her head.

"How?" Margaret asked, pushing me into the chair she had just abandoned.

"Bashed over the head in her room and hidden under the bed. It happened some time ago. The body was in a dreadful state—" I choked back a sob and buried my head in my hands. The strain of hiding from Amity the events of the evening and pretending everything was normal and well had taken a toll on me. Margaret poured me a glass of whisky and forced me to gulp it down.

"Do Marie and the other girls know?" she asked.

"Not yet. We shall have to tell them in the morning." I shared with my friends the few details we had ascertained from the scene.

"Monsieur Hargreaves is speaking to Bainbridge?" Cécile asked.

"Yes."

We all sat in silence. Finally, Margaret spoke.

"So Mr. Neville and Hélène died in the space of only a few hours. If the times were reversed, I should be inclined to say that something awful happened between them and Mr. Neville struck the fatal blow, then took his own life after realizing what he had done."

"But she was home in the morning," Cécile said. "She collected the package the butcher left her."

"Unless someone else did that," Margaret said. "Whoever went to her room could have seen the note and realized that if the roast were left, the body would be discovered earlier than perhaps the murderer would have liked."

"It occurs to me there is another scenario we ought to consider," I said. "What if Hélène killed Mr. Neville, and what if she had been operating on someone else's orders? Someone who could not risk being seen at the hotel. Once the job was done, rather than leave her as a loose end, that someone else unceremoniously dispatched her."

"Who would have wanted Mr. Neville dead?" Margaret asked.

"I could not say, but it does lead me back to another question: Who would have wanted Jeremy dead? What if Hélène killed the wrong Englishman?" I asked. "When the hotel manager came to our door that night, he said that the English duke was dead, not realizing that someone other than Jeremy might have been in his room."

"Hélène might have been murdered for having failed at her mission," Margaret said. "Which means there is still someone eager to see Jeremy dead."

"No other attempts have been made on his life," Cécile said.

"It was such a beautiful theory," Margaret said, lighting a cigarette and sighing.

"You smoke too much," Cécile said. There was a sharp knock on the door. I opened it, suspecting, correctly, that it would be my husband.

"When you weren't in our room I thought I might find you here," he said.

"What did Jeremy say?" I asked.

"He admitted to having walked with Hélène after he left the casino, but only for a very short while. Swears it was no longer than that."

"But what of his admission to having been with someone when he came into the hotel to see if Augustus was in the lobby that morning?" I asked. "That was the whole pretense of his coming in at such a strange hour and demanding more pillows. Was he with someone else?"

"He would not confide in me," Colin said. "He insists he will speak about it to no one but you, Emily. He is waiting for you downstairs."

# *Amity*

"What has happened?" Christabel asked, her mouth hanging open as her friend entered their room. "Your dress!"

"Nothing at all out of sorts," Amity said. "Jeremy and I decided to take a stroll on the beach. It is sandy and damp there." She batted at the sand clinging to her hem, revealing the fact that she was wearing no stockings as she lifted her skirt.

"But your stockings—"

"I removed them in order that I might walk barefoot. You know how unpleasant sand is in shoes." She had to admit that she found the look of horror on her friend's face vastly amusing.

"Not in front of Jeremy?"

"I did not let him see, if that's what you mean. Don't be such a prude, Christabel. Nothing untoward happened. It was rather disappointing, if you must know."

"And the casino?"

"A sadly boring place." Amity dropped onto a chair. "Not at all *too very* in the least. Do you remember all those nights in India when the heat was so fierce that we used to sleep on the roof of the house in Simla? How the air felt, so moist and warm? The way the edge of the moon was never crisp, but always covered with a gauzy haze?"

"Of course," Christabel said, closing the photograph album she had on the table in front of her. "What is making you think of that?"

"The moon tonight, I suppose. I miss India."

"You will go back."

"Yes, my duke shall take me." Amity smiled and pulled the album to her. "I see you are nostalgic tonight as well, going through your photographs. Will you follow Jack to India?"

"To Egypt, you mean," Christabel said. "That is where he shall be posted for the foreseeable future."

"He could put in for a transfer back to India," Amity said. "Especially if he knew you desired it." She flipped through her friend's pictures. "He looks rather handsome here. Like a young man in love. He would not hesitate to ask for India if he thought it were what you desire."

"You might have that sort of sway over a gentleman, but I never could," Christabel said, "so I suppose that it is fortunate I would not object to Egypt."

"Would you not?" Amity studied her friend. "Have you and the dashing captain discussed the matter?"

"No, nothing of the sort. He is all politeness and reserve."

"He is an English gentleman, a most infuriating breed," Amity said. "You shall have to use all your wiles if you want him to notice that you are interested in more than friendship."

"I could never do that," Christabel said, a small sigh escaping her lips. "If he finds he is fond of me, then—"

"You cannot sit back and wait, Christabel. A girl must take charge of her own happiness. Do you think anyone else cares about it so deeply as you? If you do not act, you will find yourself married off to whatever nobleman your parents deem worthy."

"My dowry would not attract even a minor nobleman."

"A suitable vicar then," Amity said. "There now, I got you to laugh, didn't I?"

"What would you have me do? Declare myself to Jack? The very idea is unconscionable."

"It might put him off, you are right." Amity tipped back her head as if studying the ceiling. "I shall give the matter further significant thought. We will get him for you, one way or another. I shall see to it personally. Your instincts may be right, but only for the moment and only if you take my advice. Rather than declaring yourself, try becoming ever so slightly more aloof when you are around him. How will our dear friend react when he begins to think you do not admire him above all other young gentlemen? You might even flirt with Mr. Fairchild."

"I couldn't!" Christabel exclaimed. "I would never deliberately mislead someone."

"Mr. Fairchild would enjoy the friendly attention, and it might spur the captain into action. They could duel over you."

"Amity!"

"I am only teasing. I should never approve of such a thing."

"Aloof," Christabel said slowly. "Yes, I could do that."

"We shall start tomorrow."

# 16

When I descended to the lobby I did not see Jeremy. A cursory search of the area and the lounge did not reveal him, so I stepped outside, where I found him on the stoop, smoking. His face looked haggard, and there were dark circles beneath his eyes. Whatever had happened between him and Amity that evening had affected him quite differently than it had his fiancée, who had been all glowing dishevelment when I had seen her.

"You look a wreck," I said.

"Walk with me, Em?" He offered his arm. "Can you bear the scandal if we cross La Croisette and walk to the end of the pier?"

"Given that I am married and that my husband sent me to find you, I hardly think anyone would bat an eye at seeing us."

"They don't know Hargreaves sent you. Our actions could easily be mistaken for a romantic assignation."

"I shall bear the risk with equanimity," I said. "You are delaying. What is it that you wish to speak to me about?"

He finished his cigarette and did not speak until we had reached the end of the dock. There were three other couples in our vicinity, but none of them had any interests beyond the moon and their respective partners. I rested my forearms on the railing; Jeremy leaned his back against it and crossed his arms. "Hargreaves told me about Hélène. What a terrible thing."

"You knew her?" I asked.

"What a loaded question, Em," he said. "Do you employ the biblical sense of the word?"

"Of course not." Our eyes met. His expression reminded me of the one I had seen on his face frequently when he was a naughty schoolboy. "Should I?"

"Heavens, no. I realize that I have a certain reputation. As you know better than anyone, I have carefully cultivated it," he said with a sigh. "Half the time I don't know myself why I bother. I suppose it amuses me and gives me an excuse for flirting with you, which is one of my preferred pastimes."

"You shall have to curb the habit now that you are getting married." I gave him a friendly jab on the arm.

"I find it not quite so difficult as I feared it would be," he said. "I hope that does not cause you any pain."

"Not the slightest bit," I said, laughing. "You are far too pleased with your own charms. I am delighted that you have found your happiness. Amity is—"

"She is like a dream, Em. It is as if she knows me better than I know myself. She anticipates everything I could possibly want."

"An ideal match."

"Yes, save for one thing. I fear—and you must promise you will not laugh at me—that she may in fact be even more debauched than I." He paused, bit his lip, and stared at the ground. "I adore her so very much, and I would never want to disappoint her. As a result, I have been steadily raising my game and it is exhausting me. The night of her father's party, I wanted nothing more than a quiet evening."

I pressed my lips together. "I never thought I would live to hear you admit such a thing."

"I do appreciate you managing not to laugh," he said. "The gambling was amusing for a while, and the entertainment as good as anything I've seen at the Moulin Rouge. After the show, the girls sat with us, but I took little pleasure in it, and made my excuses—as feebly as possible so that the others would think I was up to no good—and I prepared to set off for the hotel. While I was waiting at the coat check for my hat, stick, and scarf, et cetera, et cetera, Hélène appeared."

"Had she followed you?" I asked.

"She had, and at first I thought . . . er . . . This is bloody awkward."

"I can imagine what you thought."

"I was entirely wrong, however." His voice was earnest. "She told me that she saw a sadness in my eyes and wanted to make sure I was all right. Now, I may have been tired, but sad I certainly was not, and I began to worry that she might report her perceived melancholia to my friends, so I asked her if she would walk with me. She balked, thinking I was . . . er . . ."

"Yes, quite."

"But of course I wasn't," he said, the words coming rapidly, "and as soon as we had cleared that up, she agreed to a stroll. We took a turn through the gardens behind the casino and then sat on a bench and talked for perhaps a quarter of an hour, and then she left."

"Where did she go?" I asked.

"I haven't the slightest idea," he said. "I gave her some money for a cab home, but I would not have been surprised if she went back to the party."

"She didn't."

"I know that now."

"What did you do after that? You didn't turn up at the hotel until nearly five o'clock the next morning, asking for pillows."

He groaned. "Please refrain from pointing out the absurdity of it to me. I was going to hail a cab and return to the hotel right away— it must have only been a bit after midnight—but instead I decided to walk. And while I walked, I thought about some of the things Hélène said to me. She had asked me if I was married, and I told her a bit about Amity. She said she sounded a capital girl and a great deal more fun than most of the ladies she heard about. The thing is, Em, I never want to disappoint Amity. So rather than going back to the hotel, I walked up and down the beach."

"All night?"

"More or less."

"Simply to impress Amity?"

"She would be disappointed if I hadn't stayed out until dawn," he said. "The party at the casino may have been hosted by her father, but she is the one who planned it."

"So why the pillows?"

"Around about three o'clock in the morning, after I had paused to speak to some other gentlemen who were in a rather advanced state of intoxication, I grew fatigued. Once I had freed myself from what I must say was a most disappointing conversation—the drunk are never so amusing as they think they are—I started walking again, trying to keep myself awake."

"Why on earth didn't you just go to bed?"

"And disappoint Amity?"

"This is when you thought she might be in your room? I must say, as I did when you first mentioned this to me, the morning after Mr. Neville's death, that I am most shocked you could have suspected such a thing."

"It was unseemly and decidedly ungentlemanly of me, but Amity possesses extremely high spirits, and I . . . I . . . Well, it struck me that she might . . . Oh, Em, I hardly know what to say. Will you please allow me to leave the subject altogether? I believed she might be there, and did not think I ought to be alone with her. So I asked for more pillows, knowing that if she were in the room when the maid arrived with them, Amity would be alarmed at having been found by someone other than me and leave. After I asked for them to be sent up, I went back outside, with the idea of waiting for half an hour or so before returning. Instead, I fell dead asleep on a bench."

"Until ten the next morning when you found us at breakfast?"

He nodded. "And now Hélène is dead, and I have no alibi for the time of her murder."

"Do you believe you need one?" I asked.

"I may be the last person who saw her alive aside from whoever killed her."

"Why didn't you tell me all this when we discussed it the morning of Mr. Neville's death?"

"I was embarrassed."

I believed him. "I think, Jeremy, you need to be honest with Amity, not just about Hélène. You have done nothing wrong and I cannot imagine a girl like Miss Wells is going to balk at your having gone for a little walk with a dancer she had hired for the evening's entertainment. Had your walk taken a different sort of turn . . ."

He made a sound something like a growl. "Quite."

"More than that, though, you must tell Amity your true feelings. You may not be the only one pretending to be more debauched than he is."

"She is not pretending, Em," he said. "If anything, she is tempering herself. All that time she was begging me not to make that ridiculous swim—I will not tolerate a word of censure from you about it—I could see that, really, she wanted me to do it."

"Then why would she have tried to stop you?" I asked.

"Perhaps because she knows I am not worthy of her."

"Oh dear heavens, Jeremy, do not go maudlin over this. I am going to bed." I started to head back to the hotel, but he grabbed my arm and stopped me.

"You won't tell Hargreaves that I was alone all night after the party?" he asked.

"I do not understand why you didn't tell him," I said. "I can promise you, Jeremy, he is not a supporter of your dedication to debauchery."

"He's a bore. I don't know why you married him." He was pouting now, but stopped short of stamping his foot.

"Don't tease," I said.

"Oh, bloody hell, I suppose it makes no difference. You might as well tell him. He's not going to spread the word through the gentlemen's clubs of London. But it was you, Em, that I knew I could confide in, not him. Thank you for that, for listening, and for accepting me as I am."

"Accepting you as you are?" I asked and looked at him, cocking my head. "I am going back to my room to collapse, inconsolable, on my bed, weeping over the revelation that you are quite as ordinary as my own husband."

"I never said he was ordinary." He grunted. "No matter what I may claim publicly, I do admire him, even if it is against my own better judgment."

"I never said he was ordinary either." I patted him on the cheek and led him back to the hotel.

The next morning I woke before the sun had risen above the horizon, dreading the conversation that Colin and I would have to have with Marie, Violette, and Rose. We met them at the café where Margaret and I had shared rosé with them, and they wept openly when we informed them of Hélène's death. There was nothing more for them to tell us—they could not think of anyone who might have wanted to harm their friend—but they promised to contact us if that changed.

That grim task done, we stopped by the police station to see what the gendarmes had gleaned from Hélène's neighbors. An elderly woman who lived across the street reported having seen someone in a long cloak ring the bell and be admitted to the house, but she could not be certain which bell—that for Hélène's apartment or the one for the Soucy family's—or whether it was Hélène who had opened the door. Monsieur Soucy and his wife were certain they had not received any visitors that day, so the gendarmes thought it reasonable to believe the person had come to see Hélène. The neighbor took note of the incident because the cloaked person had the hood of the garment pulled up, which she took as a sign that the morning was chilly and she, herself, should dress accordingly when she went out.

"So we are looking for a person of indeterminate height and gender who owns a cloak," Colin said. "How encouraging."

"I want to question the hotel staff," I said. "Not the desk clerks, but the maids and anyone else who works behind the scenes, so to speak."

"Do you believe Bainbridge was candid with you last night?" Colin asked.

"I have no reason to doubt him."

He made a low, thinking sort of noise. "Something doesn't fit."

Back at the hotel, we consulted with the manager as to who had been working overnight on the evening in question and started to interview the staff. The night clerk, to whom we had already spoken, did not alter a word of his story. He saw nothing unusual in the English duke requesting pillows in the middle of the night and then going back outside. He was adamant that guests often make strange requests, so it had not stood out to him at the time. Among the rest—the housekeeping maid who discovered Mr. Neville's body, a handyman who slept on property in case there were any emergency repairs needed after hours, and three kitchen maids—only one had anything new to share with us, the second of the kitchen maids.

"She was very, very pretty," she said. "I only saw her because I had stepped out for a smoke—I know I shouldn't have, so please don't tell—only we were so late that night, finishing up the dishes."

"Where exactly did you see her?" Colin asked.

"She saw me. I was having my smoke, just out the staff door, and she came to me and asked if I could let her in. She gave me a handful of coins."

"Did she say where in the hotel she was going?" I asked.

The girl gave me a shrewd look. "It was quite obvious, wasn't it? Dressed the way she was, all fancy, with rouge on her face? That sort don't use the front door, do they?"

"Does this happen with some regularity?" Colin asked.

The girl shrugged. "I suppose it does, often enough. We don't mind. What business of ours is it if the grand people want a little amusement?"

"Is the manager of the hotel aware of this?" I asked.

"I believe, madame, it is not the sort of thing people like you—or the manager—like to discuss."

"Did you see where, specifically, she went in the hotel?" Colin asked. "Or did she, perhaps, ask you for directions?"

"*Non.* Our conversation was nothing more than a simple transaction."

No one else reported having seen the person in question, in or out of the hotel, and the kitchen maid's description of her was too imprecise to be of much use. It could have been Hélène, but it could have been any number of other girls. The manager confirmed that he was aware of such things going on—only occasionally, he insisted—in the hotel. This, he promised us, was not the sort of establishment that encourages such happenings, but one could not stop everything.

"So we have next to nothing," I said. "I suppose the only sensible thing to do now is interrogate every single gentleman who was staying that night. You may need to torture some of them, but I am confident that eventually someone will own up to having hosted a lady of the evening."

"Quite," Colin said. "Torture is such a reliable way to get to the truth. Would you object to a spot of tea before I begin?"

# *Amity*

Jack was sulking. They were on the hotel's back lawn, playing croquet, a game Amity adored. She admitted freely this was because she so enjoyed the satisfaction that came from sending an opponent's ball far off the court in a savage roquet. Almost more entertaining than the match were Christabel's attempts at flirting with Mr. Fairchild. She was too sweet to be obvious, and, as a result, Mr. Fairchild was rather confused, particularly as Christabel's flirtation primarily consisted of refusing to take roquets when her ball hit Mr. Fairchild's. In Christabel's mind, the earnest smile she flashed at Mr. Fairchild ought to have suggested to him that she was flirting. Instead, he was left with a feeling that she did not entirely understand the rules of the game, and he kept trying to explain them to her. In reply, she asked him if he would teach her the basics of cricket, a sport about which she felt she had in the past been most unkind.

Jack was the only person who suspected something else was afoot, and this was just as Amity had wanted it. Had Christabel possessed better skills in the art of flirtation, she would have had Mr. Fairchild paying court by the end of the afternoon. As she was barely able to handle Jack in a satisfactory manner, she would never have been able to navigate her way out of the mess caused by two suitors, which perfectly suited Amity's plan. Jack was jealous, and that would spur him to further action.

"I do not think this is working," Christabel whispered when the game had finished and they were being served lemonade. "Captain Sheffield is barely speaking to me." The pained look on her friend's face told Amity Christabel could no longer bear to take the liberty of calling him by his Christian name.

"Oh, Christabel, you are so naïve! It's charming. Truly, it is," Amity said. "That merely proves our plan is working. He has been watching you all morning and he is worried. I am confident that within the next day or so—this evening if we are lucky—he will pull me aside and ask if I am aware of you having any romantic attachments."

"And you will tell him I love him?" Her eyes brightened.

"Of course not. First, because when the time comes for that sort of revelation, you are the one who shall have to make it—"

"I don't know that I could do that." Christabel wrinkled her nose.

"Do not interrupt. It is exceedingly rude." Amity laughed and pulled her friend close. "The second reason I will not tell him that you love him is that he must suffer a little longer, otherwise he will feel a rush of relief to learn that his affections are quite safe, and he shall then immediately return to treating you exactly as he did before."

"Was that so bad?" Christabel asked.

"Had he proposed?"

"No." Her voice was quiet.

"Had he declared his love to you?"

"No," came her answer, in the barest whisper.

"Had he begged even a single kiss from you?" Amity asked.

"You know he did nothing of the sort, Amity!" Christabel looked around, embarrassed, afraid that this last question had been spoken so loudly as to have been easily overheard.

"Precisely," Amity said. "So now our darling Jack must suffer, just for a short while, before we can be guaranteed that you, my friend, will have a happy ending to your fairy tale."

"I would hardly call it a fairy tale," Christabel said.

"They always become quite ugly in the middle, Christabel. Go back and read the Brothers Grimm if you don't believe me. There is little more bleak and terrifying than an unfinished fairy tale. You must focus on the end, not this part."

# 17

Given that torturing guests—or even a little friendly interrogation—was unlikely to result in us being able to identify the girl the kitchen maid had let into the staff entrance of the hotel, Colin and I had to take a different tack. To begin with, he pulled Jeremy aside and told him what we knew. Did he now want to confess to having asked Hélène to meet him in his rooms? The answer was an emphatic no.

"Do you believe him?" I asked. I was sitting on our balcony with a pot of tea (Assam) and an assortment of pastries (divine) watching the parade of tourists walk along La Croisette. It proved immensely diverting, as I have an endless capacity for inventing stories about people when I see them. The rotund lady (American) wearing a fox wrap, replete with head and feet, could only have been new money. There was no other explanation for such a garment on such a warm day. The lanky gentleman in a straw boater running at breakneck speed had let time get away from him in the casino and was now late for an appointment with his sweetheart. And so on, until Colin returned and reported the results of his conversation.

"I do believe him," he said, helping himself to a large bite of raspberry tart. "He understands the gravity of the situation. Unfortunately, I do not see how we can identify the woman in question."

"Does this not make you think, though, that someone other than Mr. Neville poisoned that whisky?"

"I admit to the possibility, but we have no hard evidence."

"You two look very serious," Margaret said, bursting onto the balcony and taking the chair next to mine. "Meg let me in and she said to remind you that she would not tolerate your being late to dress for dinner tonight. You have turned her into quite a monster, Emily."

"It is all her own doing, I assure you," I said.

"Bring me up to date on the investigation," she said, and we did just that as she made quick work of the remaining pastries. "What a hopeless business. I don't see any way through the muck."

"Nor do I," I said. "It is rather frustrating."

"If we suspect that someone other than Neville poisoned the whisky, his object must have been to kill Bainbridge," Colin said. "Jack is the obvious suspect, as he would inherit if his brother died."

"Jack has no interest in being duke," I said.

"So he may claim," Colin said. "Or is that nothing more than a not-very-clever cover?"

"You cannot truly think—" I started.

"We must consider every possibility," he said. "He would have had ready access to his brother's room."

"It pains me to even consider it," I said, "but you are right, we must." I was staring out over the water, but a shot of red fabric caught my eyes on the drive in front of the hotel. It was Amity, running at an insupportable speed. She barely hesitated before crossing the street and turning east on La Croisette, narrowly missing being struck by a carriage. I shot out of my room, through the corridor, down the steps, through the lobby past a baffled-looking Jeremy, and out of the hotel, doing my best to catch her. Running in a corset poses a unique set of problems, but I did my best to ignore the stays poking my ribs as I struggled for breath. Fortunately, Amity was struggling against the same enemy, and I found her, less than two hundred yards down the promenade, holding onto the back of a bench, trying to catch her breath.

"Are you unwell?" I asked. "I saw you flee and was worried."

"Bloody corsets." She sat down. "They render us all but useless."

"You have been crying," I said, noting her tear-stained eyes. "What happened?"

"I have just had a rather painful conversation with my fiancé, I am afraid. I am not certain that he is going to marry me." She hugged her arms around her shoulders.

"Amity, that is impossible!" I said. "Jeremy adores you—he told me just last night how much. You are like a dream to him. I use his words."

"He told me he spoke to you. Please understand that I do not fault you in the least for what happened. I know your intentions were of the best, but I am afraid they catalyzed a most serious situation." She stretched her legs in front of her, crossed her feet at her ankles, and let out a sad sigh.

"What did he say to you?"

"I have believed, even from before I met him, that we were designed for each other. Absurd, I know, but Jack's descriptions of his brother brought him to life for me. You know how easy it is to adore Jack. How could his brother prove any less amiable? And when I met Jeremy in Cairo, everything Jack had said, and that I had hoped, was confirmed. Now, though, I begin to wonder if I am not what he wants."

"Why would you think such a thing?" I asked.

"He was speaking to me of secrets and opacity and making very little sense, but I understood the thrust of his meaning," she said. "He does not want the sort of life I do. He told me my exuberance sometimes frightens him."

"That does not mean he does not love you." I put a hand on her arm, hoping to reassure her.

"I know he loves me," she said, her gaze focused on the sea in front of us, "but can I be the sort of wife that he wants? I don't want to molder away in some damp estate while my husband is out shooting birds."

"I can assure you that Jeremy does not want that kind of life either."

"Are you certain, Emily? If that is so, why does my exuberance frighten him?"

"Did you not tell me yourself last night that the casino was not so enthralling as you had hoped?" I asked. "Perhaps he feels the same. You are both doing your best to present yourselves to each other in the most extreme ways, almost as if you mean to outdo one another. Isn't it exhausting?"

"How can I be sure that is how he feels?" She looked directly into my eyes, and I began to think her feelings for Jeremy were more sincere than I had previously believed.

"Ask him," I said. "When I spoke to him I told him to be honest with you, and it sounds as if he made a bungle of doing that."

"He did nothing but confuse me." A formidable lady, dressed in a way that can only have been intended to emulate Queen Victoria, knocked against Amity's shoes with her walking stick. Rather than pull them in out of the way, Amity stuck them out farther, glaring at the woman before she turned back to me. "She could have been polite about it. I wasn't deliberately trying to block her path. What was I saying? Yes. Jeremy made very little sense."

"Speak to him again. I can assure you he never intended for you think, even for a moment, that he does not want to marry you or that he would expect you to be a different sort of wife than he knows you will be."

"Could you talk to him, Emily? I said some terrible things and I am ashamed. Sometimes I should make a better effort at being polite." Now she pulled in her feet and tucked them under her skirts so that they were no longer blocking any part of the promenade.

"I do not think it is wise to have anyone mediating in this sort of situation, Amity," I said. "You two must deal directly with each other. It is the only way forward."

"There is something else, you know," she said. She clenched her fists, then released them. "That girl—that dancer."

"Hélène, yes."

"She's dead. He swears it wasn't him—"

"You must believe that," I said.

"I do. Augustus told me he watched him the entire night, and that he was only with her for a short while in the garden at the casino. After that, he wandered around near the beach."

"Augustus was watching him?"

"It is what Augustus likes to do, and if it makes him feel useful, what's the harm in it? At any rate, I know I can trust Jeremy in that regard. Are you certain that he can be happy with a wife like me?"

"I have never been more certain of anything." I smiled, hoping there was no hint of my true feelings visible on my face. I did know that Jeremy adored her, and that he unquestionably thought she would make a perfect wife, but I still did not feel that I really knew Amity. Something about her felt false. Perhaps it was nothing more than the posturing they were both doing, but my intuition told me it was greater than that.

"I suppose we shall never find out who sent me that hat," Amity said, changing the subject. "Not now that there is a murder to be solved."

"I have not forgot that," I said, "and you have given me an excellent idea as to what to do next. I hope I shall have answers for you before much longer. Now, are you feeling better? I think we had better return to the hotel. Jeremy is bound to be worried."

Amity cried the prettiest tears I have ever seen when she stood in front of Jeremy, his face pale and drawn, waiting for her in the lobby (precisely where I had told him to be as I raced past him in pursuit of his fiancée). I left them to it, feeling rather nauseated by the way she was now fawning over him. Before returning to Colin and Margaret, I inquired at the desk as to whether Augustus was in his room. He was not, and the concierge told me he had gone to the garden at the Villa Vallombrosa, which was open to the public each afternoon. I intended to follow him there, and Colin agreed that confronting him about what he had seen the night of Mr. Neville's death was an excellent idea.

"I did not say that is why I wanted to speak to him," I said. "I had thought to ask him about the morning of the infamous hat delivery, but I see no reason I cannot address both topics."

"I would rather you let me do it," Colin said.

"Why don't the three of us go?" Margaret asked. "When we find him, it will be natural for us to walk in twos, and he won't suspect a thing."

"What he suspects is irrelevant, Margaret," I said. "I have no intention of being less than straightforward with him."

"A little subtlety never hurts," Colin said. "Margaret may be onto something." And so it was decided. We set off for the villa, but locating Augustus in its acres of plants proved a challenge. The stunning grounds were filled with lush vegetation and towering trees: cedars of Lebanon and eucalyptus among swaying palms. Large patches of bamboo seemed to shudder in the wind, and the cool grottoes with their fountains could make a lady wish for a wrap on even the warmest summer day. Aspidistra and ficus thrived here. Roses filled the sunny spots and begonias brightened the shade, their delicate petals soft as satin. When at last we found Augustus—we identified him from a distance by the bright yellow carnation in his buttonhole—he was sitting on a sunny bench, using a magnifying glass to study a beetle of some sort.

"Do your interests extend to all insects, Mr. Wells?" Margaret asked after greeting him. "I thought you were particularly keen on butterflies."

"I am particularly keen on butterflies, although I would not choose those words to describe my pursuits," he replied, biting sarcasm lacing his tone, but he did not answer her question. He had looked up from the beetle, but had not moved the glass from its position.

"The sun is coming straight through your lens," I said. "I am afraid your multilegged friend may be suffering from the heat."

"That is the general idea," he said. "I was trying to determine how long it would take before he succumbed, but now that you have interrupted me, I have lost track of the time elapsed. I was counting, you see."

"How singular of you." I cringed. "Will you take a turn with us? Margaret and my husband have been arguing about Latin poetry, and as Greek is my area of expertise, I am feeling quite left out of the conversation. I do hope you will rescue me."

He gave me what can only be described as a look of disdain, but he rose, put the magnifying glass in his jacket pocket, and walked beside me. Colin and Margaret, as planned, pulled ahead of us. Augustus did not reply to any of my attempts to engage him in friendly conversation, but after approximately a quarter of an hour—a most uncomfortable quarter of an hour—broke his silence as we passed a tall fountain.

"What do you want from me, Lady Emily?" he asked. "I know you have as little interest in befriending me as I have in befriending you. You have come here for a specific purpose. What is it? I would prefer if you were as direct as possible so that we may end this charade in an expedient manner."

"Amity told me you were following Jeremy the night Mr. Neville died," I said, regretting that I had not followed my instincts and approached him directly. "Did you see anything out of the ordinary?"

"Do you know how many times I have been asked that question? The police are not absolute fools, you know. They did speak with us all."

"I am well aware of that, but now that we know there was a murder that night—"

"The death of some sad little prostitute is hardly any concern of mine."

"She was not a prostitute."

"However you would have it," he said, poking at a hedge with his walking stick.

"Did you see her again after she and Jeremy parted at the casino?"

"I did not. Your question, however, suggests that you suspect she was with your dear friend the duke, because you already claim to know that I was following him."

"I do not suspect him of anything untoward, but it is possible that the girl—her name is Hélène—was doing something of which he was unaware."

"You think perhaps she was following him as well? Yes, that would make things considerably more interesting, wouldn't it?"

"But you did not see her?" I asked.

"As I already said, I did not. I admire your insistence on pursuing the truth, though, and as a result will share with you this: had I seen her, whether at the hotel, or in the casino, or anywhere else, behaving in a manner that led me to believe the duke was even contemplating betraying my sister, I would have gone straight to Amity, rousing her from her bed if necessary, and made sure she knew without delay. I would not stand by and let her marry someone who I believed would not make her happy."

"Do you believe Jeremy will make her happy?" I asked.

"I have not yet reached a verdict on the situation," he said, his voice measured. "Is there anything else or will you release me now?"

"Did you see the hatbox being delivered to the hotel the day of your excursion to Monte Carlo?"

"I was on my way to Monte Carlo when Amity received the gift."

"I do, of course, realize that, but you are, if nothing else, a careful observer. The desk clerk does not remember seeing the box before I was at the desk, but I believe it was already there when I came to leave my key. That was not long after you had departed. Did you see a hatbox on the desk?"

His smile was reptilian. "I did."

"You did?"

"I had to turn in my key as well, didn't I? The box was there. I read the label."

"So you know I did not put it there."

"I know you did not put it there at the same time that you left your key. As to what you were doing prior to that, I am entirely in the dark. I will spare myself from any more of your mundane questions by telling you that I did not see the box being delivered. The only delivery person I noticed that morning was someone bringing a large bunch of flowers for a female guest of the hotel. I understand she is a well-known opera singer. Would you like further information about her?"

"That will not be necessary." I gritted my teeth. The man was infuriating. He saluted as he walked away from me, and I stood still so that the distance between us would increase. He turned back after he had covered about ten yards.

"You do know that Mr. Fairchild and Mr. Neville returned to the hotel together that evening, don't you? Perhaps you could torment him with some of your impertinent but charming questions."

# *Amity*

Jeremy did everything in his not inconsiderable powers to convince Amity that he was devoted to her, that there was nothing about her that he found short of perfect, and that he would never, ever again be the cause of her tears. The only awkwardness was caused by Amity's refusal to move even one step from where Emily had deposited her in the lobby, where she was now leaning against a marble column. Mr. and Mrs. Wells, setting off on a walk, saw them, and the concerned looks on their faces told him he would have to have a conversation with Amity's father to smooth things over.

"Now I have made you angry," Amity said, watching her parents go.

"Not at all," Jeremy said. "I shall make sure your father knows there is no trouble between us."

"He was being facetious when he said he brought a shotgun," Amity said. "He would never force you to marry me."

"No one will ever need to force me to marry you, my love." He brushed her cheek with his hand. "Please can we go somewhere more private?"

"Absolutely not," Amity said. "I can no longer trust myself alone with you until we are married. Not after our walk on the beach."

"Nothing so very untoward happened."

"But I wanted it to."

"I never meant to upset you—not then and not now."

"I believe you," Amity said. "Now go and find your friends and leave me be. I have some very important issues to discuss with Christabel concerning her own romantic happiness."

"Jack is quite fond of her," Jeremy said. "Wouldn't it be a perfect end if they married after we did? She could follow him around the world with her camera, recording his every adventure."

"I do not think we will ever see the day," Amity said. She felt a slight pang of guilt at misleading her fiancée, but there were times when one must focus on greater goals, and she could not let him go to his brother and ease his anxieties about Christabel. "You know how fond I am of Jack—never doubt it—but do you really think it is a good match? She would have to move to Cairo, and you cannot think that a girl like her would want that."

"He does not have to stay in the army forever," Jeremy said.

"But he loves it."

Jeremy shrugged. "He likes having a useful occupation, particularly one that puts him in interesting parts of the world, but I am sure he could learn to love something else. He is nothing if not adaptable."

"That is awfully cold of you," Amity said. "If he has found a situation that suits him, why should he have to leave it?"

"Marriage often requires compromise. I see the darkness crossing your face, my love, and I can assure you that I am not referring to our marriage. We shall never compromise—we won't need to, not given how similar we are."

"I think Christabel would be content in India. She did so love it there."

"Better than Egypt?"

"Without question," Amity said.

"You are suggesting that I speak to him about making a slight adjustment to his plans?"

"You know me too well," Amity said. "Just do not let him know that I have said a word about it. I would not want to raise in him any false hopes."

"It is a simple enough situation," Jeremy said. "Either Christabel loves him or she doesn't."

"Precisely, and it is not for me or you to push either—or both—of them to decide before they are ready. Playing matchmaker is always a bad idea. I would not have so much as mentioned India if I did not believe that your brother himself had been happy there. Should he transfer back, he would remain happy there, with or without Christabel."

"I do so admire you, Amity," Jeremy said, "and if we were not in the middle of this wretched hotel lobby I should sweep you up in my arms right now. Part of the reason I have—until I met you—dreaded marriage is that I could not bear the thought of dining nightly with someone bent on marrying off every young lady within her reach. I understand that to be the primary object of most wives."

"I can promise you, Jeremy, I shall never be like most wives. Now go, before I have the urge to kiss you in public and thoroughly disgrace myself." He kissed her hand and sauntered off. Amity watched him go, feeling more and more certain that Emily had been quite correct. Not only did he adore her, he would never want her to be an ordinary wife. Nothing could be more perfect.

# 18

Beautiful though I had found the gardens at the Villa Vallombrosa, my conversation with Augustus had left me frustrated and with a general feeling of unease. Nonetheless, upon our return to the hotel, I did want to set off in search of Mr. Fairchild, as Augustus had suggested I speak to him. Colin stopped me, reminding me that he had already queried him about the night of Mr. Neville's death.

"You are letting Augustus fluster you," my husband said. We had retired to our balcony, with Margaret and Cécile. "He is trying to distract you with irrelevant details. If Bainbridge was the intended victim of the so-called suicide, we can focus on that. I am going to speak with Jack, but will not let him know that I suspect his brother was—or is—at risk. I merely want to better understand him and what he wants from his life. I shall also inquire as to his finances via Scotland Yard."

"We ladies shall go back to the Soucy house and the dressing room at the casino and comb through all of Hélène's things," I said, waving away a bee that was becoming rather too interested in my hat.

"I do not want to believe that she was responsible for poisoning the whisky," Margaret said.

"You like the idea of the poor, noble girl who stands by her principles," Cécile said. "It is a romantic notion, but not often realistic."

"Even if she had poisoned it, she may not have known what she was doing," Margaret said. "Whoever ordered her to do it might have given her a vial of some mysterious liquid and told her it was something to help the duke sleep."

"Or she might have been so mortified that Bainbridge rejected her advances that she wanted him dead." Colin ran a hand through his tousled curls. "We do not know enough about her to make any assumptions. It might be useful to talk to someone who didn't consider her a friend."

"That is an excellent idea," I said. Meg stepped onto the balcony and handed me an envelope.

"This came up from the desk," she said.

I thanked her and opened it. "Amity asks if I could meet her to discuss something urgent. She is at a café not far from where we caught the ferry to Sainte-Marguerite—she rang the hotel to get me the message."

"You go meet her," Margaret said. "Cécile and I can manage without you."

Not wanting to waste any time, I left without so much as grabbing an umbrella. The cab ride to the café was short, but the place was extremely crowded. The weather looked as if it would soon turn inclement; the wind was picking up and dark clouds hung heavy in the sky, driving inside many of the tourists who wanted to be settled somewhere cozy before the rain began. The maître d' did his best to assist me, but neither of us could find Amity. I checked with waiter after waiter, asking if they had served a table with an American girl on her own, but none of them replied in the affirmative.

Wondering if the clerk who wrote the message might have garbled the address, I went back outside, and searched the cafés on either side of the one where I expected to find Amity, but to no avail. I was about to go back to the hotel, when a coarse, elderly woman sitting on a bench, dressed in the heavy black clothes one expects to see on a Greek widow, called to me. She was holding a large umbrella, open even though it was not yet raining.

"Are you the one who was supposed to meet the pretty young lady?" she asked me, her accent coarse.

"Yes," I said. "Did you see her?"

"She came running out the door, crying like anything, so I called out to her. It is painful to see someone in such a state of distress. Told me she had been waiting for someone—you, I imagine—but that she had given up hope that you would come."

"Where did she go?" I asked.

"She ran to the end of the block and then turned up the hill to Le Suquet. I believe she was in need of religious consolation."

I thanked her and waved down another cab. It dropped me in front of Notre Dame de l'Espérance a short while later, but Amity was nowhere to be found. After a thorough search of the small church, I went back outside, climbed the stairs to the parapets, and walked the length of the wall. The rain started, coming down in droves, and I wished I had brought an umbrella. The cobbles, which had been slippery when dry, proved an absolute hazard when wet, so I used the rough stones of the battlement to steady myself. Halfway along, I noticed a splash of yellow on the pavement: the sad remains of a large yellow carnation, just the sort Augustus Wells sported in his buttonhole every day without exception.

I collected the flower, and then looked down over the wall, but saw no one below outside the church. In the other direction, the wide stairs that led to the houses in Le Suquet were empty save for a solitary couple, the gentleman's one arm firmly around the lady's waist, the other arm holding an umbrella above her. Augustus was nowhere to be found. I went back into the church to search again, and then into the garden next to the remains of the castle. By now, I was soaked to the bone, and the chill in the air would not be ignored.

There were no cabs to be found up here. In my rush to reach Amity, I had neglected to ask my driver to wait for me, so I was forced to walk back down the hill in the driving rain. My progress was deliberately slow, as I did not want to slip. My straw hat had long since ceased functioning in any practical capacity and was now funneling water down my back. I had no map with me, not that it would have mattered, as it would have become soaked and useless. Devoid of guidance, the narrow streets of Le Suquet confused me. I kept heading downhill, not worrying much about where, exactly, I would come out at the bottom, figuring that once I was in a busier section of town, I would be able to hail a cab.

I paused briefly near a twelfth-century wellhead that had been built sunken into a wall, providing a small shelter. Shivering, I stood out of the rain for a few minutes, and then continued on my way. I thought I recognized the buildings around me, not far from the site of Mrs. Wells's ill-fated dinner party, and therefore only a short walk from the promenade that would take me to La Croisette. I brushed some of the water from my jacket and continued, confident that I was soon to be out of my misery. This, unfortunately, was not quite correct. Cab drivers, I have learned, are averse to stopping for ladies who are bedraggled and dripping wet, and I was forced to walk the entire way back to our hotel.

The desk clerks were horrified by my appearance, and my shoes creaked as I crossed the lobby, leaving a trail of dripping water in my wake. Colin, Mr. Fairchild, and Jack were sitting at a table near the lounge and called out to me.

"Emily! You look like an extremely elegant drowned rat," my husband said, as they all rose to greet me.

"An Englishwoman ought to know better than to face the day without an umbrella," I said. "The usually fine Côte d'Azur weather is making me weak."

"You are shivering," Colin said. "Get yourself upstairs and warm. I shall organize some soup to be sent up."

"No, thank you, I shan't require soup," I said.

"Where were you?" Jack asked.

"Looking for Amity," I said.

"Amity is over there with her mother," Mr. Fairchild said. "They have been playing cards for nearly two hours."

"Another drowned rat," Jack said, and we all turned to the door, where Jeremy had just appeared, as soaked as I was. "This one less elegant. Were you walking together?"

"No, I was on my own," I said. "I am off for a hot bath before I flood the lobby. Do hold on to this flower for me, will you? I shall tell you why it matters when I return." I put the sodden carnation on the table.

Jeremy caught up to me while I was waiting for the lift. "Have you gone lazy, Em?" he asked. "I thought you always insist on the stairs. Although in your present condition, I can imagine speed is of the essence. Were you swimming?"

"You are no better off than I," I said. "What happened to you?"

"I was to meet Augustus—dreadful bloke—and he stood me up."

"Where were you to meet him?" I asked, as the lift operator opened the door and ushered us in, looking unhappily at the puddles that had formed around us.

"A little café not far from the ferry dock. When I couldn't find him, I took a stroll along the water until the rain started. It took me ages to get a cab."

"Had you arranged in advance to meet him?" I asked.

"No, he sent a message."

"Did he ring the front desk?"

"Yes, why?"

"That is more or less what happened to me, although I thought I was to meet Amity," I said. "Come back downstairs once you are dry again. Something most peculiar is happening."

Much as I longed for a luxurious soak in a hot tub, I forced myself to hurry and, hence, was still chilled when I returned to the lobby. Jeremy was not yet there—nothing would induce him to rush his ablutions—but I quickly explained to Colin and our friends what had occurred. By this time, Margaret and Cécile had arrived, both utterly dry, I might add, Cécile being far too wise to ever let a cab get away from her.

"Has anyone seen Augustus?" Margaret asked. "So far as I know, he did not depart the Villa Vallombrosa until after us."

"He joined his parents and Amity about twenty minutes ago," Colin said, nodding toward the table near the lounge where they were all seated. He was still wearing a flower in his buttonhole, but I did not doubt he would have been meticulous enough to replace the one he had lost on the battlement.

"Where is Christabel?" I asked.

"I have not seen her all day," Jack said, "but I believe you lunched with her, did you not, Fairchild?" I detected a tone of irritation in his voice.

"She was with Mrs. Wells and Amity," Mr. Fairchild said. "They invited me to join them. I have not seen her since then."

"Is that so?" Jack dragged so hard on his cigarette it was almost as if he meant to attack it.

"Quite." Mr. Fairchild said.

"Who extended the invitation?" Jack asked.

"Does it matter?" Mr. Fairchild looked away, a smug expression on his face. "If you must know, it was Christabel." Thunder brewed in Jack's eyes, but he was too much the gentleman to do anything but bury his emotions.

"I spoke to the desk clerk who answered the telephone and took the messages for both Jeremy and myself," I said, redirecting the conversation before it became more awkward. "He did not recognize their voices, but he did insist that both callers were English."

"So not Augustus and Amity," Margaret said.

"When I pressed him on the point, he insisted that, yes, there could be no doubt that they were English, but he did not know whether they were German or Swiss."

"The words *English* and *tourist* are all but interchangeable here," Colin said. "It is one of the things I find the most charming about the Côte d'Azur. Dumas wrote about it, I believe."

"In the end, he owned that he could not identify anything about the voices other than one was a man, the other a woman," I said.

"Amity certainly did not ring the front desk. She has been in the hotel all afternoon," Mr. Fairchild said.

"Augustus could have made both calls," Margaret said. "He might have disguised his voice to make it sound feminine."

"Or he might have paid a woman to make the call for him," I said.

"Or it might not have been Augustus at all," Colin said.

"This is where our bedraggled flower becomes important," I said, poking at the sorry yellow specimen I had left on the table and explaining how it had come to be in my possession. "I cannot doubt that Augustus is the one who sent me on this useless errand."

"For what end?" Colin asked.

"I have not the slightest idea," I said.

"If he wanted to send you on a useless chase, why would he have left the flower?" Mr. Fairchild asked. "Surely he wouldn't have wanted you to identify him."

"I am not so sure about that," I said. "He may have done it with the express purpose of me knowing it was his work. It could have been a way of putting me on notice."

"Notice of what?" Jack asked. "Augustus is a bit eccentric, to be sure, but I do not believe him to be vicious. What are you suggesting, Emily?"

"Perhaps I am wrong altogether," I said. "He is not the only gentleman in Cannes, surely, to wear a yellow carnation. It could be nothing more than a coincidence." I did not feel there was any merit in arguing the point. I could not prove what had happened, and would win no friends by insisting that Augustus had deliberately tormented me. Regardless, I felt no shred of doubt that he had left the message for me, possibly to repay me for what he viewed as my impertinent questions at the Villa Vallombrosa.

Jeremy appeared and slumped into an empty chair with a long sigh. "I have directed the barman to send a hot toddy over for you, Em. You are still shivering despite your best efforts to clutch that shawl around you. You look rather like a well-to-do refugee."

"Are there such people?" Cécile asked. "I cannot believe it."

"Where have you been, my dear?" Amity asked as she crossed to us. "Jack tells me you abandoned him."

"I was off . . . er . . ." He stumbled over the words. "Nowhere of interest. When did your brother return?"

"Ages ago," Amity said. "Why do you ask?"

"I had a message to meet him," Jeremy said. Soon, we had told Amity the entire story. I watched her reaction carefully. Her face was very still, but her eyes animated, and her cheeks colored prettily when we were done.

"So you think my brother sent you both on a fool's errand?" she asked.

"I can only assume you did not leave a message asking me to meet you in the café?" I asked.

"No. I have been here all afternoon." She frowned. "Augustus does like a good joke, and he certainly did get the better of you both. You won't be too stern with him, will you? I am certain he meant no harm.

The yellow carnation might as well be his calling card. He would have left it deliberately to make you laugh."

"To make me laugh?" I asked.

"Yes," Amity said. "As I already mentioned, he likes a good joke."

"I hardly see how this could be construed as a good joke," Colin said, after Amity and Jeremy had left us for her parents' table.

"That can only mean that you have not spent much time in conversation with Augustus," I said. "He makes the weird sisters from Macbeth seem levelheaded."

"The rain has stopped," Mr. Fairchild said, glancing outside. "I wonder if that means the fireworks will be on tonight. I'm going to ask at the desk."

Jack abandoned us shortly thereafter. Christabel had reappeared, and he intercepted her before Mr. Fairchild returned.

"Alone at last," Margaret said. "Do you want to hear what Cécile and I learned while you were traipsing about in the rain?"

# *Amity*

"It really is a most singular story," Birdie said when Amity and Jeremy had joined them at their table in the hotel lobby. "My dear boy, I do hope you don't fall ill after having been so drenched. Augustus, what possessed you to do such a thing?"

"It was not me, Mother," Augustus said, closing his eyes as he spoke.

"Of course it was," Amity said. "No one else shares your eccentric sense of humor. You really are too very, Augustus, although it is bad of you. He sent Emily off as well, you know, and she was even more soaked than poor Jeremy."

"Emily?" Augustus asked, and glanced at his father.

"Evidently she was looking for me," Amity said, "and I feel unaccountably responsible, an unpleasant sensation that I blame you for entirely, my dear brother."

"I have no doubt Emily is of a hearty enough constitution to recover with very few ill effects, if any," Birdie said. "Gentlemen, do leave us alone for a moment. I want to speak to my daughter."

They acquiesced without delay. Very few people stayed when Birdie suggested they should leave. Why would they want to? "What is it, Mother?"

"I do not believe this story of theirs," Birdie said, bristling. "Do you not find it a strange coincidence that they both disappeared from the hotel and returned within moments of each other, soaked to the bone?"

"It was raining," Amity said. "Neither of them had an umbrella."

"They are hiding something and have concocted a ludicrous story to cover whatever it was they were doing."

"What are you suggesting, Mother?" Amity dropped her elbows onto the table and rested her chin on her hands.

"I do appreciate your attempts at befriending the woman, but it is beneath you, Amity," Birdie said, reaching across to remove her daughter's elbows from the surface. "Gentlemen will always have their flirtations; that is unavoidable. That is no reason to welcome the viper into your bosom."

"I find this insulting," Amity said, rising.

"Certain events from your past—events we will not revisit here or elsewhere—have led you to the delusion that you are wise with experience," Birdie said. "That is a mistake, Amity. Jeremy will make a fine husband, of that I have no doubt, but you must take him firmly in hand."

"I will hear no more of this." Amity turned on her heel, but her mother reached forward and grabbed her arm, spinning her back around.

"And I will not have this family further embarrassed," she said. "Speak to your fiancé at once or I shall have your father do it instead. I am giving you the chance to save what little face you have."

"I despise you," Amity said, her words full of venom. "How dare you?"

"You cannot play the innocent with me, my dear. It is a role that never suited you anyway. Put your house in order and stop this dalliance at once."

Amity knew she would not be able to halt the flow of tears, so when she saw Jack all but scoop up Christabel and start to walk into the games room off the lobby, she followed them, keeping her face down so that no one could see her distress. She hesitated at the door, but once she ascertained that her friends were the only ones inside, she entered the room.

"I am so sorry to intrude upon your solitude," she said. She dabbed at her eyes with her handkerchief as a little sob escaped her throat. Christabel rose from the table where she had been seated opposite of Jack, a chessboard between them, and rushed to her side.

"Whatever has happened to you?" she asked, putting an arm around Amity's shoulder.

"Mother has just said the most awful thing to me," Amity said. "It is so dreadful that—oh, Jack, will you despise me forever if I ask you to leave us? I couldn't bear for you to hear what I have to say."

"I could never despise you; you know that," he said. "Do you need anything at all? Should I have some tea sent in?"

"That would be lovely. You are so thoughtful." Amity's chin trembled as she looked up at him through damp eyelashes. Jack excused himself and she pulled Christabel to a cushion-covered settee in a corner of the room. "My mother believes that Jeremy and Emily—" She could not continue.

"No! You can't possibly think—"

"Of course not," Amity said. "She has ordered me to confront him. Can you imagine? He will think I am some sort of shrewish harpy."

"He knows you are nothing of the sort," Christabel said.

"I do not know what I shall do. They were off together walking this afternoon and got caught in the rain. Not wanting to embarrass me, they came up with some ridiculous story about Augustus tricking them both. I believed it—it did sound rather like him—until my mother pointed out the inadequacies of the explanation."

"Augustus is not much fond of Emily," Christabel said. "I could well imagine him setting into motion a plan that would leave her trapped in the rain."

"My thoughts exactly." Amity picked up a cushion and placed it on her lap. "We do not even know for sure that Jeremy was with her. It is only that they returned to the hotel one after the other."

"But they did not come in together?" Christabel asked.

"No."

"So the timing of their respective arrivals was a coincidence?"

"Exactly. It is hardly surprising given the weather. They both started back to the hotel at similar times in an effort to get out of the rain." Lines etched her brow. "You do believe me? Tell me you do not take my mother's side."

"No, I would never do such a thing." Christabel's tone was less than enthusiastic.

"I could never doubt Jeremy," Amity said.

Christabel smiled. "Nor could I. He adores you, and even if he were walking with Emily, what harm is there in that? This is nothing more than a tempest in a teapot."

"You do not think I am being naïve?" Amity asked. Christabel shook her head. "Good." She took a deep breath and released it slowly, shaking off the bad feelings her mother had drilled into her. "Now, we must discuss you and Jack. Whatever were you thinking coming in here alone with him? Do you want him to propose or not?"

Christabel's eyes brightened and she leaned toward her friend, her voice low. "I think, Amity, that is exactly what he was about to do."

"Over a chessboard? Oh, Christabel, you have so much to learn."

# 19

The sky cleared almost as quickly as it had earlier darkened, and the sunset was like a tapestry of scarlet and gold. Colin and I dined in our room but rejoined the others afterwards, and we all crossed to the hotel's dock to watch the fireworks that were being shot off a barge in the harbor. A damp chill had remained in the air after the rain, but Mrs. Wells, in a kind attempt at keeping us all comfortable, caused hot chocolate to be sent out for us, a gesture that was much appreciated.

"I have always fancied fireworks," Jeremy said, eschewing a mug of steaming chocolate for a quick sip from a flask of whisky, relying for warmth on that and the scarf wrapped firmly around his neck. "From now on, I shall insist on them nightly when I am in residence at Woodsford. Can't imagine why I didn't think of it before."

In my mind, I could hear Amity's *You are simply too very* even before she said it, but I did manage to resist rolling my eyes, which was fortunate, as no sooner were the words out of her mouth than she had turned to me and clutched my arm. "Walk with me, Emily."

"You do not want to miss the finale, do you?" I asked, hope in my voice. She did not care about the fireworks, however, and I had no choice but to walk with her the length of the dock and then turn onto the promenade at La Croisette. The pavement was crowded with other tourists, but there was little movement on it, as nearly all of them had stopped, their heads tilted up, to watch the colorful explosions in the sky.

"Christabel and my mother have been filling my head with poison—well, not Christabel so much, but I remain unconvinced she believes me," Amity said. "Please tell me, were you and Jeremy out together this afternoon?"

"I promise, hand on heart, we were not," I said, "and I have no reason to lie to you. If we had gone somewhere together, why would we hide the fact? You know we are friends. That is no secret."

"And there is nothing more?" Her voice was hesitant. I heard a loud sigh behind me.

"Are we back on to this?" Margaret said, coming up behind Amity. I shot her a look of gratitude. "Surely you must be tired of it, Amity?"

"Exhausted, in fact," Amity said. "It is so difficult to convince others that they are obsessed with a worthless rumor of their own making."

"Ignore them," Margaret said. "And come with me, now." She guided Amity back to the edge of the railing, where the others were standing. I did not follow, instead remaining at the railing of the promenade, perpendicular to them, watching the color of the fireworks bathing their faces. Jack's eyes focused not on the sky, but on Christabel. Christabel, standing awkwardly next to Mr. Fairchild, paid Jack not the slightest attention. Margaret was ribbing Jeremy about something, and Amity was looking away, past Colin.

"I have already instructed my daughter to speak with the duke about his attentions to you," Mrs. Wells said. I had not seen her approach. "I do hope you will have the decency to support me in this matter."

"Mrs. Wells, I believe I look forward to your daughter's marriage perhaps even more than you do," I said. "Let me assure you that I shall be the first to offer my best wishes to her after the happy event."

"I was certain that once you felt your own reputation was under threat—"

"My own reputation has never been under threat," I said. "You ought to better consider what your own gossip is doing to Amity. No one else sees the problems you are so keen on revealing to the world. I wonder what you can mean by it?"

"Do you have a daughter, Lady Emily?"

"No, only three sons."

"Then you shall not know the tribulations caused by a girl who—" She huffed. "I shall say no more."

"Are you concerned that Amity has done something wrong?" I asked. "Mrs. Wells, your daughter is exuberant and not particularly interested in following the conventions you may think necessary and appropriate, but she . . ." My voice trailed and I paused. On consideration, I realized that although I was not particularly fond of Amity, she was more similar to me than I cared to admit, and watching her sometimes felt like seeing a painful mirror image of myself. Like me, she pushed boundaries, in a different way, granted, but I felt I should defend her nonetheless. She might have no academic interests, but she wanted her own voice, and I ought to support that position.

"You, Lady Emily, have no inkling as to what I have dealt with, and I would be grateful if you would not encourage my daughter to flaunt the rules of decent society."

"Did something happen before you came abroad with her?"

"Did you not only just now warn me of the evils of spreading gossip, Lady Emily? Now you seek it out?" She did not wait for me to reply, but turned and marched away so quickly that I feared her enormous hat—replete with yet another of her signature stuffed and mounted birds that looked ready for flight—would fly off her head. I waited a few moments, and then followed her to my friends.

The fireworks having finished, there was general conversation about what to do next. Spirits were high, particularly amongst the gentlemen, and before long Amity was encouraging them to find rowboats and set off on a nighttime sea adventure. Knowing it was unlikely that even Jeremy would consider this appalling suggestion, I removed myself from the others, taking Margaret with me.

"Could you telegram your mother for me?" I asked. "She may be able to offer us an insight into some most intriguing comments Mrs. Wells has offered."

"Telegram? She has got a telephone in New York. Insisted Father get her one of her own so that she would never have cause to step into his office at the house. Let's ring her at once," Margaret said, as soon as I had further explained the situation. The hotel manager was not on-site, but the desk clerk agreed to let us use the office for the call, and, although I could not precisely hear Mrs. Seward's words in response to her daughter's questions, it was evident from the unbroken stream of sound coming from the receiver of the telephone that she had a great deal to say on the subject.

After Margaret had returned the earpiece to its cradle, she pushed back from the desk on which it stood and let out a long, low whistle.

"Sometimes, you know, I nearly forget that you are American," I said. "And then you whistle like a cowgirl."

Margaret grinned. "What makes you think only cowgirls know how to whistle? Amity Wells has a rather colorful history that her parents have gone to great lengths to hide."

"Do tell."

"Evidently, two seasons ago, she was deeply infatuated with the son of one of the lesser railroad barons. My mother would not tell me who, and I suppose it does not much matter. Mrs. Wells and her husband never gave the situation any serious regard, as they considered the gentleman far below their daughter's status." Margaret rolled her eyes. "When he approached Mr. Wells to ask for Amity's hand and was rebuffed, the matter would have been closed, except that Amity did not take the news lying down. She arranged to run off with him, in the dark of night, and they planned to elope somewhere upstate. She was thwarted, however, by a servant who heard her coming down the stairs with a valise she could barely carry, and the whole affair was hushed up as much as possible."

"Hence the need to take her abroad to find a suitable husband," I said.

"According to my mother, that was always Mrs. Wells's plan," Margaret said. "She has had it in her head for ages that Amity ought to marry someone with a title. The failed elopement only spurred her to act sooner than she had originally planned."

"Poor Amity," I said, feeling more sympathy for the girl than I had before. "I have been so very hard on her because I thought she was only pretending to be what she thinks Jeremy wants, but now I wonder if she is only doing what she can to help her forget the man she truly loves."

"The worst part is that the man she loved has recently announced his engagement. I have no doubt Mrs. Wells is aware of the fact, but it is possible that Amity doesn't know."

"I suppose it is hardly of consequence, is it? She has accepted that she must do as her parents wish. It is rather sad."

"Do you think she truly cares for Jeremy?" Margaret asked.

"I do believe she does, in her way," I said. "She has already been thwarted once in love and it would not surprise me to find that she is holding back a small piece of her heart. Could you blame her?"

"No," Margaret said, "although I do very much blame her for going along with her parents' scheme."

"She must think she has no choice," I said. "Given the . . . er . . . force of her personality, she would not otherwise have agreed to their plans. I am going to endeavor to be kinder to her."

"Take care that she doesn't mistake it for pity," Margaret said. "She would resent that."

"Ring your mother back, Margaret," I said. "I should like to know the name of the rejected suitor. Could it be that he is bent on disrupting her wedding and disposing of her groom? Perhaps he is trying to escape an engagement forced on him by his own parents."

"Capital idea," Margaret said, and returned to the phone. It took a considerable amount of begging for her to convince her mother to reveal the name. Mrs. Seward insisted she would not stoop to the level of forwarding gossip, but at last relinquished the information. Margaret then placed another call, this time to an old friend of hers in Manhattan, who, she insisted, knew everything about everything and everyone. After a chat of nearly a quarter of an hour—I shuddered at the thought of what these calls would cost—she could not control her excitement.

"Yes?" I prodded, knowing how she loved to prolong the anticipation of her audience when she was in possession of particularly desirable information.

"Mr. Marshall Cabot sailed for France the day following the announcement of his engagement," Margaret said. "The *Herald Tribune* reported his arrival in Paris two days before Mr. Neville's death. Should we go there directly, do you think?"

"We can make discreet inquiries," I said. "Do we know if he is still there?"

"I have the name of the hotel. Shall we ring them?"

"Not quite yet," I said. "Let us consult with Colin and Cécile. You have not yet told me what you learned this afternoon."

Margaret and I extricated Colin and Cécile from a game of poker Amity had started at a table in the lobby; while Amity looked less than pleased, Cécile made no attempt to hide her relief.

"*Mon dieu,*" she said. "Such a dreadful game. So coarse. It makes me hope to never again see a deck of cards." She had insisted that we go to her rooms, where there were two bottles of chilled champagne waiting for us. "I would rather have absinthe with dancing girls, and you know I do not drink absinthe."

"What did Marie and the others have to say to you today?" I asked.

"Unfortunately, nothing of note," Margaret said as I refused her offer of the champagne she was pouring for the others. "I do not believe they have any more information that can help us. We asked about people who were less fond of Hélène, and spoke to two waiters and a baccarat dealer. The dealer was jealous of the second waiter, whom he correctly suspected of being in love with Hélène, and his ire at the girl resulted from his incorrect belief that she returned the sentiment."

"But you made it sound as if the second waiter was also less than fond of Hélène," I said.

"Well he was," Margaret continued, "once he began to think the baccarat dealer was a serious rival. Hélène objected to his possessiveness, and quite threw him over."

"And the first waiter?" Colin asked.

"He believes that she put on airs by speaking too much about the ballet in Paris, where she felt she belonged," Margaret said. "As for neighbors, none of them spoke a word against her. They all described her as sweet."

"Sweet, *oui*," Cécile said, "but it was clear that they wished she would abandon her occupation. They feared it was too closely connected to, shall we say, undesirable outcomes. What is interesting is that they did not entirely judge her for dancing. They felt, it seems, that she could still be saved. The son of the cheesemonger, who lives two streets over from the Soucy house, had hoped to pay her court, but she refused to let him, telling him she was not worthy."

"Was he angry at the rejection?" Colin asked.

"Not in the least," Cécile said. "He viewed her response to him as nothing more than an opening gambit."

"And what about your day, Colin?" I asked. "What can you tell us about Jack?"

"Genuinely loves army life. Bainbridge has arranged things for him financially so that he never need worry, even should he leave his chosen profession. I do not believe he has any designs on his brother's title."

"I could have told you that," I said. "I did practically grow up with the two of them."

"And, as such, are a terribly biased and unreliable—although extremely charming—witness," Colin said.

"There is one more thing that we have been desperate to show you," Margaret said. "I am confident you will admire our restraint in not pulling them out with the others present. Or during the fireworks. We searched both the dressing room in the casino and Hélène's room at the Soucys' and found these hidden amongst her things." She handed me a small leather box that contained a pair of gold cuff links engraved with the arms of the Bainbridge family.

# *Amity*

"There was no need for Emily to disrupt your game," Birdie said.

"Mother, you are causing a scene," Amity said through clenched teeth. "Do sit down or go upstairs. People are beginning to stare." She flung her cards down onto the table.

"It is fortunate my own mother is not here," Jeremy said. "I am quite certain, Mrs. Wells, she would never stand for ladies playing poker. You two might have come to blows." His attempt to lighten the mood fell flat as his soon-to-be mother-in-law scowled at him.

"Are you defending Lady Emily?" Birdie asked. "Suggesting, perhaps, that your mother would have found her to have been a more suitable bride?"

"Please excuse me," Jack said, rising from the table, discomfort writ all over his face. "I quite forgot a letter I must write. Mother will never forgive me."

"Would you be so kind as to help me find a good spot for writing, Jack?" Amity asked, standing as well. "I am certain I, too, have correspondence waiting to be written." Christabel gave her a look that pleaded for rescue, but Amity was not about to risk being further censured by Birdie, and did not wait for even an instant before leaving with Jack.

"Your mother seems bent on finding controversy everywhere," he said.

"You cannot begin to understand the pathology of the woman," Amity said, rushing him along the corridor. "She is driven by dark forces."

Jack laughed. "I do so admire your flair for the dramatic."

"I feel dreadful leaving Christabel and Jeremy with her, but could not bear to stay a moment longer," she said. "I do hope they can find it in their hearts to forgive me."

"Of course they will."

"Do you really have letters to write, Jack?" Amity asked.

"No," he admitted. "I just wanted to escape. You?"

"The same."

"I am glad that we have wound up together in more or less private circumstances," Jack said, opening the door to the games room and leading Amity to the same table he had earlier occupied with Christabel. There was a group of Italians playing cards in one corner, but other than that, the room was empty. "May I broach a subject of some delicacy with you?"

"So long as it would not horrify your brother." Amity's eyes sparkled.

"I had thought that I was close to having an understanding with Christabel, but recently it seems that she . . ."

Amity did not finish the sentence for him as his voice wavered. She began returning the pieces on the chessboard between them to their starting positions, but remained silent. Finished now, she folded her hands and rested them on her lap, not removing her eyes from his.

"You are going to force me to say it?" Jack asked.

"You know, Jack, that I consider you to be one of my closest friends," she said, "but you cannot expect that I would betray the confidence of another so dear to my heart."

"Is Christabel in love with me?" His eyes brightened as he spoke and color rose in his cheeks. "I begin to worry that Fairchild—"

"You must take this up with Christabel. I cannot—"

"Please, Amity. I am very nearly your brother, and I only want to know if there is any hope that I can make Christabel happy. If her affections are no longer what they used to be, I shall trouble her no further."

"Your love must not run very deep if you are so quick to abandon it," Amity said, moving the chess pieces to random positions on the board. "Would you like me to tell that to Christabel?"

"I would not be quick to abandon it, but I would always respect her feelings, and if she is not—"

"You want me to give you private and extremely sensitive information so that you can best decide how to act without risking embarrassment." She plopped the white queen down in the center of the board.

"Is that so wrong?"

"Love, Jack, is full of risk and embarrassment. If you do not have the stomach for it . . ."

"So you are telling me she does not love me?"

"I never said any such thing. It sounds to me as if you need to search your heart and decide what it is you want. We are to remain here in Cannes for several more days. I would hope that by the time we depart, you will know yourself well enough to speak to Christabel without confusing her."

"Can you offer me no words of encouragement?" Jack's eyes bulged and he looked rather desperate.

"Do you love her only if she loves you?" Amity asked. "If so, that is a very poor sort of love. I will not betray your confidence by telling Christabel anything about it, and for that you should thank me. It would bring her nothing but disappointment."

# 20

Cécile, noticing that I had refused her champagne, took the much-appreciated liberty of ordering for me a pot of tea. I had never quite warmed up after my time in the rain. I took the cuff links from Margaret and removed them from their box so that I might better study them. "Jeremy does not wear these with evening kit," I said. "He always insists on his ruby and diamond quatrefoil cluster set—he goes on about them at such length it is impossible not to notice. She must have taken these from his room."

"Which would mean that she poisoned the whisky," Margaret said.

"Not necessarily," Colin said, "but it does mean she was almost certainly in his room. We have nothing firm beyond that."

"And what does that mean, Monsieur Hargreaves?" Cécile asked. "Are we to believe she was there without his knowledge?"

"I think we must," I said. "Jeremy would have confessed if he had brought her there." Cécile raised her hands to object, but Colin silenced her.

"Emily is correct concerning this matter. I do not believe Bainbridge brought the girl to his room."

"So how did she get in to take the cuff links?" Margaret asked.

"I have not the slightest idea," Colin said. "I shall see what I can find out about Marshall Cabot, however. The Sûreté in Paris may be able to help us on that count. Was there anything else of note in Hélène's room? Letters? Papers?"

"Nothing at all," Cécile said. "Their very absence struck me as odd."

"I quite agree," I said. "Her mother, at least, would have written to her. The person who murdered her must have taken or destroyed all of her correspondence, which suggests that that individual may have used letters to communicate with Hélène."

"Which, in turn, suggests that individual is the person who wanted Jeremy dead!" Margaret slammed her hand onto the table in front of her. It would have made for a more effective punctuation to her statement if the table had not been so much lower than the divan on which she was sitting, causing her to nearly topple over.

Colin and I looked at each other. "It is as viable a theory as any we have at present," I said.

My husband's colleagues at the Sûreté, with whom he had worked on our case in France the year before, agreed to make inquiries about Marshall Cabot, and before noon the next day, Colin rang them to hear the results. Cabot was still in Paris, traveling with two of his friends. They had not left the city since, even to go so far as Versailles, and none of them had received any mail at the hotel, nor had they sent any telegrams.

"He could have sent a telegram from somewhere else in the city," I said as Meg was fighting with my hair to make it respectable looking before I went downstairs for lunch. We had taken breakfast—an extremely long breakfast—in our rooms.

"Of course," Colin said, leaning against the wall in the dressing room, his long legs crossed at the ankles. "They are going to continue to watch him, but I think it will be difficult for us to uncover any connection to Hélène. The best thing now will be for us to give them a few days to trail him."

"Is there anything more we can do here in the meantime?" I asked. "Inquire as to whether he is known at the casino here, perhaps?"

"I will do that this afternoon," he said.

"Will you require my assistance?"

"No, it will be easier for me to do what I need to alone."

"Then perhaps I will organize that trip to Cimiez I have been promising Amity. I still feel a bit guilty for having lied to her about Margaret and me going to the ruins."

It was too late to go to Nice that day, but I spoke to Amity, and we agreed that two days hence would be perfect. The gentlemen were planning a sailing excursion for tomorrow, and we did not want to conflict with that. "I only wish I had thought to write to the director of the excavations there," I said. "He might have been able to give us a tour himself. I suppose I could send him a telegram."

"We don't need that," Amity said. "I'm sure he would be a fine man, but you must admit that the odds of him being anything other than, well, boring, are unlikely. I want to explore the ruins on my own, running through them and imagining what it would have been like for a Roman girl. Should we wear togas, do you think?"

"Ladies did not wear togas," Margaret said, disgust straining the features of her face. "They wore tunics, a peplos or a chiton if they wanted sleeves. A married woman might wear a stola over another tunic, but I have always thought they look a bit frumpy. You might instead focus on a Roman hairstyle, Amity. They were quite elaborate and spectacular. The manner favored by the Flavian empresses would suit you."

I covered my mouth with my hand and shot Margaret what I hoped she would interpret as an evil look. The Flavian ladies' coiffure consisted of a tall mass of curls heaped up on the front of the head, almost like a crown, with the rest of the hair pinned into place smoothly in the back, so that the difference of height, if viewed in profile, was astonishing. It could be described in any number of ways, but attractive was not one of them, and it was very bad of Margaret to mention it to Amity. Her motive was perfectly clear to me, and although I did, secretly, applaud it, I knew Amity wearing Flavian coiffure could be nothing but a bad idea.

"I don't suppose, Margaret, you have a book that includes an illustration of the style," Amity said. "I have quite an idea forming."

"Indeed, I do," Margaret said. "I shall run upstairs and fetch it for you, but only if you first tell me your idea."

"I am going to throw a real Roman banquet for us in Nice, and you all shall have to dress accordingly. No more House of Worth for you, Emily."

"I am confident the messieurs Worth could produce a worthy costume, but not in so little time," I said. "What a marvelous idea, Amity." Colin might not agree, but I thought he would look rather well in a toga.

By the end of the day, our plans were firm. Rather than attempt to get to the ruins and back in a single day, we would go to Nice tomorrow after lunch, taking a train that would get us there in plenty of time for Amity to set into motion plans for her Roman banquet. She would have the remainder of the afternoon to solidify the arrangements, and the following day, after a leisurely tour of the ruins at Cimiez, we would dine as *nobilitas Romana*. We would leave the bulk of our luggage in our rooms in Cannes, taking only what we would need for this short trip.

"She cannot be serious about this," Cécile said. She, Margaret, and I had sequestered ourselves in a private train compartment for the trip. Colin, wisely, had gone with Jeremy, Jack, and Mr. Fairchild, leaving the Wells family and Christabel together. Mrs. Wells, in particular, approved of the arrangements.

"Margaret bears all the responsibility," I said. "It was she who put the idea into Amity's head."

"I admit it is my fault entirely, and was due to a misguided attempt to convince her to adopt the Flavian coiffure," Margaret said. "I pointed how out exotically beautiful she would look reclining on a dining couch, her hair jutting up far above the top of her head . . ."

"A dreamy image to be sure," I said.

"I am not, reclining or otherwise, dining on a couch," Cécile said.

"*Jutting* was a poor choice of word," Margaret said. "Fortunately, it did not seem to put off Amity."

"You are evil, Margaret," I said. "She is going to wear it and will know the instant she sees how everyone responds that you have tricked her into looking like a fool."

"Then you shall owe me thanks, Emily," Margaret said. "It will distract her from going back to being angry with you."

Because it was so late in the season, it had not been a simple matter to find a sufficient quantity of available hotel rooms in Nice. Fortunately—or unfortunately, depending on one's point of view— Queen Victoria was there, having taken rooms at the Hôtel Excelsior Regina, which had opened only the year before after having been built with the royal party in mind. Colin, a longstanding favorite of the queen's, had sent a telegram, requesting assistance, and with a wave of the royal hand (I speak figuratively, of course), rooms were made available for us. The hotel was only a short walk from the ruins, situated on a hill overlooking the city. Soon after we had all checked in and gone upstairs to freshen up, Meg stepped away from the thankless task of attempting to tame my hair to answer a knock a the door and returned to announce that a Monsieur Guérin had arrived in the hopes of seeing me.

"How exciting," I said, urging her to hurry with my hair. "He is the director of the excavations at Cimiez. I did not expect to have the opportunity to see him."

Monsieur Guérin, a broad affable man whose tanned face bore evidence of one who spent much time digging in the sun, was perhaps more coarse than I expected to find him, but he apologized profusely for having descended upon me without a formal introduction. "I hoped you would not object, despite the fact that I am unable to accommodate the request you made in your telegram. As I said, I am leaving town tomorrow, and cannot take you and your friends through the ruins. However, my wife and I are hosting a small dinner party this evening. Regrettably, one of our guests has just sent word that his wife is indisposed and unable to attend. You are aware, I am sure, of how this would have sent my own dear spouse into a flurry of concern. She is afraid her table will now be unbalanced. Our gathering is not a fashionable one. We are all scholars of ancient Rome, but I do hope I can entice you to join us. You would be doing my wife a kindness, and I could take you for a quick turn around the ruins before the other guests arrive."

"What a delightful invitation," I said. "I should love to accept. Thank you so much for thinking of me."

"You have made her happier than you can imagine," Colin said. "Now she will not only have had a superior tour of the site, she will be able to lecture all of us on what she learned when she takes us there in the morning."

"I shall do my best to be as entertaining as possible," Monsieur Guérin said, smiling to reveal a wide gap between his front teeth. We set a time to meet, bid him adieu, and headed downstairs to find our friends. Everyone had gathered except for Amity and Jeremy, who, Christabel explained, were seeing to the final details of tomorrow's Roman banquet. They would meet us as soon as they could. After piling into carriages, we were driven down the hill to the sea, where we strolled along the Promenade des Anglais. Lest anyone believe the city of Nice owes its prominence to any other group of travelers, the name of this famous walk should disabuse said person of his erroneous notion.

The sea views from the wide promenade were nothing short of

spectacular, but I was more taken with the views back over the city, where, past the hills, the snow-covered Alps thrust toward the sky. It was as beautiful a sight as could be found anywhere in the world. The promenade itself was lovely as well, with gleaming white benches placed all along it beneath a wide pergola, the harmonious simplicity of it complementing the whitecaps of the waves crashing against the pebble-filled beach. Tourists, decked out in their finest garb, processed along, some of them better pleased with themselves than their surroundings, but that is not to say that many of them did not stand, breathless, watching the sea before turning around and taking in the mountains and the elegant villas and hotels beneath them.

"Everything is set for tomorrow night," Amity said, looking up adoringly at Jeremy as they walked toward us. "I cannot tell you what a help my darling boy has been." She gave every appearance of brimming with excitement. Her face was flushed, her eyes shining, and her lips were so red I wondered if she had used something to color them. "Although I am confident that nothing we can do will even approach the splendor of what I have planned for tomorrow, I am consumed with the notion that we must find something spectacular to do this evening."

"I am quite in agreement," Margaret said. "What do you propose?"

"The theater, perhaps?" Christabel suggested. "I saw several notices in the hotel lobby that looked interesting."

"Pedestrian," Margaret said, her nostrils flaring.

"Not if it is the operetta at the casino," Jeremy said. Margaret raised a skeptical eyebrow.

"What are they playing?" she asked.

"I am afraid that whatever you decide, you shall have to count me out," I said. "I have had an invitation to dine with the director of the excavations at Cimiez."

"That is not pedestrian in the least," Margaret said. "You must take me with you!"

"I am afraid the invitation was extended only to me," I said, and recounted for her Monsieur Guérin's visit. "I am dreadfully sorry, Margaret."

"I told her you would be fiercely angry," Colin said. "I do hope having said that in front of Monsieur Guérin was not what dissuaded him from including you in the party."

"Colin!" Margaret whacked him on the arm. "How could you?"

"He did nothing of the sort," I said. "He is merely tormenting you."

Margaret threw up her hands in despair. "You are a scholar of Greece, not Rome! This is wholly unfair."

"That it is," Amity said, coming close to Margaret and taking her by the arm. "Shall we insist on going without an invitation? It would be simply too very."

"We could follow Emily in disguise if she refuses to let us accompany her," Margaret said.

"We could wear our Roman gowns!"

Now Amity was getting carried away, and I scowled at Margaret. "What would Mr. Michaels say if word reached him of such a breech of etiquette?" I asked. "Indeed, what would the scholars of classical Rome think of him once his wife's ill-breeding was so revealed?"

"You know as well as I that neither Mr. Michaels nor the scholars of classical Rome would even notice," Margaret said. "I would never show up uninvited and am wounded you suggest I am capable of such a thing, but I am certain that, somehow, I shall find it in the depths of my soul—the very deep depths, the deepest of all depths—to forgive you. Eventually. At any rate, I have just discovered an idea for tonight that is far better even than dining with Monsieur Guérin. Look!" She pointed above us, where a hot air balloon floated, its large basket full of passengers. "That is what I want to do."

"I should be terrified," Christabel said. Jack started and stepped forward, as if he meant to offer her comfort, but retreated when he saw Mr. Fairchild already at her side.

"Nonsense," Margaret said. "My parents rode in one in Paris at the 1878 exhibition. I have never forgiven them for insisting I was too small to accompany them." She took Colin by the wrist. "Come and help me arrange it." As no one other than Christabel objected—I am confident Mr. and Mrs. Wells would not approve, but as they had stayed behind at the Regina, they had no say in the matter—it was soon agreed.

Colin and Margaret returned half an hour later. The ride could not take place for nearly two more hours—the balloon was a popular attraction—so it was determined that we would sit and listen to one of the small orchestras playing a program of Mozart and Strauss in a nearby park to pass the time. Because I would need to dress for dinner, I left the others there, leaving before the concert was over. Back at the hotel, a message awaited me, informing me that Her Majesty requested my presence at breakfast the following morning. This came as no surprise. My mother's relationship with the queen, whom she had served for years as a lady-in-waiting, made the summons a foregone conclusion. They were still close friends. As much as Victoria Regina adored my husband, she shared my mother's low opinion of myself, and I had no doubt that I would be treated to a stern lecture over porridge. Still, it was not to be avoided.

I would worry about the queen later; now I had to decide what to wear this evening. A dinner dress would not be practical for exploring ruins, so I instead donned a smartly tailored suit and a pair of sturdy boots, assuming that the wives of archaeologists and scholars would not balk at the lack of formality. Meg, however, did not approve. "No matter what you are doing first, you ought to be dressed properly for dinner, madam," she said.

"Just wait until you see what Miss Wells is requiring for tomorrow night's banquet," I said.

"That is entirely different, madam," Meg said. "When the hostess has given specific directions—"

"Thank you, Meg." I said. "That will be all."

I set off from the hotel a little after eight o'clock. Twilight had drenched the sky in indigo, but there were still traces of pink in the scattered clouds. A bright moon had risen, and I was anticipating with a thrill of delight the effect it would have on the ancient stones I was about to see. There was an iron gate at the entrance to the site, and a chain and open padlock hung on it.

"*Bienvenue*, Lady Emily!" I could not quite make out Monsieur Guérin's face in the dim light, but I recognized his voice, cheerful and strong, and followed the sound through the gate. Before I had taken no more than six steps, pain exploded in the back of my neck and everything around me went black.

# Amity

─────◆◇◉◇◆─────

The balloon ride proved a spectacular success. Amity could not have been more delighted. She had disappointed herself, though, by not being able to muster the courage to step into the basket. Instead, she was forced to watch from below, waving as her friends floated above her. If Jeremy considered this a weakness, he showed no sign of it. He offered, gallantly, to remain behind with her.

"I only said I would go because I thought you wanted to," he confessed, standing next to her watching the balloon. "It is much more pleasant to have a few moments alone, is it not?"

"I could not agree more," Amity said. "Do you think they are high enough now that I could kiss you without anyone we know seeing? Had I realized the potential of this situation, I would have engineered the entire scheme just for this purpose."

"I am willing to take the risk." He lowered his face to hers. "Our wedding cannot come soon enough." They stepped back from the railing and sat on one of the benches that stood on the Promenade des Anglais, facing the sea. There was almost no breeze now, a happy circumstance for the ballooners, and fortunate for the gentlemen who often had to cling to their hats as they walked along the shore. The sun was setting, filling the western edge of the sky with bright streaks of vermillion, while the east fought to remain blue, even as the shade grew more and more pale before retreating in the face of dusky twilight.

"Where shall we go on our honeymoon?" Amity asked. "The sky is so lovely here it makes me feel quite romantic."

"Anywhere and everywhere that strikes your fancy, my love," Jeremy said. "India, perhaps? You say you came to adore it, and I have never been there."

"There is nowhere I would rather go." She let her head drop onto his shoulder. "I should very much like to hold my husband's hand and gaze with him at the beauty of the Taj Mahal. I suppose that makes me sound very boring and predictable, doesn't it?"

"Amity, my dear, I do not think most ladies would brave a trip to India, even for the Taj Mahal," Jeremy said. "You stand so far above your peers it seems wrong to even classify them with you. I do apologize, I am not good with words, but I do hope you catch my meaning." Amity smiled and opened her mouth to reply, but stopped when a man appeared in front of them.

"Monsieur le duc?" he asked, whipping the hat from his head and holding it in front of his chest. "Are you the Duke of Bainbridge?"

"I am," Jeremy said, rising.

"A message for you, sir." He smiled, revealing a gap between his front teeth, gave Jeremy an envelope, bowed awkwardly, and gestured for him to follow.

# 21

When I opened my eyes, pain at the base of my skull consumed me. Something felt as if it were oozing, but when I went to reach up to see if I was bleeding, I found that my hands had been bound behind my back and my ankles tied. I was somewhere in the ruins, on the ground next to the wall of what remained of a semicircular space. Above me, there was no longer any trace of sunset left in the sky, only the moon, now fighting with clouds, and darkness. Wriggling, I managed to sit up and assess my situation. By kicking, I was able to loosen the rope around my ankles enough to free my feet. This gave me better control over my posture, and I compensated for the awkwardness of the position of my hands. Much though I struggled, I could not make any headway toward releasing them. My eyes, well adjusted to the low light, could make out scattered rock over the ground, and the bruises I could feel developing over my body told me that I had been flung into this pit.

When I stood, I discovered it was not a pit, just what was left of an ancient room, now without a ceiling and in possession of walls that stood only a few feet taller than I. My shoulders aching from the position into which they had been wrenched, I started to search for a stone, or brick, or bit of column that had an edge rough enough to work its way through the twine around my wrists. The action was more than awkward, as I could not see what I was doing with my arms behind my back. I rubbed and rubbed, hoping I was making progress.

The repetitive motion seemed to be taking more of a toll on my hands and wrists than on the rope, but eventually I felt it start to give, and I applied myself to the task with an increased vigor. When the bonds fell away, my hands were raw and battered, and my arms cramped. I shook them to throw off the pain and stretched as best I could before trying to get a sense of my bearings.

Because I had not before been in the ruins, I had little way of taking stock of the situation. The moon was much higher in the sky than it had been, so some considerable amount of time had passed. I did know, as well, that the site was not enormous, and I hoped it would be easy enough to find my way out. The chamber, for lack of a better word, into which I had been thrown, had neither door nor window, but I used the bricks that formed the walls as a makeshift ladder, and climbed to the top. This effort put me above a longer passage that, so far as I could see—which was not far, given the darkness of the night now that the moon was partially covered with clouds—had on its far end a doorwaylike opening. I tried to lower myself from my perch, but my hands were too shredded to hold my weight while I tried to find a purchase for my boots, and I slipped, down to the bottom of the wall.

At least I landed, more or less, on my feet. I wished I had a candle or something that might illuminate my progress, but even as the thought entered my mind, it occurred to me that I did not know if I was alone in the ruins. Was my captor lingering somewhere nearby? If so, light would give away the route of my escape. I moved ahead slowly, careful to avoid tripping over any debris strewn in my path. Knowing what little I did from having read about the site, it consisted of thermal baths, some sort of an early Christian church (my Baedeker's described it as a Temple of Apollo; perhaps the precise details of the structure was a subject of some debate), and an amphitheater. All of these would have been discovered well below the street level of our present day, so I would have to somehow climb my way up and out when, if ever, I reached the end of what was beginning to feel like a never-ending maze.

I could see a wall in front of me now, and I felt my way to an opening in it. It wasn't a door, as it did not go all the way to the ground, so rather than directly climbing through it, I inspected the room to see if there was a door somewhere else. There was not, so I swung my leg through what appeared to be a window and heaved myself to the other side. The clouds were moving above me, and I stopped to watch them, hoping the moon would reappear and better illuminate my efforts. It did, which was helpful, but as soon as the silvery light fell on the stones, creating an eerie contrast with the dark shadows, I heard a sound, something like footsteps, but not quite. I froze and pressed myself flat against the nearest wall, my heart pounding.

It came again, this time accompanied by the rattle of scattering stone, as if someone had dropped a handful of pebbles. I held my breath, listening. Whoever it was, I wanted to be ready. I squatted on the ground, feeling around for something I could use as a makeshift weapon, settling upon a broken brick whose sharp edge, as well as its solid weight, recommended it.

The sound was moving closer, and whoever was making it seemed to be picking up speed. I braced myself and raised the brick above my head, ready for anything. That is, almost anything. Anything, in fact other than the appearance of a sleek cat, whose silvery fur was spotted almost like a leopard's. It leapt off the wall, landing directly in front of me, gave me a look of feline disdain and meowed loudly before pawing at my boots. I looked back at it sternly and continued to make my way carefully through the ruins. The creature followed me for a while, until, apparently frustrated by my lack of progress, it raced ahead and out of sight. I had never before then had much of an opinion one way or another about cats, but I found now that I wished it had stayed with me. Its presence, oddly enough, had been reassuring.

Eventually, I reached a room that had no ready exit. The walls were tall—a good four or five feet above my head—but I saw no option other than to attempt to scale them. I tore strips from my petticoat and wrapped them around my palms to protect them, then dug the toe of my boot into a convenient space between bricks, pulling myself up as I went. When I reached the top, the moonlight revealed my surroundings to me. I was two-thirds of the way through a large complex of ruins. To my left were the passages from which I had just emerged. To my right, below me, the space was more open. The remains of standing columns suggested a courtyard or atrium of some sort, beyond which stood a much taller wall than the one I was currently sitting atop, so high that it must have been the edifice of a building with more than a single story. The walls were dotted with a series of archways and a considerable number of windows. The height made visible more features of the walls, which had been fashioned from white stones and bands of narrow red bricks.

I heard the cat again, meowing, but then something else. This time there could be no question: it was footsteps, and the low rumbling of voices, coming from the far end of the site, the direction from whence I had emerged, and, I surmised, most likely toward the gate through which I had entered. If my abductor had returned for me, he would soon discover my absence, and the current spot which I occupied, on the top of a wall, did not strike me as a decent hiding place. The height would have made for a dangerous drop, so I scrambled to climb down, straining my ears in an attempt to determine whether one or more persons were speaking.

The fabric from my petticoat served its purpose well, and I was able to cling to the wall until I had found a spot into which I could wedge the toe of one of my boots. I made my way down slowly and deliberately, careful to be as quiet as the circumstances allowed. One of the voices was louder now, closer, and I could identify it: Jeremy was carrying on what sounded like an ordinary conversation.

# Amity

Amity remained alone on a bench after Jeremy left, watching the path of the balloon that carried her friends high above the white-capped waters of the Mediterranean. Their ride over, they tumbled out of the balloon's basket, while Amity, who had walked over to greet them, applauded and threw at them flowers she had purchased from a vendor.

"How I wish I were as brave as the rest of you," she said. "Now that it is over and you are back safely, I am regretting my cowardice."

"You were not a coward," Christabel said. "It was terrifying. I spent the entire time clinging to the basket and wishing I was safe on the ground with you."

"But the view must have been incomparable," Amity said, noticing that Mr. Fairchild had helped Christabel descend from the basket.

"It was," Jack said. "Next time, Amity, you are coming." Amity smiled. Was he now playing at Christabel's game? Flirting to make her jealous? Foolish boy.

"Count on it," she said, and let him take her arm, bestowing on him her loveliest smile.

"Where is Jeremy?" Margaret asked.

"A message was delivered, summoning him," Amity said.

"Where?" Madame du Lac asked. "And by whom?"

"He did not say. It appeared to be a matter of some urgency."

"He rushed off, without so much as a word about the content of the message?" Colin asked, his brow creasing. He stepped closer to Amity.

"Yes," she said. "I did not like to press him for details. He looked rather upset."

"He did not tell you whom the message was from?" Margaret asked.

"He did not." A stricken look clouded Amity's pretty face. "You all think I am very foolish, don't you? I should have asked more questions. I can tell by your response you think something is wrong."

"*Non*, Mademoiselle Wells," Madame du Lac said. "Bainbridge is not much of a mystery. I should not be surprised in the least if this concerned some part of his costume for tomorrow night. I heard him saying that he would not wear a toga and was trying to find a Roman general's uniform instead." This coaxed a weak smile from Amity. "You must promise to act surprised."

"Of course," she murmured.

"We had no fixed plan for dinner, did we?" Christabel asked. Jack glared angrily at Mr. Fairchild, who hadn't left her side from the moment they stepped onto the balloon.

"We did not," Mr. Fairchild said. "Why don't we see if we can get a table at the West End Hotel? It is a short walk along the promenade and I understand has a decent reputation."

"I am going to the casino," Augustus said. "Not hungry." Without waiting for a response, he gave his sister a quick kiss on the cheek and disappeared into the crowd.

"He cannot abide any of us, can he?" Margaret asked.

Amity laughed. "Augustus has always been a man unto himself, even when he was a little boy. Do not take the slight personally. Do you really believe I ought not worry about Jeremy, Margaret?"

"I am positively certain," Margaret said and took her by the hand, pulling her in the direction of the West End, one of a long row of fashionable hotels that lined the Promenade des Anglais, offering their guests unparalleled views of the sea. Amity tolerated this for a short while, then freed her hand and let Colin take her arm, after which she slowed her pace so that the others pulled ahead.

"May I ask you a terrible question?" She looked up at him through her long, thick lashes.

"I can hardly refuse," Colin said, "terrible though it may be."

"It is only that . . . well . . . you are the only other person on earth who might understand what I am feeling. Emily is not with us because she got invited to dinner, correct? Just this morning, at breakfast, she told us all that Monsieur Guérin was leaving Nice tomorrow. That is why he would not be able to show us the ruins himself."

"Yes."

"But then this unexpected invitation comes, and she abandons us tonight. Are we really to believe he is hosting a dinner party just before leaving town?"

"It would not be wholly unusual," Colin said. He was dreadfully handsome. The wind had picked up again and was tousling his thick hair. His hat was in his hand. "And at any rate, his wife will have made all the arrangements, not him. She may not be leaving town tomorrow. He seemed wholly unconcerned with the plan when he called on us at the hotel. Why is this troubling you?"

"It is troubling me, Colin, because only a short while after she deserted us . . ." Her voice trailed, and she looked up at him again, now with tears pooling in her eyes. Colin handed her his handkerchief without a word. "Thank you," she said, pressing it daintily to her face. "Jeremy gets a mysterious summons and flies off without a word of explanation. I can hardly say what I suspect."

"Emily did not summon Jeremy," Colin said. His voice, firm and decisive, ought to have inspired confidence in Amity, but she found she could not believe quite so readily as he.

"You trust her so very much."

"I would never doubt her."

"Where else could he have gone?" She dabbed at the corners of her eyes with the handkerchief. "I know there is no one else with the power to induce him to do whatever she needs. And I am not so naïve as to believe that he received an urgent message about a costume for a Roman banquet."

"You are falling prey to vicious gossip promulgated by your own mother."

"Can you really tell me, hand on heart, that my fiancé is not in love with your wife?" Amity stopped walking and stood squarely in front of him, her little hands clenched in hard fists.

Colin did not reply immediately. He looked at Amity, her trembling lips, her tear-stained cheeks, and he did the only thing a gentleman could in such a circumstance. He lied.

"I can, Miss Wells," he said. "Bainbridge is not in love with my wife. Come now, we have almost lost sight of the others. What you need is a nice meal and some lively conversation to restore your spirits. If you would like, I shall send word to the Excelsior telling them to alert Bainbridge to our location, so that he will know where to come meet us should he wind up back at the hotel."

"You are very kind," Amity said, "but I fear I am in no state for social discourse. Would you be so good as to find me a cab? I should like to return to the hotel and rest for a while."

"I shall take you there myself."

"No, please, Colin. I can hardly criticize my own fiancé for flirting if I am willing to be seen entering and exiting a cab with someone else's husband. It would not be appropriate, and I think it is time I begin to give more consideration to my actions."

As a gentleman, there was no way Colin could argue with that.

# 22

When I first heard Jeremy's voice resonating from above the ruins, I felt relief. Someone had come for me! But the sensation did not last. If he were looking for me, why was he not calling my name? And if my friends knew me to be missing, would not my husband have come himself? I almost called out, but bit back the words, knowing it would be foolish to reveal my position, particularly if Jeremy had been brought here against his will or, like me, lured under false pretenses. I scuttled across a more open section of the site, where the walls were considerably lower, doing my best to use the occasional column to hide my progress, and made my way to the tall edifice, having decided it could offer me both protection from being seen and an excellent vantage point from which to better observe how I might get back up to modern street level and away from this place.

Jeremy was speaking again. I thought I heard him laugh, but no amount of straining could enable me to see him. From the direction of his voice, it was apparent he was still above me. The smell of cigar smoke wafted from the general direction of the entrance to the ruins, and I started to wonder if he had even the slightest idea that I was here. Had he and Amity—and, no doubt, Margaret—decided to steal into the site? It seemed unlikely, and I did not hear any female voices. If Margaret were with him, she would be (loudly) reciting Virgil in Latin, but surely Jeremy would never have come on his own, unless—no, that thought was too dire even for my current circumstance.

I was tempted to try to move closer to him in order to hear what he was saying, but knew I ought not. Instead, I climbed to one of the arched doorways partway up the façade, at what would have been the first floor, pressed my body against the side not illuminated by the moon, and waited. The height of my perch would protect me, for anyone searching would be likely to assume I had remained at ground level. Every instant felt like a lifetime. The voice—or voices—had stopped, and the silence was oddly terrifying. I tried to distract myself from an impending sense of doom by considering why these archways were so far above the courtyard. Had there originally been a terrace of some sort that looked over the more open space below? The cat was now sprawled out on the top of one of the shorter walls, meowing loudly. Then, in the snap of a second, I heard a cracking sound, a cry, and a dull thud. The sickening feeling in my stomach told me Jeremy was being treated to the same warm hospitality I had enjoyed upon my entrance to the site.

The sound of a grunt was followed by footsteps coming closer, and soon a hulking figure appeared in the moonlight. Monsieur Guérin—although at this point I could no longer believe the person who had introduced himself to me as such was actually the archaeologist—carrying a lifeless form over his shoulder. Jeremy. A second form appeared a few yards behind him.

"There," Amity said, pointing, her voice a hoarse whisper. "Tie him to that column and then go get the other one and bring her to me."

The man dropped Jeremy at the base of the column, took a large coil of rope that had been slung over the shoulder opposite the one that had carried my friend, and moved him into a sitting position before wrapping the rope around his chest and the column, again and again. He tied what appeared to be an enormous knot. "That will hold him." He spoke to her in heavily accented English.

"Good," she said. "Now get her, quickly."

The man took a lantern from her and slunk away, back toward the entrance, which I could now see was accessible from the courtyard via a modern, if somewhat haphazard-looking, staircase, without going through the stone maze into which I had been flung. As soon as he was out of sight, Amity stood directly in front of Jeremy and pulled something from her reticule.

"I am very sorry to have to do this," she said. "You must understand you give me no choice. It is nothing personal, I assure you, and I am grateful that you made it so easy. Anyone could see that you love Emily, and no matter what her devoted husband claims, it will be easy enough to convince the world that she loved you as well."

Jeremy moved his head, moaning as he regained consciousness. "Amity?"

"I do wish you could forgive me, but it hardly matters, does it? We cannot always have icing for our cake. She will be with us at any moment and then—"

"Put the gun away, Amity," Jeremy said, his voice rough.

"What should it be, do you think?" she asked, circling him, her arms raised in front of her, the weapon firmly in her grip. "A lover's pact ending in mutual self-destruction or, rather, murder-suicide? I had settled on murder-suicide myself, because I do not think these days anyone would believe in double suicide. It is not dramatic enough and hardly necessary when everyone is having affairs."

"What are you talking about?" Jeremy asked. "Amity, untie this rope."

"She's gone!" The man's voice boomed through the air and Amity spun around.

"Find her!" she cried. Amity lowered the object, which I could now identify as a small pistol, and looked around. Raising the gun again, she walked the perimeter of the grassy area near the edifice where

I was hiding. "Emily! You might as well come out. I know you are still here. There is only one exit and it has been under constant guard."

She was fewer than thirty yards from me, but fortunately had her eyes focused on ground level, and had not looked up, so I remained securely hidden. My decision to go up had been sound. I could not stay, however, as I had to do something to get Jeremy away from her. I wished I had not been forced to abandon the broken brick when I had climbed the wall. There was nothing that could replace it in the archway where I now stood, but regardless, I was too far from Amity to be able to throw something with reliable aim. I would have to make my way back down the edifice, keeping out of her sight, find another suitable stone, and somehow get close enough to strike her. What would be the wiser course of action? Should I target her head, hoping to render her unconscious, or try to knock the gun from her hand?

Then there was the matter of her henchman. I presumed he would be armed as well. Neutralizing him could prove even more difficult. Furthermore, she had said the gate had been guarded. Was he the guard, or was there a third man? The clouds were moving back toward the moon, so I waited until the light dimmed again, and then, carefully and quietly, I crouched down in the archway, keeping to the darkest corner, and lowered myself along the side of the wall away from the open space across which, so far as I could tell, Amity was still pacing. She would not be able to see me unless she walked behind the remains of the building. So far, she had not gone in that direction, but now I would no longer be able to follow her movements.

When my boots touched the ground I bent down and felt around for a new weapon. There was no brick handy, but I picked up an uneven hunk of white stone. Its weight could do a significant amount of damage, but its cumbersome shape would make it difficult to hurl through the air with any hope of accuracy. I would be better off with something easier to wield.

"I don't see her!" The voice sounded far away. The fact that no one else joined in the henchman's chorus encouraged me. If there were a third person, surely he would be joining the search for me, or at least shouting out to confirm I had not left the site.

"Do not lose focus," Amity said. "Start where you left her and try to retrace her steps."

"You want me to go down into the ruins, room by room?"

"How else would you propose to do it?" Amity's voice raged with frustration. Her partner did not reply. I could hear the sound of her shoes on one of the patches of marble pavement scattered over the site. She was not far from me now. I lifted the less than satisfactory stone and clutched it to my chest, figuring it was better to have something rather than nothing, and quietly made my way along the length of the ancient façade until I reached a small, low opening in the wall. I ducked through it, knowing that now I would be on the side of the building facing where Jeremy was being held. Having studied all that was below me while I had hidden in the higher archway, I was aware that there were three rectangular spaces enclosed by walls of varying heights between me and the column to which my friend was tied. If I could make my way through them, I might be able to approach Amity from behind.

The trouble came from not being able to scale walls while carrying my would-be weapon, so I abandoned it, confident that I would be able to replace it as I came nearer to my target. As I shifted my weight over the first wall, I heard, from the general direction of Jeremy's column, a strangled cry followed by the shuffling of feet and a single shot. Half over the top, I stopped, unable to breathe. Had she killed him?

"It was a cat, Amity, nothing but a cat," Jeremy said. "Please, you must let me go."

I opened my mouth in a silent scream of relief at the sound of his voice and lowered myself back to the ground on the other side of the wall, wondering if she had shot the cat. Almost as if the creature anticipated my thought, it meowed, and I would swear it sounded almost bored.

"Do you hear something else?" Amity asked. "I hear her. She is nearby."

"Who? Emily?" Jeremy asked. "Why would she be nearby? If she is not where you left her, you can be sure she is long gone. She is probably back at the hotel having a hot bath right now." He was trying to distract her. "Let's go find her together, Amity. If you would just—"

"Silence! I hear something."

I had made good use of their conversation, covering the remaining ground—and walls—that stood between me and the column, and was now just on the other side from where my friend was being held. The wall separating us was solid and high, too high for me to feel confident about using it effectively. I would not be able to carry a heavy projectile to the top, and, once there, would be exposed to my enemy. If I tried either to throw something down or to lower myself, she would spot me at once and I would be an easy target. Assuming most Americans (Margaret being an obvious exception) to be partly civilized cowboys, I had no reason to doubt Amity's skills with a firearm.

As a result, I decided to stay as far away as possible from her and her gun for as long as I could. I climbed over a shorter wall parallel to the other. Beyond it was a grassy area littered with stones. I selected what seemed, in the rush of the moment, the best choice to arm myself, and made my way around the outside of the structure, keeping as close to the walls as possible. I paused at the final corner, knowing that another step would render me vulnerable to attack. I could now see Jeremy again. Blood had stained his collar but he was conscious and alert. Amity was not in my field of vision.

What one needed in such a moment was a berserker rage, so fierce and so violent that one might overcome one's opponent in a blinding flash. Unfortunately, despite my father's insistence that the Bromley family were descended from Viking stock, I was unable to rise to the occasion. I watched, hoping to catch a glimpse of Amity so that I might at least ascertain what direction I should head. I took the slightest step away from the wall, hoping for a clearer view. I still could not see Amity, but my movement caught Jeremy's attention, and his eyes widened.

"What are you looking at?" Amity's voice was sharp. "Do you see her?"

"I heard something," Jeremy said, gesturing with his head in the direction away from me. "It was probably the cat."

"You looked the other way."

"I was startled."

"I am afraid, my darling boy, that I am going to have to end this without further delay."

"You have already fired one shot," he said. "Another is likely to raise alarm, and there is a villa in plain sight beyond those trees. You will have to give up on finding Emily, but perhaps it was I who was your target all along."

"Of course you were." She stood still, several yards from him, searching for any sign of me while she spoke. "How was I ever going to convince my parents to let me marry Jack with you alive? I must have a duke, you know. They decreed it."

"Jack?" His voice sounded strangled. "You want to marry my brother?"

"Almost from the moment I met him," she said, her tone turning soft. "When he told me about you, the plan came to me with so little effort it was all but miraculous." She was moving closer now. "If you had only gone back to your room and had a nightcap, your darling Emily wouldn't be in the slightest danger now. You have quite let her down. Not very gentlemanly of you."

I could see her shadow now. She was very near to Jeremy. If I attacked now, she would have a clear shot at close range, but if I waited, she would probably still have that. I stepped back, well out of sight, protected by the wall, and grabbed a second stone, this one smaller. Then, in a fluid motion, I flung it with all my strength over the wall behind me and ran toward her shadow.

The noise startled her, and she turned around, but only for a moment. It was enough, however, for I was already upon her and smashed a second rock against the side of her head. The force of the blow knocked her to the ground, but she did not drop the pistol and was now swinging it wildly, trying to point it at me as she struggled to get back on her feet. Fortunately, as archaeological sites have no shortage of convenient blocks of stone, I reached for another one and threw it at her. It cast only a glancing blow, but to her face, and this gave me the time I needed to stomp on her arm until she released her grip on the gun.

I scooped up the weapon, surprised to find that my hands were not shaking, and leveled it at her. A strange calm came over me. "Untie him," I said.

"I will not." She spat the words at me, her eyes wild.

"I will shoot you."

"You won't. And even if you tried, it would amount to nothing. Jeremy told me what a terrible shot you are."

"You believed him?" I laughed. "Amity, my dear, I am an excellent shot. If your fiancé—or perhaps I should say former fiancé, as I think it very likely he shall call off the engagement after this—told you otherwise, it must only have been to hide his admiration for me."

"You are wrong if you think I am jealous of you," Amity said. "I never wanted him."

"Yes, I heard it all. It wasn't a very interesting story, I'm afraid." I was circling closer to her. "At least the way you told it. In more skilled hands it might make for a rather diverting, if somewhat sensational, novel. Just the sort of thing my husband despises." Footsteps, hurried, warned me that her henchman was drawing near. I had to incapacitate her so that I could deal with him. I bit my lip, steadied my breath, and pulled the trigger. She cried out and I looked away, searching for her accomplice. He was not yet in sight, so I turned my attention to Jeremy, but the knot restraining him appeared all but impossible to untie. I would need something to cut it.

"No, I do not have a knife with me," he said in answer to the question I posed him. "I thought I was going to have a rather different sort of evening and did not arm myself. You shot her, Em." We both looked at her crumpled body.

"Yes, I am well aware of that. We need to get away from here before—" But it was already too late. The hulking form appeared once again from the shadows. "Time to screw your courage to the sticking place," I said, my voice choked. "Never thought I would have the occasion to feel such sympathy for Lady Macbeth."

"Don't joke, Em."

They were the last words I heard before I pulled the trigger again. This time, I did not hit my target and I braced myself for return fire, but none came. Instead, the man turned and ran. Amity must not have thought he would need to be armed with anything other than the cudgel he had used on both Jeremy and myself. Or perhaps his loyalty to Amity's cause proved insufficient. I applied myself again to freeing my friend, and found that without the threat of imminent disruption, and possible destruction, I was able at last to loosen it. Jeremy stood, took me by the shoulders, and looked deep into my eyes.

"I do think this will get me entirely over loving you, Em. I should have been the one rescuing you. How ever will I live down this embarrassment?" I appreciated his attempt at humor, but the pain in his voice was evident. He crossed to Amity's motionless body. I could not bear to look. "She is still breathing."

"I aimed for her shoulder," I said. "I have read countless novels in which the hero lives relatively unscathed after a bullet goes clean

through the fleshy part. It seemed a decent enough strategy." The pre-
ternatural calm that had come over me so unexpectedly now vanished, and I stood, shaking rather violently. Shouts came from the
direction of the gate, and soon half a dozen gendarmes had descended
upon us. They told us, later, that the owners of the nearby villa had
summoned them the moment they heard the first shot. Never have I
been more grateful for my fluency in French, as the situation looked
rather awkward: me, standing, holding a pistol, and Amity bleeding
on the ground. I explained what had happened, Jeremy corroborat-
ing my story, and, perhaps more importantly, Amity's henchman,
whom they had caught fleeing from the scene, had confessed to
everything. She had hired him to lure me to the site, and had given
him explicit instructions to introduce himself both to my husband and
me, so that there would be no question that I would meet him at the
ruins. That task finished, he was to come to a predetermined spot on
the Promenade des Anglais and deliver a note to the Duke of Bainbridge. He did not avoid looking at either Jeremy or me as he spoke.
The affability I had noted upon first meeting him now seemed to mask
something more sinister. All the while, the cat, who had reappeared
after I fired my last shot, sat approximately six feet from Amity, staring at her accusingly.

We followed as they carried Amity away, putting her in a wagon
that would take her to the hospital. Much as I wanted to find Colin, I
decided we should accompany her, and asked if we could give our official statements there, rather than at the police station. Ironic though
it may sound, I wanted to be sure I had caused her no irreparable harm.
The gendarmes did not object. Just before he helped me into the second police vehicle, Jeremy put his arm around my waist and pulled
me close to him.

"All things being equal, Em, I much prefer Cannes to Nice."

"Is that so?" I asked, doing my best to restore both of our spirits.

"It seems to me you ought to rethink your position. I am beginning to believe that your life was threatened multiple times in Cannes, yet only once in Nice."

"Multiple times?" he asked, sitting next to me on the hard bench against the wall of the wagon. "I am not certain about that. Regardless, the attempt here was far more dramatic. You know I have no stomach for drama. And my head may never recover from that fellow's blow. Yes, I blame Nice entirely. Much prefer Cannes."

I took his hand and smiled before letting my head drop onto his shoulder. "The ruins are lovely," I said, "yet I find myself forced to agree with you. Cannes was much better."

# 23

It did not take long for the doctors at the hospital to treat Amity. Despite my lack of skills when it came to firearms, the bullet, as I had intended, passed cleanly through her shoulder, and she required nothing more than stitches to close the wound. I insisted that the police allow Jeremy and me to be in the room when they questioned her, pointing out that we had more information about the full extent of her crimes than they. She did not look at Jeremy even once while she spoke, but her eyes were full of hate when she met mine. She had already confessed to having poisoned the whisky in Jeremy's room, and, hence, to Mr. Neville's murder, but I was still confused about something.

"Why did you kill Hélène?" I asked.

"She was insurance," Amity said. "Although I believed my plan to be sound, I worried there was a slim possibility that something would go awry. I knew any one of the dancers would serve my purpose, so I went to the casino a few days before the party, after my father had arranged for the girls to dance, and paid Hélène a little extra to make sure she would shower special attention on his grace. She did try to insist she wasn't *that* sort of a girl, but she did not hesitate to take my money. I asked Augustus to let me know when he returned from the casino that night, and to tell me whether his grace"—

apparently she would no longer say Jeremy's name—"had spoken to her." Her voice was shockingly cold.

"Was Augustus aware of what you were doing when you waited up for him that evening?" I asked.

"No. Why would I have wanted anyone to know what I was doing? Taking someone into my confidence would have served only to make me vulnerable to that person. I am not foolish enough to have done that, and I needed very little help to complete my tasks. It only took a matter of minutes to prepare everything in his grace's room. While I was still in Cairo, I bought a set of tools and taught myself to pick locks—it is not so difficult as you might expect—and also procured the poison. I had prepared the whisky earlier in the day, so had only to place it on the bedside table and remove every other beverage from the room to ensure his grace wouldn't be able to choose something else to drink. That done, I went and sat in the lobby until I saw my brother, who confirmed his grace was no longer with the girl."

"When did you kill her?" I asked.

"Early the next morning. When I paid her for the extra services at the party, I insisted that she tell me where she lived. If she thought it was an odd request, she didn't show it, and certainly didn't object. The early morning strolls I made a point of telling you all I took were in fact drives to her neighborhood. I watched her to learn her habits. She always went back upstairs after she breakfasted with her landlady. That morning, when she was downstairs eating, I slipped to her room, picked the lock, and hid, waiting for her to return. I took her completely by surprise. She didn't even see me. I came upon her from behind and bashed in—"

"I do not need further details," I said, swallowing bile.

"It was simple to slip out of her rooms unnoticed. The butcher was busy with customers and his wife saddled with washing the dishes." Amity scowled. "I had hoped the girl's death would have been noticed sooner. Perhaps I should have left her valise at the bottom of the stairs instead of taking it with me and disposing of it so that someone would have gone upstairs to look for her. That was my one mistake. I should have figured out a better way to draw attention to her demise."

"*That* was your one mistake?" Jeremy's eyes bulged and the thick veins in his neck pulsed. Amity only turned her head farther away from him.

"What about the cuff links?" I asked.

"I took them when I left the whisky and then hid them in the girl's room after I took care of her. If his grace's death were ruled a suicide, that would be that, but if it weren't, the cuff links could connect the two crimes."

"How so?" I asked. "Did you want the gendarmes to believe that Jeremy had murdered Hélène after she stole his cuff links?"

"Yes," Amity said. "And then gone back and, consumed with guilt over his rash act, taken his own life. I was a bit concerned about not being able to deal with the girl until the following morning, but I did not think it would be possible for the coroner to determine the time of death with enough precision that a few hours would prove problematic."

"If Jeremy had gone to her room surely he would have recovered the cuff links?" I asked.

"Not if he couldn't find them. Everyone would believe that he had known that they had been stolen and that she was the only one who had the opportunity to take them. The police would have found them eventually, though, and then if people—like you—started asking questions about why his grace had killed himself, their investigations would lead to the dancer with whom his grace had left the casino."

"But of course none of this went according to plan, and poor Neville—" Jeremy's voice cracked and he turned to the wall. "I can listen to no more." He left the room. I followed soon thereafter, once Amity had answered my few remaining questions.

Mr. and Mrs. Wells made no comment as we passed them in the

hospital corridor. They were standing, speaking to the physician who had treated their daughter, and I could hear him telling them he was confident she would make a full recovery. The look on Mrs. Wells's face left me to wonder whether she considered that a favorable outcome. Augustus was nowhere to be seen; he might not yet know what had transpired.

A gendarme took Jeremy and me back to the hotel, where outside the entrance to the lobby, the cat from the ruins was standing. She followed us inside, keeping very close to my skirts. How she knew to wait for us there is inexplicable, but I do not think it possible to interpret her actions as anything but deliberate. The desk clerk told us our friends had not yet returned, so I instructed him to send them up the moment they arrived and to also have a bottle of whisky delivered to the room. Jeremy clasped my hand in his and led me to the elevator. "I know you prefer the stairs," he said.

"I do not think either of us is in any condition to do much walking," I replied.

"I told the clerk, when your back was turned, to send up port as well as whisky. I am not the only one in dire need of fortification."

When we reached my room, we sat in silence, Jeremy with his whisky, me with my port, the cat purring contentedly in my lap. After what felt like an eternity, he spoke. "You are a terrible shot, Em. You have always been a terrible shot."

"I know."

"But your aim was true tonight."

"I am so sorry, Jeremy. I never meant—"

"To shoot my fiancée?" He gave me a wry smile. "No, I would imagine not, although I had the distinct impression all along you were not fond of her."

"No, that is not true. I—" He waved his hand to stop me.

"This will make for quite a scandal, won't it?" he asked. "And only think—the queen is occupying rooms two floors above us. What will your mother say?"

"Something far worse than whatever Her Majesty says. I wonder if she will still expect me to breakfast with her in the morning?"

Keys rattled in the lock and Jeremy looked up at me, pain over his face. "I thought Amity loved me, Em. What a fool I am."

"You are not a fool," I said. "She is an excellent player. She had everyone fooled."

"Except you—"

The door burst open before he could finish his thought, and Colin and Jack were all but fighting to be the first to enter the room. The hotel physician came next, followed by the rest of our friends. Neither Jeremy nor I was willing to succumb to medical inspection—we had already refused it at the hospital—and the fierceness of our stance on the matter convinced the man that our health was not in imminent danger. He left without further pressing his case.

"Tell us everything," Margaret said. "The desk clerk said the police brought you to the hotel and that the two of you looked a fright. We knew something dreadful must have happened, especially once we learned Amity never returned to her room. How did you find Emily, Jeremy?"

"Do not give me any of the credit for our rescue," he said. "The message that came for me at the Promenade des Anglais—Amity had sent it herself—purported to be from Emily. It said she had twisted her ankle at the ruins and required my immediate assistance. I will thank you, Hargreaves, to refrain from commenting on my reaction to this."

Colin crossed his arms, but remained silent.

"The man claiming to have been Monsieur Guérin brought me the note and took me to the ruins himself. He said that he did not think Emily's injuries were serious in the least, but that his wife had insisted he fetch me at once. I should have known at once something was wrong. She would have sent for you, Hargreaves, but sometimes we choose to believe . . ." Jeremy's voice trailed and pain crossed his face. "He offered me a cigar as we went into the ruins, and the next thing I knew, he was whacking me on the head and leaving me tied to a column."

"Were you there already, Emily?" Colin asked, sitting by my side as I recounted the story, his dark eyes full of concern as he listened, doing his best to remain perfectly still. The cat had, at first, objected to his presence, but accepted it after I explained the situation. She was much happier when Colin, unable to contain himself any longer, rose from his seat and started to pace, as was his habit when he was stressed. When I reached the end of my narrative—Jeremy interjecting only occasionally—I turned to my husband. "You will agree, after this, that I ought to learn how to shoot?"

"I will shoot Monsieur Hargreaves myself if he does not," Cécile said. "And you know that I am, in fact, an excellent shot."

"I know the futility of arguing with either of you," Colin said.

"The poison was intended for my brother all along?" Jack's face had gone ghost pale as we revealed the details of our adventure. "And Amity thought I would marry her after she killed him?"

"No one was ever to suspect anything other than suicide," I said. "You and Amity were already close friends, and it would be natural for you to console her after the tragic death of her fiancé left her devastated."

"From there, it would not have been difficult to convince you to marry her," Jeremy said, "or so she believed. After all, there is plenty of precedent for younger brothers stepping in after such an event. Princess May of Teck married Prince George after his elder brother died, and that was only a few years ago."

"That does not mean I would marry her," Jack said, his face turning crimson.

"She wanted to live in India with you," I said, "and admitted that she was concerned that such an outcome might not be possible if you were duke, as there was the estate to be run, but she decided you were worth more to her than India." Jack cringed. "Regardless, when Mr. Neville succumbed to her poison instead of Jeremy, she had to try something else. She was not about to give up on her dream of marrying Jack—not after she had already had to abandon her previous love, Marshall Cabot."

"Marshall Cabot?" Christabel asked. "I never heard her mention that name."

"Amity loved him, long before she went to India, but her parents did not consider him to be a worthy husband," I said. "They refused to let her marry him and stopped her planned elopement. The next time she fancied herself in love, this time with an equally unsuitable younger son, she decided to take matters firmly into her own hands, and to do whatever she deemed necessary to make the object of her affection a catch certain to meet with her parents' approval. When Mr. Neville drank the poison instead of Jeremy, she pressed on with her plan. She tried again to achieve her desired result, first on the parapet by the castle in Cannes, where she pretended to trip and fall against Jeremy. The force of her weight was not nearly enough to send him careening over the edge as she had hoped, but she thought it worth a try."

"Then," I continued, "she made another attempt, on the boat. She had hoped that Jeremy's swim would result either in him drowning or in him falling ill."

"Evidently she felt she could help me along my way, so to speak, if the illness weren't enough to kill me on its own," Jeremy said. "She planned to insist on nursing me back to health, or, well, somewhere else."

Margaret, sitting next to him, took his hand. "I cannot tell you how sorry I am—how sorry I know we all are—"

"Please, don't," he said. "Having lived through it is embarrassment enough."

"Are you sure that was her intention?" Christabel asked. "Amity was trying to convince Jeremy not to swim."

"That is what she wanted us all to think," I said, "but she knew Jeremy well enough to know that if she goaded him in just the right way, he would decide on his own that the swim was a good idea."

"She goaded him the way she accused you of having done," Christabel said, tears springing to her eyes.

"I am afraid that is all too true," Jeremy said. "It was she who brought up the story of Colin swimming the Bosphorus, going on at length about how dangerous it had been and how brave—but foolish—he must be and how Emily's heart must have . . . Well, you get the general idea. I took the bait with little coaxing. The moment she tried to forbid me from leaping overboard was the moment I set my mind to the task. The more she tried to stop me, the more certain it was that I would go through with the action. Had I been thinking clearly I should have taken this as a sign she would prefer Jack to me. He's the chap for feats of physical strength."

"If only there were some catalog of accounts of ridiculous actions taken by gentlemen solely as a result of their own stubbornness," Margaret said. "I should very much like to read it."

"I do appreciate your attempt at humor," Jeremy said. "When the swim did not kill me—no thanks to you, Hargreaves, for leaping in to rescue me (truly this has been a terrible time for my ego)—she decided to change tactics. Her direct attempts had failed, and she worried that if she continued, she might start to appear suspicious, so she targeted Emily instead."

"She tried to kill Emily?" Colin asked.

"No, but she tried to turn you all against me," I said. "This was in preparation for the final part of her plan. She locked me in the cell on

Sainte-Marguerite, and hoped you all would come to the conclusion that I had done it myself to get attention."

"But the barrel was far too heavy for her to move," Mr. Fairchild said. "She must have had assistance with that."

"Evidently a few kisses were enough to convince one of the guards to help her," Jeremy said, his face a terrible shade of grey. "She told him it was all to be a good joke."

"And then she switched the invitation to her mother's dinner to a card she had written herself, with the wrong time, so that I would look rude and inconsiderate," I said. "Following that, she sent herself the crushed hat. The conclusion to be drawn then was that not only had I been behaving badly, I had now revealed my jealousy."

"Of course," Colin said. "You are secretly in love with Bainbridge, and he with you. We would be helped to that conclusion when the two of you, in rapid succession, returned to the hotel soaked from the rain."

"Precisely," I said. "She arranged for the telephone messages to be left for both of us."

"I only had to make my way back from the café," Jeremy said. "Poor Em got the added treat of racing through the city to the church and back. Amity never was particularly fond of you, Em. I will admit that now."

"And the yellow carnation on the walls?" Margaret asked. "Surely she had not gone all the way up there to leave it?"

"She claims she did not, and I am inclined to believe her," I said. "It would have been nearly impossible for her to have done so with time left to return to the hotel in a timely fashion, and we know she was there, in the lobby, for much of the afternoon. Either Augustus had been there himself and lost the buttonhole, or it was nothing more than a coincidence."

"But surely she noticed that none of us blamed you for the hat or any of these other things?" Mr. Fairchild turned to me. "I regret very much that I did not defend you publicly. You deserved better support from your friends."

"You are kind to say so," I said. "She did realize that the plan wasn't working particularly well, as there was no wholesale turning against me by any of you—and I thank you all for your loyalty and assure you that defending me more staunchly would not have changed the outcome of the situation—but that did not worry her much. Each of those events remained, more or less, unexplained, which was just what she wanted. When Jeremy and I turned up dead at the ruins, they would help to reveal why I had decided to kill him and then myself."

"What a horrible woman," Cécile said. "You, Kallista, have encountered many—too many—disgusting criminals, but I do believe Mademoiselle Wells is the worst of them all. So cold-blooded and calculating. A very devil of a person."

"And at the same time a product of a society that cares about nothing but money and rank," Colin said.

"If her parents had let her marry that Cabot fellow—" Jack began.

"No," I interrupted. "Amity is not a victim of circumstance. She is a selfish, manipulative person without any sort of a moral compass. I have not one ounce of sympathy for her."

"Nor would anyone suggest you should," Colin said. "Although, were she here with us now, she might use your impassioned critique of her as further evidence to convince us that you are well and thoroughly in love with Bainbridge."

"It is only a matter of time, Hargreaves, before you accept reality," Jeremy said. "Emily has loved me since she was three."

"The reality, my dear man, is that this entire incident has left you a priceless gift," Colin said. "You have never really wanted to be married—you have held that position for all the many years I have known you. And now, after having been engaged to a woman who tried multiple times to kill you, you can hardly be expected to even consider approaching the altar anytime soon. I should think no one, even your own mother, would dare broach the subject for a solid five years at least."

"Hargreaves, what a brilliant observation," Jeremy said, leaping to his feet. "And as I am certain I never would have reached it on my own, I do believe I am now obligated to you in a way that even yesterday I would have found intolerable. I may, in fact, be fonder of you than I am of your wife."

"High praise indeed," Colin said. "At the risk of dooming myself to having to bear with equanimity even more of your goodwill, I shall take things a step further and suggest that if your brother, whom I am thoroughly convinced was well on his way to proposing to a certain young lady even before arriving in Cannes, would now follow through on his ambitions, you might no longer have to consider marriage as a necessity for yourself."

"My brother?" Jeremy asked.

Jack looked at his boots. "I—I—you all are very kind, but I am afraid that my hopes—"

"You, my dear boy, have fallen victim to Amity as well," Margaret said. "Forgive me for speaking about it so publicly, but you are among friends, and I am not about to let another minute go by without correcting your misapprehensions, particularly as what you have suffered is not nearly so . . . er . . . humiliating as what your brother has gone through."

"You are kindness itself, Margaret," Jeremy said. His tone was pointed but he was smiling.

"I do not think you understand—" Jack started, but this time Christabel interrupted him.

"Amity told me to push you away," she said. "She was certain you would never propose to me if I didn't make you suffer just a bit."

"It was another layer to her scheme," I said. "She couldn't very well have you proposing to Christabel before things were settled, so to speak, with Jeremy, so she convinced Christabel to pull away from you."

"She told her she ought to flirt with me," Mr. Fairchild said. "Christabel confessed everything to me at once, because she is too dear a creature to lead a man on. Perhaps I ought not have gone along with her plan, but I thought you might need a bit of prodding to get a proposal out of you."

"I have been a fool," Jack said.

"You are not half so foolish as I was to have listened to Amity," Christabel said. "And I am most heartily sorry if I caused you any pain, Jack."

"My dear girl—" He crossed to her and pulled her to her feet.

"That is quite enough," Colin said. "Take her somewhere else to propose, will you? And the rest of you, go downstairs and order champagne to toast the happy couple. Emily and I will see you at breakfast. We have had more than enough excitement for one night."

They protested as one, but it was Jeremy who ushered them out of our room. No one was about to argue with him after what he had gone through. When Colin had closed and locked the door behind them, he took my face in his hands and began to examine the various bruises and scrapes that covered it. "My dearest, darling girl, I hardly know what to say. Are you truly all right?"

"A little battered and somewhat the worse for wear, but nothing serious," I said.

"You have distinguished yourself tonight," he said, encircling me with his arms. "I could not be more proud. Moreover, I could not have handled the situation better myself. You are as capable as anyone with whom I have ever worked, and I hope you know that I have long considered you my full equal."

"There is nothing you could say that would mean more to me." I buried my face in his chest.

"That pleases me no end," he said. "I do hope you realize, however, that your actions may cause you to soon find yourself in an interesting situation."

"Of what sort?" I asked, pulling back from him. "I was rather hoping for a steaming bath. I am filthy and sore and have already asked Meg to fill the tub."

"I would not describe that as an interesting situation, but you shall have it at once," he said. "While you are soaking consider this: you have saved the life of a duke, a peer of the realm. Whatever will Her Majesty say? I shouldn't be surprised if she gives you some sort of official recognition. You are after all having breakfast with her tomorrow."

"I suppose it would be too much to wish for a reprieve on that count. Has anyone been named a Lady of the Garter since Margaret Beaufort?" I asked. "I am no admirer of Henry Tudor, but he did have the sense to elevate his mother to the position. Perhaps Her Majesty could do the same for me?"

"I would not set my sights quite so high," Colin said. "I may consider you my equal, but the queen—"

"Yes, yes, the queen. I doubt very much I will receive any sort of honor from her. More likely, she will reprimand me tomorrow morning and somehow have twisted events so as to blame me for the ensuing scandal."

"You are almost certainly correct," he said. "What could I have been thinking? Rejoice, however, that there is not time for your mother to come down from Kent before breakfast."

The cat hissed. I took this as a sign of superior intelligence as it was clear the creature was objecting to the very idea of my mother. I decided at once that we would take her home with us. She would amuse the boys.

"I shall rejoice in that knowledge," I said. "You ought to as well because there is no risk of any honors or worse for me. Only consider if she made me a peeress in my own right—she could at last call you lord, even if it were only a courtesy title."

"No, my dear, your mother would never stand for that. Can you imagine?"

"The mortification? The horror? Oh, to have a daughter recognized for service and given a peerage. One shudders at the very thought."

"Quite," Colin said. "And that is more than enough shuddering for you tonight. Meg must have your bath ready by now."

"I would never take a peerage, you know," I said, as he scooped me up and carried me to the bath. "You have corrupted me too thoroughly for me to believe that to be a good idea. The aristocracy, that is. But I would very much like to live in a world where such a thing was possible. Ladies recognized the way men are."

"It will come, Emily, it will come. We are only a few years from the dawn of a new century."

"I have great hopes for it," I said. The cat meowed as if in agreement. I found myself already unaccountably fond of her.

The queen was not fierce with me the next morning. In fact, she sent down word that we would delay breakfast by half an hour so that I would have time to recover from my travails. I appreciated the gesture even as I was amused by the idea that thirty minutes would be ample time to recover from having been knocked unconscious, kidnapped, and having shot someone. To her credit, though, Her Majesty was horrified by the dangers that had threatened Jeremy and me, and she praised the courage with which I had faced them, saying that she would expect nothing less from a noble Englishwoman. The whole affair took less than an hour, and when I returned to my friends I was delighted to be able to congratulate Jack and Christabel on their engagement. Cécile had already taken the bride under her wing, and had telegrammed Christabel's parents to inform them she would be traveling to Paris, where together they would see to her trousseau. Mr. Fairchild booked himself onto the first train out of Nice, saying he could no longer tolerate the Côte d'Azur, and I was sorry that he could not separate the lovely towns from the brutal events that had taken place there.

Margaret, however, had no such problems. She had sent a telegram as well, to Mr. Michaels, whom she had ordered to meet her in Nice as soon as possible. "You didn't take *me* to the ruins, Emily," she said, "so I shall have to make him do it."

I thought it unlikely we would see Mr. or Mrs. Wells again, and on that count I was correct, but Augustus was waiting for me in the lobby of the hotel that evening when Colin and I returned from a quiet dinner at a restaurant in town. He presented me with a small package, bowing ever so slightly as he gave it to me.

"I believe you prefer them unbound," he said, and slipped away. I unwrapped the parcel. Inside was a glass box, the sort used by scientists to display entomological specimens. Within it was a single pin, stuck through nothing but the white backing that filled the case. Next to it was a label, written in a neat hand: *Iolana iolas.* I unfolded the small piece of paper that accompanied it. The note said *I am not so bad as you think.*

"I may have misjudged him," I admitted, as Colin read over my shoulder.

"Either way, I am very glad to be done with the Wells family," he said. "I am not, however, certain that I am done with Cannes. Let's go back, today. I have already contacted the hotel."

"What a marvelous idea," I said. "We could wait for Margaret and Mr. Michaels—"

"Not a chance," he said, slipping his arm through mine and pulling me close. "I want you all to myself. No more parties, boat excursions, fireworks, dinners, prisons. Just the two of us, no interruptions."

"I do rather like fireworks," I said.

"Then you shall have them in spades," he said.

"What about Roman banquets? Do you object to them?"

"Not in principle, but if you think I am going to willingly don a toga, you could not be more wrong."

It had taken a considerable effort to persuade him to let me bring the cat home with us. I decided to keep the toga in reserve for future use.

# AUTHOR'S NOTE

The seeds of the story of *The Adventuress* were first sown while I was writing *A Fatal Waltz,* a novel in which Emily and Jeremy's friendship blossoms even as it becomes complicated. While they are in Vienna, he talks about an uncle who has always coveted the Bainbridge estate, and wonders aloud if he might ever have bastard children who might challenge their cousins for the title.

Part of the inspiration for Jeremy's character came from William Cavendish, the sixth Duke of Devonshire, commonly referred to as the Bachelor Duke, who never married after Lady Caroline Ponsoby chose William Lamb over him, but Jeremy's commitment to debauchery is his own. He does not mention his brother in *A Fatal Waltz* because I had not yet decided exactly how his story would transpire. All I knew at the time was that Jeremy's brother had no interest in the dukedom. It was only when Amity Wells made her presence known to me in the last scene of *The Counterfeit Heiress* that it all started to fall into place. As soon as I had I finished writing that book, I was compelled to tell the rest of the story.

The Hotel Britannia does not exist in Cannes. It is based largely on the lovely Carlton, where I stayed when researching this book. The Hôtel Excelsior Regina in Nice, however, is real, and was built with Queen Victoria in mind. Her majesty adored Nice, and spent a great deal of time there. Louisa, Countess of Antrim, a lady-in-waiting to the queen, left in her diary a marvelous collection of photographs and souvenirs to accompany her memories of her experiences. They proved invaluable when researching the Victorians' (and Victoria's) love of the Côte d'Azur.

I explored the ruins at Cimiez in detail, knowing the instant I saw them that this was the place where Amity would at last confront Emily, just as I knew, when I stepped into it, that the Man in the Iron Mask's cell had a place in this book. Emily's feelings about the island and the prison are my own; it is a place at once beautiful and horrifying.

We first met Christabel Peabody, named by reader Linda Kimmel, in *The Counterfeit Heiress*. Linda adores Elizabeth Peters's wonderful Amelia Peabody novels as much as I do, and she chose the name partly to honor Peters's heroine. Fans of Amelia will not be surprised to have read that Christabel's distant relation was not interested in forming an acquaintance in Egypt. And surely Amelia's husband would have objected in the strongest of terms.

Finally, I hope that Andrew and Jane recognize the reference to the Cannois on occasion carrying a live chicken in a bag. We saw a fashionable lady of a certain age strolling along La Croisette with what only could have been a well-cared-for pet chicken comfortably ensconced in an Hermes bag. The chicken appeared to be just as delighted with the display in the Dior boutique's window as his owner. I will never forget either of them.

10/15